# A Gift of Flowers

"Shame on you, my lord," she chided gaily. "Don't you know that only females are supposed to catch a bride's bouquet? Now you have deprived some poor girl of the romantic fantasy of imminent wedding bells for herself."

"From what I know of your aunt, Miss Wetherby, I wouldn't hesitate to say she meant the bouquet for you. So here it is, with my compliments."

His eyes contained a tenderness and shared amusement Diana had never thought to see in them. Resolutely, she tore her gaze from his face and wished her heart would cease doing unconscionable things in her breast. With considerable effort, she maintained a semblance of composure as he thrust the posy into her nerveless fingers . . .

# The Scandalous Wager

## Olivia Fontayne

JOVE BOOKS, NEW YORK

THE SCANDALOUS WAGER

A Jove Book / published by arrangement with
the author

PRINTING HISTORY
Jove edition / November 1992

ISBN: 0-515-10978-9

Jove Books are published by The Berkley Publishing Group,
200 Madison Avenue, New York, New York 10016.
The name ''JOVE'' and the ''J'' logo
are trademarks belonging to Jove Publications, Inc.

PRINTED IN THE UNITED STATES OF AMERICA

10  9  8  7  6  5  4  3  2  1

# The Scandalous Wager

# The Wager

"THE DEVIL TAKE you, Rotherham," a thick voice exploded in utter disgust, interrupting the animated discussion among the other guests at the Earl of Rotherham's hunting lodge. "You've left me without a feather to fly with, ol' boy. What in Hades shall I use for stakes the rest of the week? Can you tell me?" the voice added with a touch of petulance.

"Give it up, Tottlefield," someone suggested facetiously. "You ain't cut out for gambling, anyway."

"Try reading a book, Toby," another voice called out in jocular tones. "Improve your mind, old boy. Daresay it could use it, too."

"Take up meditation," someone else put in laconically. "They say it's good for the digestion. More in your line, Toby, if you ask me."

Amid the general laughter that greeted these witticisms, the Honourable Tobias Tottlefield, profligate scion of an otherwise blameless family, swivelled his portly frame around to confront the group of fashionably dressed bucks gathered before the enormous fireplace at the far end of the room.

"I'll have you know, gentlemen," he enunciated carefully, the expression of affronted dignity on his plump countenance somewhat marred by his thickened speech, "that, unlike others I could name, I am not in any immediate need of harebrained advice from a pack of wit-crackers. On the contrary, my neckties are, as you well know, the envy of every buck in town. Furthermore," he added ponderously, ignoring the shouts of derision that greeted this irrelevant statement, "I read two or three books when I was up at Oxford—"

"How many years ago?" someone shouted rudely amid the howls of laughter provoked by Tottlefield's claim to literacy.

"Sure that wasn't one and a half, old man?" inquired a lean, rugged individual with a ginger moustache springing aggressively from his upper lip.

"You may well be right, Chatham; you may be right," Toby responded, nodding his head owlishly. "But in any case, it was more than enough to last me the rest of my life, I can tell you. Swore never to touch another. Gave me an intolerable headache, as I remember. No sense in ruining your health, I always say. Wouldn't you agree, Rotherham?" he added, turning his ruddy, moon-shaped face to his host, who lounged on the opposite side of the table, long legs encased in exquisitely cut riding breeches stretched out before him.

"Quite so," replied Rotherham, amusement softening the harsh lines of his dark, aristocratic features. "But to answer your original question, Tottlefield, we can always change the stakes, if you wish. Anything you care to name."

"What a splendid notion, Chris," cut in the ginger-whiskered gentleman impulsively, striding over to the table and pulling up a chair for himself. "Tell you what, Toby," he added, an irresistible grin spreading over his tanned face. "Let's reverse the wagers and get rid of things we don't want, the way we used to over on the Peninsula when old Rotherham here, with his intolerable luck, had taken our last sou. Remember the time I had to do your guard duty for a whole week?"

"Ah, yes!" exclaimed Toby, his face brightening. "I spent that week in bed, if I remember rightly. But then I got stuck with that spavined breakdown of Coxville's. Hardest mouth of any horse I ever threw a leg over, but I had to ride it on manoeuvres for a month. Sorely tried my patience, Dick, and no mistake."

"Not nearly as much as the time you had to go into town and tell Middleton's ladybird that he had found a replacement. Remember? You came back with your face scratched in a dozen places."

"Lord, yes!" exclaimed Toby hotly. "And Middleton had the infernal gall to laugh at me. I should have called him out," he added belligerently, his usually merry countenance clouding at the thought. "Can't recall why I didn't do so."

"I can." Dick Chatham grinned. "Too close to dinnertime and Middleton was sporting the blunt." He gave Rotherham a sly wink.

Their host let out a crack of laughter which crinkled the corners of his eyes and momentarily dispelled the expression of aloofness he habitually wore.

Toby joined in good-naturedly, then raised his glass. "Here's to old Middleton. I hope his wife's a shrew," he added and drained his brandy noisily.

Attracted by this bantering exchange, several of the other gentlemen had wandered over to the table and were soon engaged in drawing Chatham and Tottlefield out about their gambling days in the army, amid a great deal of laughter and friendly jesting stimulated by generous potions of the excellent brandy Christopher Morville always provided for his houseguests.

One of these gentlemen, whose dark, intense good looks and modishly cut riding coat proclaimed his French heritage, stood behind Richard Chatham's chair, one pale hand resting lightly on the smooth wood, the other negligently fingering a jewelled fob on his waistcoat. He was considerably younger than his companions, who were all in their early or middle thirties, and he owed his inclusion in the Earl of Rotherham's hunting party—a privilege of which he seemed blissfully ignorant—to the happy coincidence of his distant relationship to Captain Richard Chatham, one of the earl's intimate friends. The two cousins had met quite accidentally in Paris during the spring of 1817 at a reception in honour of the Duke of Wellington, commander of the army of occupation. Chatham, always kind and warmhearted despite his reputation as a charming rake, had invited the young *vicomte* Ferdinand Duvalier to visit him in England.

An only son who was accustomed to being the centre of attention during the entire span of his nineteen years, the young *vicomte* had spent a somewhat trying week listening to his fellow guests exchange military reminiscences about the Iron Duke, under whom they had all served at one time or another.

Duvalier automatically raised his glass as the fat gentleman in preposterously tight-fitting clothes and an enormous cascade of lace spilling gracefully over a gorgeous yellow waistcoat called for yet another toast to another comrade-in-arms who had won what appeared to the bored Frenchman a totally ridiculous and senseless wager.

Through the haze of tobacco smoke, Duvalier suddenly noticed that the Earl of Rotherham had taken up the cards and was dealing again. The Englishmen crowded round the table, all talking at once, while Richard Chatham busily recorded their bets in the wager book.

"I have to post down to Bath next week to escort my aunt and her tiresome brood up to London," exclaimed a tall, balding gentleman whose severe, starched-up demeanour had relaxed to a point bordering on boisterousness. "Any takers?" he shouted above the hubbub.

"Done, Forsdyke," replied a youngish blond gentleman, whose neckcloth had been yanked until its highly starched points showed signs of unfashionable limpness. "I'll take you up on that if you'll take on my dashed tailor's bills. The wretch will be the death of me, and you are full of blunt. What do you say?"

"I'll take it," Lord Henry Forsdyke replied enthusiastically. "Got that, Chatham?" he demanded, turning to the ginger-whiskered record keeper.

"Got it," said Chatham laconically.

The cards were dealt and a debt changed hands amidst a loud outburst of laughter and friendly backslapping.

Ferdinand Duvalier watched the play with a puzzled frown which had not disappeared an hour later after a bewildering medley of wagers had been won or lost—he was not at all sure which.

There was a slight lull in the proceedings which were held up while the company at large, most of whom were now decidedly in their cups, quibbled in total seriousness over the relative merits of playing host to a boisterous ten-year-old schoolboy during the entire summer or tooling an antiquated family travelling coach and four around London for a season. Duvalier leaned forward rather unsteadily and demanded to know what kind of game this was in which one could only win someone else's bills, outdated vehicles, or bothersome relatives.

The Earl of Rotherham, who had been listening with cynical amusement to the heated argument among his now highly rambunctious guests, heard the Frenchman's query and turned his bored gaze upon the puzzled youth.

"My dear *vicomte*," he drawled in a languid, faintly supercilious tone which made Duvalier bristle, "I can't believe that you are not saddled with at least something that you would like to be rid of. I know that I am," added the earl, with a short laugh which did nothing to make his countenance less condescending.

"For example, I have a small estate on the Irish coast, half of it under water for six months out of the year; the rest is so low lying that it is practically worthless. But can I sell it? No, I cannot even give it away. But I plan to get rid of it tonight if I can find an unwary taker." The earl paused, his languid gaze sizing up the Frenchman.

"Have you nothing of this annoying, superfluous, or embarrassing nature tucked away in your cupboards or under holland covers over in Paris, *monsieur*?" he drawled gently, a faint smile on his well-shaped lips. "Because if you do, now is the time to put it on the table, figuratively speaking, naturally, and no doubt one of these gentlemen"—he waved a jewelled hand negligently around the smoke-filled room—"will be only too glad to relieve you of it. If you win, that is."

During the earl's speech, the babble of voices had subsided, and the young *vicomte* suddenly found himself the centre of attention. The guests stared at him expectantly, and the French youth flushed uncomfortably, partly from the heat of the wine he had drunk, partly from resentment at the earl's condescending tone which, Duvalier felt sure, implied a certain amused tolerance of a foreigner's youth and ignorance. He had a suspicion he was being baited, and his frustration increased as his own befuddled brain refused to come up with a suitable rejoinder.

Sensing his cousin's discomfort, Chatham came to his rescue.

"Do not tell me, Ferdinand," he said pleasantly, turning to Duvalier with an encouraging smile, "that you have nothing at all you wish to be rid of, because I shall believe you are hoaxing me. Only think what an opportunity you are missing, my dear boy, to unload some burden or obligation which encumbers you. Take Rotherham up on his Irish bog and give him a French one on top of it."

This suggestion met with vociferous approval from the other guests, who were eager for fresh amusement and capriciously swung their support to Duvalier, encouraging him to take on the earl and show him that he could not palm off his old bogs on others with impunity.

"After all, m'boy," Tottlefield informed his host in a stage whisper, his eyes slightly out of focus and his words slurring noticeably, "one good bog deserves another!"

When the uproar that greeted this piece of facetious wit had subsided, Tottlefield turned his ruddy face to Duvalier and peered up at him through half-shut lids.

"Come now, m'lad," he roared in his genial bellow. "Don't disappoint us. I'll back your bog against Rotherham's any day. Just put it on the table, lad, and let Chatham here do the dealing."

During this exchange, the Frenchman's face had lost its petulant expression and now fairly glowed in response to the flattering comments and encouragement heaped upon him by his noisy drinking companions. His self-confidence had returned, fortified by wine and flattery, and as he stared defiantly across the table at his host, he cast about in his mind furiously for a suitable wager.

Suddenly he smiled. His handsome face took on an expression of smug complacency tinged with a hint of secret astonishment as if he were surprised at his own daring.

"*Monsieur le comte* still wishes to dispose of this bog, or whatever you call it?" he asked his host insolently, unable to keep the excitement out of his voice.

"Certainly," the earl replied. "I have never reneged on a bet in my life."

"Perhaps, sir," Duvalier remarked with feigned nonchalance, sensing the growing tension around the table and responding to it with an increasing air of recklessness, "you may wish to change your mind after you hear what I propose to wager." He smiled condescendingly at his host, delighted at the chance to put this odiously superior English lord in his place.

Rotherham, who was already beginning to be bored with the whole affair, chose to ignore this impertinent remark but shot a speaking glance across the table at Richard Chatham, who grimaced in reply and suppressed a rueful grin.

"Consider your wager accepted," the earl said in neutral tones. "My bog is on the table, so to speak. What do you put up in exchange?"

"Unfortunately, I have no French bog to offer you, milord," Duvalier replied unctuously. "For some reason, we French are sadly lacking in bogs." The brandy he had consumed, topped by his present unexpected sense of importance, made him loquacious. "But I do have an encumbrance, as you call it, which is far worse than any bog. Like your bog, milord, I can neither sell it nor give it away."

Here he paused to survey the company through the haze of smoke, a sly gleam in his eyes. Predictably, his fellow guests responded with hoots of encouragement; only the earl remained impassive, a saturnine smile flickering on his thin lips.

"Get on with it, man," bellowed Tottlefield in acute agony. "I cannot bear this suspense any longer." Several of the other gentlemen loudly took up his plea, and Duvalier raised a hand to quiet their noisy protestations.

"It is past its prime, for one thing," he continued, still dallying with his audience. "Past the age when it could have served a useful purpose. Nobody wants it now, but perhaps milord can find some place for it among his other useless possessions.''

''Hang me if this fellow ain't about to jaw us all to death,'' bellowed Tottlefield, exasperated beyond human endurance. ''Tell us at once what it is or we'll tar and feather you.''

Duvalier looked around the circle of faces and savoured his triumph. ''Gentlemen,'' he began, grasping his cousin's chair more firmly with one hand, for the room suddenly seemed to sway before his eyes. ''I wish to wager . . .'' He paused to take up his glass with unsteady fingers.

''An old jade, no doubt,'' someone shouted in disgust.

''Not in the sense you mean, *monsieur*''—Duvalier laughed delightedly—''but you come close. Milord.'' He raised his glass and with visible effort focused his heated gaze on his host across the table. ''I put my maiden aunt on the table! Figuratively speaking, naturally.''

This bizarre announcement was followed by a stunned silence. ''Damn me if that don't take the cake!'' Sir James Langton, the earl's brother-in-law, muttered after he had recovered from his initial amazement. Toby Tottlefield was seized by a violent paroxysm of coughing, while several other gentlemen cleared their throats uneasily.

''Do I understand you to say, *monsieur,* that you wish to dispose of a blood relative on the gambling table?'' the earl inquired without raising his voice but in tones so chilled that Duvalier glanced around him uncomfortably.

''P-precisely,'' he stammered, glaring mulishly into his host's grim face. ''That is precisely what I wish to do, milord,'' he added with an attempt at bravado, deliberately ignoring a warning glance from Chatham, who had turned in his chair at Duvalier's unexpected announcement.

''Very well,'' said the earl in a voice that dripped ice. ''Deal the cards, Chatham.''

''Chris, do not, I pray you, do anything you will later regret,'' pleaded Chatham earnestly. ''After all, we are all pretty well foxed, old man.''

''Speak for yourself, cousin,'' cut in the Frenchman impulsively, his face flushed at the idea of being thwarted. ''And in case you had not heard, a Duvalier never goes back on his word. Now if others wish to do so,'' he babbled on in a burst of temerity that left the company—who knew only too well their host's reputation as a crack marksman—shocked and breathless, "that is entirely another matter."

The earl had gone very white and his eyes glittered dangerously, but he had himself under tight control.

"Deal, Chatham," he repeated softly, his eyes never leaving Duvalier's face.

"I'd rather not be involved in this foolishness," Chatham replied shortly, and passed the cards over to Tottlefield who picked them up gingerly as though they might bite him.

His chubby fingers trembled slightly as he shuffled the deck, and the room suddenly became so still that the slap of the cards sounded unnaturally loud and even faintly ominous, as if the Fates, who had for thirty-five years smiled indulgently on the Earl of Rotherham, had decided to take a perverse hand in the game.

# 1 ·····
# The Arrival

ON A RAW January afternoon, two months later, a hired travelling chaise drew up in front of a rambling sixteenth-century country house in the heart of Dorsetshire, deposited a solitary female, two small trunks, an old-fashioned dressing case, and a large covered bird cage on the elegant marble stairway, and departed—after a brief but pithy altercation between the driver and the passenger over the size of the tip—in a flurry of angry whip cracks and flying gravel.

With a wry smile on her weary face, the traveller trod resolutely up the wide stairs and had raised her gloved hand to knock when the ornate oaken door swung slowly open. A shrivelled, pixie-faced butler, who looked at least as old as the house though not as well preserved, peered out at her suspiciously from beneath tangled clumps of grizzled eyebrows.

"I am looking for the Earl of Rotherham," announced the strange female in a crisp, faintly foreign voice which did not betray by so much as a quiver the apprehension she was feeling.

The butler blinked in surprise, his dry lips puckering critically. In over sixty-five years of service in the Morville establishment, Fortham had seen many females come and go, inquiring for one Rotherham or another, but few of them arrived unannounced and unattended in hired chaises. Those who did were usually directed to the servants' entrance or sent about their business.

But the lady who now stood before him did not fit into either category. Her pelisse and bonnet, though devoid of all but the barest fur trimming and a long way from being in the first stare of fashion, had an air of quiet elegance about them which the butler's practised eye detected instantly. What impressed him most forcibly, however, was the cool air of authority in the visitor's wide hazel eyes which were now focused upon him expectantly.

9

"The earl is not in residence, ma'am," he replied with prim satisfaction in a voice that creaked with age or lack of use, or so the traveller, who enjoyed a lively sense of humour, thought to herself in grim amusement.

"So much the better for both of us," she declared in a firm voice, and the startled butler stared at her, unable, as he told the housekeeper, Mrs. Collins, in the servants' hall that evening, to believe his ears.

"I will see Lady Ephigenia Morville instead," added the visitor, taking advantage of Fortham's amazement to step past him into the hall. "Be so good as to have my luggage brought in before it snows and Bijou catches his death of cold," she continued briskly, for all the world, Fortham would later relay to the housekeeper, as if she were the lady of the house returning from a season in London.

"Whom shall I say is calling, ma'am?" the butler inquired, his voice rigid with disapproval at this high-handed behaviour.

The visitor, apparently wise in the ways of servants, flashed him a conciliatory smile. "Please tell Lady Ephigenia that Miss Diana Wetherby has arrived from Paris. She is expecting me, I believe."

Five minutes later, Miss Wetherby, having followed the butler's painful progress up the thickly carpeted stairs, was ushered into a small, elegantly appointed drawing-room where a bright fire burned invitingly in the wide hearth. At first glance, she imagined the room to be empty, but as she approached the fire with the intention of warming her chilled hands, a tiny figure bounced out of a deep armchair beside the hearth and rushed to greet her effusively.

"My dear Miss Wetherby," exclaimed this diminutive figure enthusiastically. "I'm so glad . . ." But the greeting died on her lips and she stopped abruptly, staring at Diana Wetherby in disbelief.

"There must be some mistake," her ladyship murmured distractedly. "You cannot be Miss Wetherby." She looked so disappointed that her visitor could not resist smiling.

"Oh, but I am indeed, ma'am. I have it on the highest authority, too," she added, letting her amusement get the better of her. "So you may rest easy on that account. After all, why should my poor dear Mama deceive me on an issue of such relatively minor importance?"

"Oh, dear me!" exclaimed her ladyship, slightly flushed at the very thought of such a thing. "I don't doubt it for a minute, my dear. Not for a single moment.'' Then she stopped and broke into a sudden tinkling laugh. "But that is not true at all, is it? Because I certainly did doubt, didn't I? But I meant no offense, my dear, no offense at all. Only it did strike me as highly unlikely, that is to say . . .''

She faltered, and a gleam of amusement crept into her sharp blue eyes. "To tell you the plain truth, my dear, you look far too young,'' she blurted out with another gurgle of laughter and drew her visitor forward towards the warmth of the fire and helped her remove her bonnet and pelisse.

"You will hardly call six and twenty young, ma'am,'' protested Miss Wetherby, as her hostess settled her into a comfortable chair and rang the bell vigorously for the tea tray. "After all, I have been at my last prayers for ages,'' she added, luxuriating in the attention that her ladyship seemed determined to lavish upon her.

"Fiddle!'' exclaimed her hostess, fixing her lively gaze on Miss Wetherby. "You are no simpering schoolroom chit, I will admit, but you hardly look a day over twenty, my dear, and I was led to believe by that pesky nephew of mine, although he didn't actually say so, now that I come to think of it,'' she put in hastily, "that our visitor from Paris was an old parrot-faced Tabby like me, and I was quite looking forward to a cosy exchange of crim-con. stories.''

Miss Wetherby felt quite overcome by this startling frankness, which she imagined might well be one of her ladyship's most endearing traits. Her sense of humour prompted her to reply with equal openness.

"I would never call you parrot-faced, Lady Ephigenia,'' she ventured with a teasing smile. "And I always thought of a Tabby as an old harridan which, I assure you, my lady, you are not. I do hope, however,'' she added apprehensively, "that you are not too disappointed in me. I will do my best to—''

"No, no, no! Not at all,'' interrupted her ladyship impetuously, jumping up to supervise the placing of the tea-tray on a low table in front of the fire. "I never meant to imply anything so addle-pated, my dear, although I know I said so,'' she added illogically. "You just took me by surprise, that is all.''

Diana could only be thankful that she had passed this first hurdle. Her dear Aunt Sophy, whom she had left safely installed with an old school friend in London, had been anxious about her ability to impersonate a maiden aunt of advanced years.

"But I *am* a maiden aunt of advanced years,'' Diana had

insisted patiently. "And I'm sure the Morvilles will not even care which maiden aunt they get. It's not as if we are deceiving them, dearest. I *am* Miss Wetherby, maiden aunt to Ferdinand Duvalier."

"That's cutting it rather fine, my love," Aunt Sophy had protested. "I wish you would listen to reason and let me go to Morville Grange as both your nephew and that heartless brother of yours intended."

Diana had dismissed this suggestion out of hand. Aunt Sophy had not been in good health and the inordinately rough crossing from Calais to Dover had left her prostrate. So Diana had overridden her aunt's scruples and posted down to Morville Grange to take on the role of resident maiden aunt in her place.

She was roused from her musing by her hostess's animated chatter.

"On second thought, I can see we shall deal famously together." Lady Ephigenia smiled, and a delightful dimple appeared on her chin. "It will be such a relief to have someone intelligent to talk to," she confessed candidly. "We are so quiet here at the Grange this time of the year, although my nephew, Lord Rotherham, sometimes brings a hunting party down during the season for a week or two and fills the house with dogs, guns, and tobacco smoke."

The mention of Lord Rotherham brought a slight frown to Miss Wetherby's face and the animation died out of it. She needed to know just how much her hostess knew of the true nature of her presence at the Grange.

"I assume, Lady Ephigenia," she said in a sober voice, "that you are aware of the circumstances of my presence here?"

"Of course, my dear," exclaimed her ladyship, who had caught the bleak look in her guest's fine hazel eyes and wondered at it. "Christopher . . . Lord Rotherham, that is, told me all about you. In fact, he was quite loquacious, which surprised me. He is not usually one for explaining why he does things, you know." Here she paused to share a smile with her guest.

"He did say you were a relative of Richard Chatham's and are going through a very distressing time," she continued. "And everyone knows how close Christopher and Dick are—they grew up together, you see. The Chathams have an estate on the other side of Melbury, almost as old as Morville Grange but not so solidly built. They have had to make extensive repairs over the years, while the Grange is exactly as it was when I was a girl. I was born here, my dear, and that was a good many years ago, I can tell you,'' she added with a wry laugh. "So was Christopher. In fact, most of the Morvilles for the past two hundred years were born here; it is a family tradition, except that . . .''

Here her ladyship paused to stare abstractedly into the fire, her hands clasped tightly in the lap of her green figured-silk afternoon dress. Then, with a little shake of her crimped curls, she turned back to her guest with an elfin smile on her kind face.

"Here I am, rambling on as usual''—she laughed—"when what I wanted to say is that Christopher and Dick are such good friends, almost brothers you could say, so it is hardly surprising that my nephew should invite you to the Grange to recuperate. He is so thoughtful. Chatham House is closed most of the year, you see, because Lady Chatham prefers Town life to the quiet of the country. And I was delighted with the idea, of course, even though you have turned out to be only half my age.'' She chuckled, her blue eyes twinkling with good humour.

While Diana Wetherby digested this unexpected information which gave a rather different picture of the earl's character than the one she had received from her nephew, Ferdinand Duvalier, and convinced her that her charming hostess knew nothing of the real nature of her arrival at Morville Grange, her ladyship jumped up again to wait on her guest.

"Have some more tea, my dear Miss Wetherby,'' she said in a motherly tone. "Or may I call you Diana, my love? As you can see, I am not one to stand on points.''

"Please do, ma'am,'' her guest hastened to reply, as her ladyship poured the tea.

"Such a pretty name, I have always thought,'' her ladyship rattled on. "So woodsy and mythological, although I don't hold with bathing without a stitch on in the moonlight,'' she added incongruously. "One never knows who might happen to be in the neighbourhood. Poachers and other riffraff, I mean. Besides, it is not quite the accepted thing, even for a goddess, don't you agree, my dear? I cannot imagine what inspired her to indulge in such a caper . . . and I always felt rather sorry for Actaeon. He sounded like such an innocent, well-behaved boy, if you know what I mean, dear . . .''

While her loquacious hostess prattled on about the unseemly and capricious behaviour of Greek goddesses in general and Miss Wetherby's namesake in particular, Diana had been struggling with an uneasy conscience.

She had not bargained on having to sustain a double imposture. It was clear that her hostess had accepted her identity as the genuine maiden aunt without question. Should she, however, remove the second deception by revealing the true circumstances of her presence under Lord Rotherham's roof or allow her ladyship to continue in the belief that this visit was purely a recuperative one?

A natural honesty urged her to take the former course, in spite of the embarrassing position in which such a confession would certainly place her. Yet, she also felt strongly tempted to let this particular sleeping dog lie, at least for the time being, since Lord Rotherham himself had obviously gone to some trouble to conceal the shocking truth from his aunt.

Perhaps, Diana thought ruefully, the earl had experienced a pang of conscience for having contributed to her present highly compromising situation. Although this explanation for his devious behaviour seemed decidedly suspect, she reasoned, if one were to believe—and she was only too ready to believe them—half the stories her unscrupulous nephew, Ferdinand, had told her about the Earl of Rotherham's notorious reputation. She could not suppress a shudder of disgust at the thought of being in the power of such a man.

"Good gracious! You are shivering, child," her ladyship exclaimed, handing Diana a fresh cup of steaming tea. "Draw your chair closer to the fire, my dear," she insisted solicitously and with such genuine kindness that Diana, tired, heartsore, and very apprehensive about her future, felt a sudden uncharacteristic desire to burst into tears.

She was saved from this embarrassing show of missishness by Fortham, who shuffled into the room at that point to demand, in tones of offended dignity, what Miss desired him to do with the parrot.

"Parrot?" exclaimed her ladyship delightedly. "Don't tell me you have brought a parrot all the way from Paris, my dear. How exciting! Do bring it in here, Fortham. I simply must see it," she cried with such childish enthusiasm that Diana was distracted from her own heavy thoughts.

Fortham presently returned with a liveried footman carrying the covered cage which had arrived with Miss Wetherby and from which issued a series of piercing whistles, punctuated by cracks of diabolical laughter.

"He seems very lively," her ladyship commented nervously, an understatement that the butler acknowledged by casting his eyes heavenwards in a gesture full of martyred resignation as he closed the door.

"Oh, he always gets excited when he travels, my lady," Diana explained as she removed the cover from the cage.

The noise ceased abruptly as the bird, a handsome white cockatoo with a flamboyant yellow crest curling defiantly on top of his head, eyed her ladyship curiously.

"Oh, how beautiful!" she exclaimed. "I have never seen such a gorgeous creature. What do you call him, dear?"

"Bijou, Bijou, Bijou, and who are you?" said the parrot so clearly that her ladyship jumped.

Diana laughed. "As you see, Bijou has no manners at all, and he can be quite a chatterbox if you encourage him," she warned.

"Fudge!" said the parrot conversationally and sidled across his perch to stare up at her ladyship with bright obsidian eyes. *"Quelle sottise!"* he added, shaking his head from side to side.

"He is absolutely charming," her ladyship exclaimed in admiration. "Is he tame, though?"

"Yes, indeed," replied Diana, as they sat down before the fire again. "Bijou has been with me forever. My father brought him home from India for my dear Mama's birthday when I was still in the schoolroom and he quickly became one of the family. In fact, now that both my parents are gone, old Bijou is all that I have left. Except for an elderly aunt on my father's side of the family," she added, determined to tell as much of the truth as possible.

"But Rotherham mentioned something about a half brother if I remember rightly," began her ladyship in a puzzled voice.

"Oh, yes. That is Jean-Pierre, my mother's son from her first marriage with the *comte* Duvalier. But he doesn't count, you see, for we have never been close. He is so much older and besides, as head of the family, Jean-Pierre bitterly resented Mama's second marriage to Colonel Wetherby, so it was only natural that he should resent me too. Especially since I take after the Wetherby side of the family."

"Fiddle!" interrupted Bijou loudly.

"I couldn't agree more, Bijou," her ladyship said, an indignant frown on her merry face. "Fiddle, indeed! There is nothing natural about that, let me tell you. After all, you were hardly in a position to have any say in the matter, much less prevent your mother from marrying whomever she chose, my dear."

"And if I *had* been," Diana declared with irrational fervour, "I would most certainly never have opposed it. Mama's second marriage was a true love match, you see," she added, a sweet smile suddenly transforming her rather serious features. "Not at all like her marriage to Duvalier, which was arranged by her father when she was barely seventeen."

Lady Ephigenia clicked her tongue sympathetically. "My two sisters were disposed of in the same fashion," she said, shaking her head at the recollection. "Excellent alliances, both of them, for my father had a great sense of his own consequence; he was a true Morville in that respect. They are all sticklers for propriety . . . particularly in others," she added, with a mischievous twinkle which caused Diana to smile again.

"That sounds exactly like Jean-Pierre." She laughed. "Except that he is stuffy and starched up too, and he married a woman who is worse than he is: a regular pattern card of respectability. Anne-Marie always disapproved of Papa, who was gay and fun loving like Mama, and she never missed a chance to make poor Mama feel miserable by pointing out that he was also improvident.

"Which, of course, he was," she added after a small pause. "There is no denying it. But I cannot find it in my heart to blame him, for he made us both so happy, especially dear Mama. When I look back, I realize he must have spent a fortune on her clothes alone, not to mention the extravagant baubles he was forever giving her. And then, poor dear, she had to sell everything and live with those two fustian nip-cheeses, in a house Papa had given them, furthermore."

Her ladyship made sympathetic noises and poured them each another cup of tea.

"Oh, it was just too lowering," Diana burst out impulsively. "No wonder she faded away into a shadow and died of a broken heart. It was like taking an orchid out of the hothouse and trying to grow it in a woodshed. Poor, dear Mama! I blame myself for not getting married when I had the chance . . .

"But please forgive me, my lady," she broke off in sudden embarrassment. "I shouldn't burden you with all these tedious family details. I cannot imagine what came over me, it's just that . . ."

"Rubbish!" cut in Bijou energetically.

"Exactly so!" agreed her ladyship, her blue eyes snapping angrily as indignation at a son's unfeeling treatment of his own mother welled up in her tender heart. "What a perfectly awful, shabby-genteel thing to do, my love. That brother of yours sounds like a regular loose screw if you ask me," she added hotly. "A thoroughly odious creature, my dear, with no sense of propriety at all."

"Oh, but the worst part is that his intentions were good, or so he always claimed," Diana pointed out. "He felt that he was helping poor Mama to overcome her weakness for finery and extravagant living."

"That is the most outrageous piece of nonsense I have ever heard," retorted her ladyship acidly. "And I do object to people whose good intentions always seem to benefit them and inconvenience everyone else. I only wonder that you did not go into a decline yourself, my love. Did they not attempt to reform you as well with these so-called good intentions?"

"Can you doubt it, ma'am?" Diana laughed, her spirits revived by the tea and the friendliness of this cheerful creature who seemed to know instinctively how to make a person comfortable. "But I am afraid I made it rather difficult for them. I am not as good-natured as Mama, by a long way, and Anne-Marie was always coming to cuffs with me about something. She particularly objected to Bijou, for instance, and I have to admit that he can be noisy. But the children—I really am on the shelf, you know, for I have five nieces and a nephew—anyway, they would tease him so, which naturally made me furious."

"Those Duvaliers sound like thoroughly disagreeable people to me and I imagine they were thankful to see you leave, my dear," her hostess observed dryly and was startled to see that sudden bleak look cross Diana's face again.

Little did she know that her casual remark had brought back very unpleasant memories for her guest. As Diana stared moodily into the fire, she was remembering Jean-Pierre's heavy-jowled face, set in rigid indignation at her refusal to accept an offer from an old friend of his who had been pestering her with his attentions.

"You will do as I say, my girl," Jean-Pierre had shouted at her. "Or you and that antiquated aunt of yours will no longer be welcome in my house."

When Diana had pointed out that the suitor in question was more than twice her age, he had exploded into a tirade of abuse which had left her pale and trembling with anger and frustration. She was to have no choice in the matter. It was either accept a husband old enough to be her father or both she and her dear Aunt Sophy would be thrown out on the street.

Jean-Pierre had been adamant. Diana had realized that she

would eventually have to accept his terms. Luckily, before she actually committed herself, she learned of Ferdinand's absurd wager with the English earl. She had naturally assumed that it would be set aside as preposterous and insulting to her Aunt Sophy, since the latter had, although unrelated by blood, always treated Ferdinand as her nephew.

But Jean-Pierre, in his narrow selfishness, had only been able to see his son's predicament. The Duvalier honour was at stake, he had declared in his pompous, sententious voice. And when she had asked how that same honour could be salvaged by condemning her aunt to live out the rest of her days in the custody of a strange man without the benefit of a marriage license, he had accused her of being ungrateful and of using feminine logic.

The last straw, however, had been the spiteful remark from her sister-in-law that Aunt Sophy possessed neither the face nor the figure to be in any danger from anyone of such immense wealth and good breeding as the Earl of Rotherham. "And if you wish to escape the same fate, Diana, you had best listen to your brother's advice," she had added maliciously. "He only wants the best for you; besides which, you are already long past your prime, *cherie.*"

Diana knew this to be true, but it was one thing to know one is on the shelf and quite another for her self-righteous sister-in-law to tell her so in that odiously smug way of hers.

Diana closed her eyes briefly to dispel these painful memories and opened them again to find Lady Ephigenia gazing at her quizzically, her blue eyes full of concern.

"Why, yes," Diana said with a faint smile. "I can well imagine they were indeed only too happy to see the last of us. Right, Bijou?"

"Good night," echoed the parrot solemnly.

Diana refrained from clarifying that she had failed to consult her brother and had escaped from the house with a minimum of luggage and her precious Bijou to join Aunt Sophy in the dilapidated chaise hired to convey her to Calais.

"*Pshaw!* You are well rid of them, my love," snorted her ladyship, visibly incensed by this callousness. "And even though they *are* your relatives, dear, I find it extremely improper of them to allow you to junket all over England by yourself."

"At my advanced age, there is hardly need for a chaperone," murmured Diana mendaciously. "And besides—"

"Oh, fiddle!" exclaimed her ladyship. "I don't want to hear any more of that cockle-headed flummery. Now, come along, my love,'' she added brightly, jumping to her feet and catching Diana by the hand. "I'll take you upstairs and help you get settled in. And once you get that foolish notion out of your head that you are some kind of superannuated old maiden aunt, I think you are going to enjoy yourself here at the Grange.''

Later that night, as Diana lay snugly in her warm feather bed, she had to admit that Lady Ephigenia, or Aunt Effie, as she had been instructed to call her hostess, was probably right.

In the space of a few short hours, she already felt the soothing effects of Morville Grange, a well-run establishment where servants were discreet, efficient, and practically invisible, and the food was not cold by the time it got to the table. She particularly appreciated the fire in her bedchamber (an unheard-of luxury in her brother's house) and the warming pan wielded by a pleasant, rosy-faced girl in a mobcap. Her only regret was that dear Aunt Sophy was not there to enjoy these comforts with her.

But it was Lady Ephigenia herself, Diana realized, with her cheerful friendliness and quick sympathy, who had given her unhappy guest reason to believe that perhaps the Fates had tempered their sentence with a touch of unexpected compassion and that her future at Morville Grange as Lord Rotherham's pensioner might not be quite so bleak as she had anticipated.

# 2 .....

# Accidental Encounter

By the end of January, Diana felt even more inclined to believe that the Fates had been lenient with her, and by mid-March, thanks to a growing affection for her hostess, she was certain of it.

Lady Ephigenia proved to be an amusing and indefatigable companion and, as a firm believer in fresh air and plenty of exercise, she had an immediate influence on Diana's sense of well-being. Rarely an afternoon passed, weather permitting, when the two ladies did not don their fur-lined boots, warm cloaks, and mufflers and spend two or three happy hours trudging along country lanes, exploring the Home Wood or following the many bridle paths that crisscrossed the extensive Morville estate.

If they felt like roaming further afield, Lady Ephigenia would order her yellow tilbury brought round, and they would drive off at a smart pace behind a mettlesome roan cob that her ladyship handled with aplomb and easy competence, to run errands in nearby Melbury, pay afternoon calls on the local gentry, visit one or another of the earl's tenants with baskets of food from the Grange kitchens, or stop in for tea and crumpets with the vicar.

This worthy gentleman, Jonathan Fenley, and his elderly sister, Josephine, had become fast friends with Miss Wetherby, and she was often a guest for tea at their pleasant cottage next to the vicarage in Melbury. In fact, the vicar was beginning to show a marked deference to Miss Wetherby's opinion on various matters concerning the parish, and his sister had already enlisted the visitor's assistance in selecting materials for the small school she had started for the village children.

When Lady Ephigenia discovered quite by accident that Diana was a notable whip and horsewoman, who had been taught by Colonel Wetherby to be at home to a peg both in the saddle and at the reins of his curricle-and-four, Lady Ephigenia was quite content to allow her guest to take over the driving of the roan cob on their little expeditions around the countryside.

"It is a pleasure to see you handle the ribbons, my love," she remarked one afternoon after watching Diana manoeuvre the tilbury down Melbury's crowded High Street in grand style.

As she spoke, her ladyship observed her companion affectionately and noted with deep satisfaction that life at Morville Grange had done wonders for the pale, thin-faced young woman who had arrived there a little over two months ago. Diana Wetherby would never be a great Beauty, her ladyship had to admit, especially in an age when fair-haired, ethereal creatures with die-away airs were all the rage. Her features were pleasant, however, and she had laughing, expressive hazel eyes, an easy self-assured elegance, and a truly charming smile. And now that she had lost that peaked look around her well-shaped mouth and allowed her ladyship's dresser to arrange her dark auburn hair in a more flattering style, Miss Wetherby had begun to attract admiring glances among the local swains.

But it was her guest's ready wit and superior intellect that had won Lady Effie's respect and admiration. An avid reader herself, she had been delighted to find a fellow bibliophile in Diana, and the two ladies spent many a rainy afternoon discussing the merits of a particular novel before a cosy fire in the library.

Diana's enjoyment of this pleasant occupation was interrupted late one afternoon by the disturbing news, delivered in a lugubrious voice by the worthy Fortham, that the Earl of Rotherham had sent down a message with his man Clintock announcing his arrival for a few weeks of hunting at the Grange with a small party of friends.

Diana could not share Lady Ephigenia's happy anticipation of this event and spent a restless night. Her vivid imagination caused a riot of conflicting emotions to keep her wide awake long after the grandfather clock in the hall downstairs tolled the hour of midnight. Even after she managed to fall into an uneasy sleep, the alarming news of the Earl of Rotherham's imminent arrival filled her dreams. And when she woke at an unusually early hour the next morning, the apprehension she had felt the night before had abated very little.

Perhaps I have misjudged him after all, she tried to tell herself, braving the chill morning air to reach out and pull the tasselled bell rope hanging next to her bed to summon the maid Lady Ephigenia had insisted she needed.

When Molly bustled into the room with a steaming cup of chocolate and a kettle of hot water for her young mistress's morning ablutions, Diana had climbed out of bed and was inspecting her old riding habit with a rueful eye.

Compared to the fashionable brown velvet habit worn by Lady Ephigenia the previous afternoon, her own, much faded, green habit gave her a momentary feeling of despair at the unfairness of her fate.

If only, she thought, I had accepted one of the many offers from those dashing officers in Papa's regiment. Although she knew that most of them had been second sons and in straightened circumstances, as was Colonel Wetherby himself when he had married her dear Mama, she might have achieved the happiness her mother had enjoyed. If only . . .

She shook herself impatiently. No use crying over what might have been. What I need now is a good gallop in the park to clear away all these doleful thoughts.

An hour later, she was cantering across the wide park, mounted on Perseus, the sleek bay gelding Lady Ephigenia had encouraged her to ride once she discovered that Diana was well able to handle such a mettlesome horse.

The sun was barely showing itself behind the Home Wood, the dew sparkled on the well-kept grass, and a thrush practised a series of trills in the hawthorn hedgerow bordering the lane beyond the impressive stone entrance to the Grange.

Diana felt better already.

Perseus seemed to sense the exuberance and optimism that surged through her veins at the thrill and promise of a new day. His canter lengthened to a gallop and his ears pricked up expectantly as they neared the stone gateway.

On impulse, Diana decided to ride down to the village. She knew it was probably improper of her to do so without the protective presence of Lady Ephigenia or Ben, the old groom who had been hired many years ago expressly to accompany the impetuous young Lady Ephigenia Morville on her dashing excursions in her high-perch phaeton.

But this morning Diana felt daring and rejoiced in her superbly responsive mount and the exhilarating caress of the morning air on her cheeks. For a moment she felt she was back in Paris putting one of her dear Papa's thoroughbreds through its paces in the Bois de Boulogne, to the great delight of her retinue of admirers from among his junior officers.

Carried away by these happy thoughts, Diana momentarily relaxed her control over Perseus, and the horse, sensing the abandon in its rider, surged out of the entrance and streaked down the lane in a thunder of hooves and flying mud.

Unfazed by these developments, Diana settled herself firmly in the saddle and let Perseus have his head. After all, there would be nobody in the lane at this early hour. And it stretched for nearly five miles before it entered the village. She would have plenty of time to bring Perseus back to a sedate canter before then, she told herself. And it's been so long since I have enjoyed the thrill of a race, she reasoned.

At the back of her mind, a nagging little voice murmured that such ramshackle behaviour was to be condemned in a young lady of quality, but Diana pushed the thought impatiently aside and bent lower over Perseus's neck to urge him to greater speed.

The horse responded willingly and, in what seemed to his exuberant rider no time at all, had covered the two-mile stretch running parallel to the Morville estate and was approaching the curve which branched off towards the little village of Melbury.

At the sight of the curve in the lane ahead, Diana gathered up the reins and tried to slacken her horse's breakneck pace. Perseus, however, had other ideas. He fought the bit and Diana found that, pull as she might, he refused to resume a more prudent gait.

It never occurred to her to be frightened. As an experienced horsewoman she had dealt with runaway mounts before. So she kept her head and sat tight, waiting for Perseus to run himself out as she knew he would eventually.

And so he would have if, at that precise moment, a curricle and four beautifully matched greys had not materialized in the lane ahead of him going at a pace calculated to arouse the envy of every member of the Four-in-Hand Club.

So concentrated was she on her own precarious situation that Diana did not see the oncoming vehicle until it was almost on top of her. When she did perceive the danger, it was too late to avoid disaster.

The four greys, taking violent exception to the bay gelding hurtling towards them, broke their perfect formation and swerved towards the ditch, rearing and pawing in a tangle of twisted traces.

As Diana pulled a suddenly docile Perseus to a prancing halt beside them, she had a confused glimpse of a many-caped gentleman fighting desperately with the reins. She watched in horror as the right wheel of the curricle hit a large stone and the whole equipage toppled over, dumping the driver unceremoniously in the ditch.

A small Tiger who had been riding behind his master was thrown clear of the carriage but landed with such a resounding thump that Diana was sure he must be either dead or unconscious, until she saw him get quickly to his feet.

Leaving him to attend to the driver of the curricle, Diana quickly dismounted and rushed to pacify the greys. She knew that such highly strung cattle could easily break their legs if not extracted immediately from the tangle of traces. She didn't want that on her conscience as well. By the time she had soothed the trembling, snorting horses, she was joined by the small groom, who seemed none the worse for his fall.

"I'll take 'em, miss," he said. "You see about his lordship. He ain't so much as twitched since he went into that ditch. Lor' love us, miss, I 'ope he ain't gone and died on us."

He rubbed a torn sleeve across his brow and glared at Diana with such belligerence that she felt the need to justify herself.

"If he has, he may blame himself for it," she retorted curtly. "I never saw such an irresponsible whipster. I have a good mind to report him to the local magistrate for endangering the lives of innocent travellers. He could have killed me."

She paused after this somewhat illogical pronouncement, unable to account for the sly grin that appeared on the Tiger's sharp face.

"Better see if he's alive first, miss," was his laconic response, accompanied by a nod in the direction of the overturned curricle.

Diana picked her way through the weeds and peered around the still spinning wheels of the vehicle. What she saw made her gasp and throw herself on her knees beside the prone form of the driver.

Gingerly she unbuttoned his many-caped driving cloak and loosened the elegantly tied cravat which was now stained with blood from an ugly looking cut on the gentleman's left cheek. At the sight of the blood, she felt a moment of queasiness but forgot it the next instant when her tentative touch on the gentleman's muscular chest revealed that the unconscious driver's heart was still beating.

"I'll need some water here," she called to the groom, mildly surprised at the steadiness of her voice.

"Got me 'ands full, miss," came the curt reply. "There's a

flask of brandy around someplace, if it ain't got broke. His lordship never travels nowheres without it.''

Glancing around the wreckage of the carriage, Diana spotted the silver flask under a tangle of rugs and pulled it out. After assuring herself, as best she could, that the driver had no broken bones, Diana sat on the damp grass and, settling the dazed gentleman's head comfortably in her lap, opened the flask and poured a small amount of brandy between his clenched teeth.

The results were encouraging.

After several swallows, which brought on a severe bout of coughing, the gentleman's eyes flickered open and he gazed up at Diana with a bemused expression. Diana could not control a great sigh of relief.

"I'm so glad you are not dead, sir," she exclaimed impulsively. "It would have been an impossible coil if you had been. Most inconvenient and untimely," she rushed on, too relieved at his escape and disturbed by the amused appraisal in the gentleman's intense gaze to pay much attention to what she was saying.

"For you or for me?" came the droll reply.

Diana gave an embarrassed laugh. "For all of us, I meant. Although you especially don't deserve to be so lucky, the way you were racing those beautiful greys. Shame on you, sir. You should know better."

"My God, the greys." The gentleman suddenly seemed to remember where he was and struggled into a reclining position. "Where are they? Did they come to any harm? And what about Jeremy? Where's that rogue? Not dead, I hope?"

"The greys are safe, sir. So is your groom. Here, let me help you," she cried as the gentleman struggled to sit up. "You may have broken or twisted something."

"Nonsense," he exclaimed impatiently. "Merely a few bumps and bruises, I assure you." He pulled away from Diana's solicitous grasp on his elbow, but when he tried to rise, he had to clutch the side of the upturned curricle with a suppressed groan of pain.

"What did I tell you," Diana told him crisply. "You are hurt more than you realize. Here, lean on me and don't be so stubborn, sir. It serves no useful purpose."

"Jeremy," the gentleman called weakly, ignoring Diana's proffered arm. "Where the devil are you, man?"

Diana had by now scrambled to her feet and took the time to examine the driver of the curricle more closely. It did not take her more than a quick perusal of his person, from his unruly dark hair and aristocratic profile, down to his superbly cut boots to decide that he was definitely a member of the *ton* and quite impossibly handsome. His temper, however, left much to be desired, she felt.

He is obnoxiously toplofty and full of his own consequence into the bargain, she thought ruefully, brushing off her riding skirt and tucking several stray curls back into place under her practical bonnet. She was a bit miffed that he had completely ignored her offer of assistance, although he was obviously in some pain. He reminded her forcibly of the young officers in her father's regiment who would come back from battle with serious wounds their sense of honour would not permit them to acknowledge as anything more than scratches.

She considered such behaviour the height of foolishness and was about to say so to this imperious gentleman, who had finally allowed her to help him sit against the turn of an old oak tree, his mouth twisted into a grimace of pain, when a commotion in the lane drew her attention in that direction.

She saw that Jeremy had managed to calm the greys into comparative quiet, but they were now eyeing the approach of a farm wagon piled high with hay with snorts of incipient panic. Instinctively taking the initiative, she stepped into the lane and, signalling the wagon to halt, quickly persuaded the two stalwart lads in charge of it to pull the curricle out of the ditch and set it upright in the lane.

Diana was relieved to see that the dashing-looking vehicle had suffered little real damage and she was able, with Jeremy's help, to get the reluctant greys back into the traces.

She had had to ask the two farm lads to lift the gentleman—in spite of his feeble protests—into the curricle, for he was patently unable to get into it himself, having lapsed into a semicoma. When he was settled to her satisfaction, a warm rug around his shoulders and another tucked over his knees, she calmly took up the reins of the restive greys.

"You can ride my horse, Jeremy, and follow along behind us. I am taking his lordship to Morville Grange where we can summon a doctor to look him over. I greatly fear he may have sustained some serious injuries."

Jeremy gaped at her. "Nobody drives them greys but his lordship," he stated categorically. "And certainly no female. Perish the thought." He grasped the leaders by their halters and

glared up at her. "It's worth me job it is, miss," he added in a
pleading voice.

"Kindly bring up my horse, then," Diana said, appearing to
concede to the groom's request.

No sooner had Jeremy caught up Perseus's reins, however, than
he heard the sound of nervous hooves and turned to see the
curricle rattle off down the lane at a fine pace.

Cursing under his breath at all the tribe of female busybodies
who insisted on making his life impossible, Jeremy swung up on
Perseus and galloped after the curricle. He fully expected the greys
to bolt with that meddling minx and hoped it would teach her a
lesson. He was surprised and a little disappointed when the
curricle swung neatly into the great stone entrance of Morville
Grange and bowled up the wide drive, the greys apparently on
their best behaviour.

Fortham had the door open when the carriage pulled up in the
porte-cochère, and Miss Wetherby hurriedly explained the situation to him, before running upstairs to remove her soiled habit. By
the time she had changed into a soft green afternoon gown of
twilled silk, the now unconscious gentleman had been carried
upstairs, undressed, and placed into a hastily warmed bed under
the watchful eye of the housekeeper herself.

Having dispatched a footman to summon Dr. Porter from the
village and the housekeeper to break the news to her ladyship, who
was still in her boudoir, Diana ordered everyone out of the room
and stood at the foot of the bed gazing down at the still face of the
injured gentleman.

Her first impression of him had been correct. His face, its harsh
lines softened in sleep, was one of almost sculptured male beauty.
The grimace of pain was now erased from the generous mouth,
giving it an aura of such awesome masculinity that Diana felt an
unaccustomed surge of warmth flood through her veins. Forcing
her eyes downwards, she smiled slightly at the imposing chin
which, even at rest, gave every indication of authority and
self-possession.

She would not care to come into conflict with a man possessed
of such a chin, she thought. She knew herself to be strong willed
to a fault, but she recognized in the unconscious form before her
a will perhaps even stronger than her own.

She had no memory of just how long she stood contemplating
that handsome face which, for some reason beyond her control,
had triggered memories of romantic moments in her carefree life

in Paris. He would have looked dashing in uniform, she mused irrationally, lifting her gaze to his eyes.

It came as something of a shock to find those eyes now half open and staring at her from beneath hooded lids. She felt herself pierced by the coolest, most penetrating gaze she had ever been subjected to, and for some unknown reason her heart raced uncomfortably.

"Ah, you are awake, my lord," she murmured, trying to control her strange nervousness. "The doctor will be here shortly, but I do not believe you have any broken bones."

Since this soothing comment brought no response, Diana shook off her nostalgic reverie, picked up a damp cloth, and was busy applying it to the patient's feverish brow when the door burst open and her ladyship flew into the room.

"Christopher," she cried excitedly. "Mrs. Collins tells me you have had an accident, dear boy. I am so glad to see you," she added, somewhat disjointedly. "But I do wish you had not—quite literally—fallen in upon us like this. So inconsiderate of you, dear—"

This affectionate tirade was interrupted by a crash as the bowl of cool lemon water used to bathe the invalid's brow dropped from Diana's nerveless fingers.

"L-Lord Rotherham?" she stammered, color draining from her face and her glance nervously meeting the cool stare from the silent gentleman, whose lips, she was certain, had twitched in a sardonic smile.

Her ladyship stared at her in surprise. "You did not know, my love? How very droll." Her twinkling eyes took in Diana's embarrassment and she hastened to jump into the breach.

"My dear"—she smiled—"I want to make you known to my favorite nephew, Christopher Morville, sixth Earl of Rotherham. Christopher, this is Miss Diana Wetherby.

"From Paris," she added, after an awkward pause, when a puzzled frown appeared on the earl's brow. "How quaint that neither of you thought to introduce yourself."

Diana pulled herself together with an effort and answered with a semblance of her normal demeanour. "It all happened so suddenly, my lady. Everything was in such a hurly-burly there was no time for the usual niceties." She stopped and then added stiffly, "It's a pleasure to meet you, my lord."

The earl had transferred his cool gaze to her face and was studying her with some perplexity.

"Miss Wetherby?" he repeated.

"Yes, dear," her ladyship broke in. "I see you are just as confused as I was when I first set eyes upon darling Diana. She is not at all what you had led me to expect, you naughty boy."

"She is not at all what I was led to expect myself," the earl said dryly. "In fact . . ." But here he paused, reluctant to repeat the highly unflattering description he had received from that puppy Duvalier. *Past the age when it could have served a useful purpose . . . nobody wants it . . . find a place for it among your other useless possessions.* The words rang through his head as if they had just been uttered.

His lips twitched into a reluctant smile as his gaze took in the young woman standing beside his bed. As a long-time connoisseur of the fairer sex, Lord Rotherham was not fooled by the simple afternoon gown Miss Wetherby was wearing which did nothing to hide the slim form beneath it, nor by the severity with which her glossy auburn curls had been confined.

Diana returned his gaze defiantly. "In fact *what*, my lord?" she queried brusquely. "Did my precious nephew describe me as being at my last prayers or perhaps as a gossipy old Tabby?" She glared at him coldly, her hazel eyes meeting his without flinching.

"At least he never warned me that you would pose a serious threat to unsuspecting travellers, Miss Wetherby," he replied smoothly, a flicker of irritation in his eyes.

"I would say the shoe is on the other foot," Diana retorted before stopping to consider the temerity of taking on an opponent whose chin spoke volumes, all of them clearly authoritarian.

Her ladyship looked from one to the other in astonishment. "What are you talking about," she cried. "Do you mean to tell me, Christopher, that Diana had something to do with your accident?"

"She had everything to do with it, Aunt Effie," replied the earl. "And by the way, please have Jeremy come up immediately. I want to find out what damage the greys have suffered."

"The greys didn't even get a scratch," Diana interrupted. "They are sweet goers, my lord. If they were mine, I'd take better care of them."

The earl looked at her in surprise for several moments. "Am I to understand that you actually *drove* the greys?" he inquired softly but with such sternness that Diana quailed inwardly.

"Fortham, send Jeremy to me at once," he snapped at the

ancient butler, who had at that moment entered the room to announce the arrival of Dr. Porter.

Diana felt impelled to come to the unfortunate groom's rescue. "It was all my fault, my lord. I . . . I must confess I tricked him."

"That I can well believe, my girl," muttered the earl, signs of exhaustion clearly visible on his drawn face.

Further discussion was impeded by the arrival of Dr. Porter, a small wiry individual who quickly banished everyone from the sickroom, much to Diana's relief.

Later that morning, over a tray of fresh tea and cinnamon toast in Lady Ephigenia's sitting-room, Diana was persuaded to relate the whole story of that first disastrous encounter with her reluctant host, the Earl of Rotherham.

Her ladyship clucked her tongue sympathetically during this rambling recital. When it was over, she patted Diana's clasped hands affectionately. "You acted just as you ought, dear. And don't mind Christopher. He is quick to fly up into the boughs, but he also prides himself on being scrupulously fair, so when he sees that his precious greys came to no harm—even if they *were* driven by a female," she added with a flash of sarcasm—"he will be more reasonable. Take my word for it."

Diana was not so sure. Try as she might, she could not banish the conviction that she had seriously alienated the one person who now controlled her fate. She was far more reluctant to admit, even to herself, that the prospect of remaining as the earl's pensioner might entail more self-control and heartache than she had anticipated.

Naturally she revealed none of these misgivings to her ladyship, and that night, snug and safe in her feather bed, she vowed to keep a tighter rein on her temper and her heart, and control her tongue at all costs. She would endeavour to become more like her namesake, that cool, chaste, self-possessed goddess Diana. Only by doing so could she hope to avoid the emotional pitfalls she had glimpsed opening up before her in the days to come.

# 3 .....

# Sir Rudolph

DIANA HAD EVERY opportunity to put this new resolve into practice the following afternoon as the ladies were returning from their weekly visit to the small but well-stocked circulating library in Melbury. As they turned off High Street and into the lane that led to the Grange, Diana set the cob at a spanking trot and glanced at her friend with a smile.

"There is no need to be apprehensive, Aunt Effie." She laughed. "I promise not to put us in the ditch."

"I have complete confidence in your driving, dear. Unlike my nephew, I have absolutely no reason to accuse you of recklessness."

"*He* was the reckless one, but of course he won't admit it," Diana responded with some spirit. "And if the tales I have heard are true, Aunt Effie, you used to cut quite a dash in these parts yourself with a high-perch phaeton and matched team. Now *that* must have been something to see on these country lanes. I wish I could have seen you," she added impulsively, her eyes sparkling with animation. "I imagine that driving Jupiter here," she gestured at the roan with her whip, "must seem very tame after handling a team of blooded horses."

Lady Ephigenia laughed. "Yes, it was all very exciting at the time, my love. But Jupiter is more my style now, I'm afraid. My dashing days are over and that phaeton was sold over twenty years ago. My dear papa gave it to me on my nineteenth birthday to coax me into accepting an old hunting crony of his. Sometimes I wonder if perhaps I shouldn't have married him after all."

She paused, looking at her guest speculatively. Then she added, with a hint of irony in her tone, "He was killed two years later in a curricle accident, right here in this very lane, so perhaps it wouldn't have been too painful. And, as you know, for some odd reason it is so much more respectable to be a widow than a spinster.''

"Nonsense!" burst out Diana indignantly. "How can you say such a thing, Aunt Effie?"

"Because it is true, child." Her ladyship laughed. "You'll have to agree that a husband confers an almost visible aura of consequence on a woman."

"Not if he is a Captain Sharp, a confirmed rake, or a clodpole who is forever in his cups," Diana replied so hotly that she startled Jupiter, who made a halfhearted attempt to bolt.

After bringing him expertly under control, Diana glanced at Lady Effie expectantly.

"I hate to pull caps with you, love," her companion said with a smile. "But you must be a peagoose if you think that the *ton* will censure a gentleman merely because he is addicted to the rites of Bacchus and Venus. And no real gentleman would be a Captain Sharp, so that does not apply, dear."

"True," agreed Diana reluctantly. "But there is a vast difference between a Bond Street Beau ogling an actress who is an acknowledged high-flyer and some ancient coxcomb leering at a chit barely out of the schoolroom, don't you think, Lady Effie?"

"Perhaps," her ladyship conceded grudgingly. "But although poor old Lord Penthurst might have ogled actresses in his salad days, he certainly never leered at me, my dear, so that hardly signifies. If anything, he was quite the opposite of a rake, and a dead bore who felt he was doing my father a great favour in offering for me and didn't hesitate to say so at least once a day."

"How very lowering," exclaimed Diana, amused at the prospect of a union between such a tactless, stolid creature and a young lady accustomed to tool a sporting vehicle and four around the countryside.

"And only think, Aunt Effie," she added with a gleam of devilry in her hazel eyes. "Perhaps if you had married him, he might have stayed at home instead of gone off racing around in his curricle. He might even be alive today."

"I rather think not." Her ladyship chuckled. "He was sixty at the time, if he was a day, and that was thirty years ago. And besides, my love, Lord Penthurst *never* raced; he was far too dignified."

"He does sound like a dull old gager," Diana stated frankly. "And I think you did the right thing in not getting riveted to him. Besides, I like you the way you are," she added shyly, two charming dimples appearing suddenly in her cheeks as she smiled at her companion.

Dear Aunt Sophy would have liked you too, she thought to herself. In fact, her ladyship was like her aunt in so many ways that Diana occasionally had to watch what she said. She was not yet ready to reveal all her secrets to her hostess, although she hoped to do so eventually.

Diana was startled out of her musings on the deception she was practising on Lady Ephigenia by an old-fashioned travelling coach which, approaching from the opposite direction, created a diversion by nearly running them into the ditch as it passed the tilbury on the narrow road without giving so much as an inch.

By the time Diana had quietened the nervous cob and set the tilbury bowling along the lane again, her spirits were somewhat restored and she had almost convinced herself that perhaps she was refining too much on a situation which her hostess, in whose judgement Diana had the greatest confidence, would undoubtedly blame entirely on Lord Rotherham.

"That was old Mrs. Robinson, an addle-pated Eccentric if ever I saw one," snorted her ladyship, glaring angrily after the lumbering coach. "She insists on driving about in that monstrous relic of her married days, when she can perfectly well afford a decent-sized carriage."

Diana had to smile at the picture Lady Ephigenia was painting of one of her close neighbours.

"And her coachman is about a hundred years old and as blind as a mole. He sees nothing smaller than the Mail Coach, which luckily does not come down these lanes or we would have a rare tangle, believe me. Why, only last Christmas he drove straight through a flock of sheep right here on this very lane and killed six prime ewes. Claimed he never saw nor heard a thing."

"Did Mrs. Robinson's coachman have anything to do with Lord Penthurst's curricle accident?" inquired Diana, quite diverted from her somber thoughts by Lady Ephigenia's lively chatter.

"Why no, dear," replied her ladyship with a laugh. "Old Crofts was only half blind at that time, as far as I remember, and managed to miss most vehicles except for a farmer's gig or two and a few geese."

The rest of the journey passed very pleasantly with Lady Ephigenia recounting various local anecdotes with wry humour until they turned in at the wrought-iron gates of Morville Grange. At this point they were startled by a smart curricle, driven by a very large gentleman, which swept round a curve in the lane ahead and approached them at a breakneck pace.

"Oh! Do stop a moment, Diana, if you please," her ladyship cried out excitedly. "That is Sir Rudolph Potter back from Ireland. He is bound to stop when he sees us."

This prediction proved to be correct. As Diana brought the tilbury to a standstill under the arched entrance to the Grange, in spite of strenuous resistance from Jupiter who wanted to get back to his warm stall, she heard the fretting team come to a sudden, prancing halt in the lane beside them and a gruff, masculine voice call out heartily to her hostess.

"My very dear Lady Effie, what a delightful coincidence. I had planned to call on you tomorrow. I hope I find you well?"

"Oh, in excellent spirits, Sir Rudolph. Thank you. I didn't know you were back from Ireland."

"Just got back last night, dear lady. The roads are mighty sticky because of all the rain, but the girls insisted that we push on home. They were not too happy at my brother's old house, you know. It's said to be haunted." He laughed good-naturedly at such childish nonsense.

"Come and take tea with us tomorrow afternoon, then. Rotherham arrived from London yesterday and will be glad of the company. That will give us more time to hear all about your travels, Sir Rudolph."

"Thank you, my dear lady. Glad to." As he spoke, Sir Rudolph Potter had been rather openly casting admiring glances at Diana, who was busy trying to curb Jupiter's eagerness to continue up the driveway.

"And who, pray, is this charming young creature?"

Since this remark clearly referred to her, Diana swung her gaze round and looked up, over Lady Ephigenia's fur-clad head, into a pair of appraising blue eyes set in a tanned, leathery face, lined with age or mirth, she could not immediately decide which.

As her ladyship performed the necessary introductions and made polite inquiries about each one of Sir Rudolph's five young daughters, who had accompanied him to visit his brother in Ireland, Diana was able to scrutinize the large stranger at her leisure.

The first thing her critical gaze discovered was that the gentleman was both older and better looking than she had first imagined. Those admiring blue eyes were so merry that they distracted the observer from the myriad of small, insistent lines around the eyes and mouth which suggested that their owner was rather older than he tried to appear. At rest, Sir Rudolph's mouth, somewhat dwarfed by an impressively large nose, was generous and well shaped, but it was rarely relaxed and more often than not showed a lamentable tendency to curl up at the corners in an engaging grin.

Diana had to admit, however, that in spite of these minor and, to the uncritical eye, inconsequential blemishes, Sir Rudolph Potter cut a very dashing figure indeed, albeit an exceedingly large one. His chocolate-brown velvet driving coat, embellished with numerous capes, showed off his enormous shoulders to advantage. His untidy, windblown hair escaped from beneath his oversized beaver in curly ginger strands, giving his craggy face a youthfulness belied by closer examination. Although he lacked Rotherham's classic good looks and air of unmistakable breeding, Sir Rudolph was, Diana decided, far more amiable than the enigmatic earl.

Diana was unusually silent after Sir Rudolph had driven off towards Melbury at the same reckless pace, promising faithfully to attend the ladies at Morville Grange the following afternoon for tea. She tried to ignore the sudden glow of pleasure she had derived from the unmistakable admiration in his merry eyes. When she unexpectedly found herself wondering what it might feel like to have Rotherham look at her so warmly, however, she chided herself for being foolish beyond bearing.

Wordlessly, she guided Jupiter at a sober trot up the winding oak-lined drive to the front door, handed the reins to the waiting groom, and ran upstairs to take off her bonnet and plain pelisse, both more notable for their warmth and practicality than for their elegance, she observed with an unfamiliar stab of regret.

Crossing the main hall a short time later, Diana was informed by Fortham that three young gentlemen had arrived at the Grange not an hour since and were even now closeted with the earl in his sitting room upstairs.

"Trying to persuade his lordship to come down to dinner with them tonight, they are," he grumbled. "When Dr. Porter expressly forbade any activity at all for the rest of the week." He stared morosely at Diana as if expecting her to enforce the good doctor's orders.

"Don't worry, Fortham," she replied. "I expect Lady Ephigenia will have something to say about that."

"No doubt," the butler answered primly. "But whether Master Christopher will pay any attention to her is another matter. Right willful he was as a lad and hasn't changed a jot since." He seemed to derive a grim satisfaction from the fact.

This was an extraordinarily long speech from the dour butler, and Diana saw it as a sign of the changes which had already occurred in the Morville household since the unexpected arrival of the head of the family. She could not help being apprehensive about the changes in her own daily routine the presence of the earl and several other London gentlemen of fashion would undoubtedly precipitate.

She found herself taking particular care with her appearance that evening, choosing a long-sleeved gown of yellow sarcenet, the sleeves buttoned tightly round her wrists, unadorned by frills of lace or other embellishments except for a demure lace ruffle around a moderately low neckline. She gathered her auburn curls into a simple cluster confined by a yellow satin ribbon, and was pleased with the air of quiet elegance and propriety she had achieved.

Slipping into her hostess's sitting-room after a discreet knock, she found that lady already dressed in one of her simple yet elegant evening gowns. Tonight, perhaps in celebration of her nephew's homecoming, she had chosen a recently acquired emerald-green silk confection, trimmed with blond lace and worn over a pale ivory satin slip, which gave her diminutive figure a slim, youthful appearance. She looked immensely pleased with her reflection in the ornate cheval mirror and chattered animatedly, as they descended the wide stairs together, about the happy coincidence of having no less than four fashionable gentlemen to entertain that evening.

Diana could not share her hostess's bubbling excitement at the prospect of entertaining the three new arrivals. Furthermore, for some reason she had not been able to fathom, she dreaded the thought of spending a whole evening under the sardonic gaze of the Earl of Rotherham. Therefore, it was with no small trepidation that she followed Lady Ephigenia's sprightly figure into the downstairs drawing room where the gentlemen awaited them. In fact, she felt decidedly inhibited—a state quite foreign to her nature—as she watched the effusive reception accorded to her hostess by the three newcomers, who all seemed to be on very easy terms with her.

Under cover of the general hubbub, Diana glanced around the

elegant room and was unaccountably pleased to see the earl comfortably ensconced in a plush wing-chair near the open fire. He acknowledged her presence with such a slight bow, however, that her pleasure evaporated. She bowed stiffly in return before turning her attention back to the group of gentlemen crowding around her hostess.

Breaking away from the affectionate bear hug of a tall, ginger-haired gentleman with a military bearing, Lady Ephigenia turned to Diana and drew her into the boisterous circle.

"Quiet, everyone. Quiet!" she exclaimed briskly. "And do behave yourselves, boys. I don't want Miss Wetherby to think you are a pack of mannerless jackstraws."

After the good-natured protests that followed this remark had subsided, her ladyship made the necessary introductions. She accompanied each one with a few pithy observations about each young gentleman, whom she had known, she claimed, ever since they were in short coats.

"This one here is your nephew Richard Chatham, my dear," she began, indicating the ginger-haired gentleman, who promptly captured her hand and kissed her fingers soundly.

Diana looked up into a lean, ruggedly handsome face dominated by a pair of twinkling blue eyes.

"Absolutely enchanted to make your acquaintance, Aunt," Chatham remarked warmly, a touch of humour in his voice as he emphasized the last word. "Morville had warned us we were in for a surprise and I can see why. Never in a million years had I expected to discover I have a Nonpareil for a relative."

"That's doing it a little too brown, sir," Diana replied with a smile. "I am not a schoolroom chit to be taken in by such flummery, you know. And besides, her ladyship has warned me about your reputation."

"Ah. Lady Effie, how could you betray me so," Chatham wailed in mock despair. "Whatever have I done to deserve such shabby treatment?"

"Fiddle!" exclaimed that lady with her customary outspokenness. "Pay no attention to this gibble-gabble, my dear. It's all a hum."

She drew Diana's attention to a second gentleman who had been eyeing her all this while with obvious approval. "This is Tobias Tottlefield—Toby to his friends—who practically lived in our pockets while he was growing up on his uncle's estate near here."

Diana smiled kindly at this robust, jolly-faced gentleman and offered her hand which he immediately clasped and raised to his lips with an exaggerated bow.

"Your servant, Miss Wetherby, I'm sure. And I beg you will not judge me by the company I am forced to keep." He made a sweeping gesture which took in the other three gentlemen present. "It's hardly my fault that I was born in such close proximity to these incorrigibly rag-mannered rakes. Why, the stories I could tell about their antics in the army would curl your toes, miss."

"I sincerely hope you do not intend anything so indiscreet, Toby," put in the earl, who had sat in his armchair, a rug tucked around his knees, observing with some amusement Miss Wetherby's reaction to his friends' gallantries. He had fulfilled Fortham's dire predictions by overriding his aunt's objections to his appearance at the dinner table. His sole concession to his twisted shoulder and bruised knee was to allow his aunt to tuck a rug around his knees and arrange a light sling around his neck to support his arm should it pain him.

After learning from Lord Henry Forsdyke, the last guest to be introduced to her, that the four gentlemen had not only been up at Oxford at the same time, but had also served together in the Seventh Hussars during the Peninsular War, Diana quite lost her initial reserve. Encouraged by the lively interest of the gentlemen, she launched into a series of anecdotes concerning her father's regiment, the Sixth Dragoons, which had been stationed in Paris when she made her come-out at seventeen.

By the time Fortham came to announce dinner, she had begun to feel that, in spite of the unspoken disapproval she felt in the earl's glance every time she caught his eyes upon her, it might indeed be a pleasant change to have the benefit of male company at the Grange during the coming weeks. The gentlemen's interest in military events and their casual references to officers whom she either knew or had heard her father speak of produced an air of easy camaraderie similar to that she had shared with Colonel Wetherby's junior officers in Paris. This fact did much to dispel her misgivings about her future role in the Morville household.

# 4 ·····

# An Accusation

THE FOLLOWING MORNING, rising at an early hour for her usual canter in the Home Park on Perseus, she was surprised to find Captain Chatham already in the stable yard supervising the saddling of a big roan gelding.

"I trust you slept well, Diana," he said when he saw her approach. "And I do hope you will allow me to call you Diana," he added with an engaging smile. "Aunt doesn't suit you at all. Dashed unsettling, you know, having to address you in such a fustian manner, when it's plain to see you are bang up to the nines. And I insist that you call me Dick; everybody does."

Diana could not find a suitable argument against this arrangement. Besides, she was not immune to the captain's undeniable charm, and what harm could it do? After all, they were related; a remote relationship, it is true, but nevertheless, related.

"Do you always ride this early in the morning?" she inquired as the captain swung her easily up onto a restive Perseus old Ben had already saddled for her.

"Not usually," Chatham replied. "I learned from Ben here that you were in the habit of exercising in the early mornings, so I thought I might join you. If you have no objection, that is. You see"—he lowered his voice conspiratorially—"we have to talk."

If Diana was surprised by this announcement, she did not show it, and it was only after they had galloped their horses through the Park and onto a bridle path leading through the Home Wood that Chatham brought up the subject again.

"I cannot tell you how much I regret the circumstances which brought you to this unhappy pass, Diana," he said finally in a serious voice. "You see, I was under the impression . . . at least Ferdinand led us all to believe that you . . . Well, to put it bluntly," he tried again, meeting her quizzical gaze with a rueful

41

grin, "we all thought you were much more advanced in years than you obviously are."

"What difference does that make?" Diana inquired rather coolly, wondering at precisely which point during this odd conversation Aunt Sophy would have given the captain one of her famous set-downs.

"Oh, none at all. And I didn't mean to imply that it was not a dashed addle-pated thing to do—"

"That's reassuring to hear you admit it," Diana cut in with more than a little sharpness.

"I tried to reason with Rotherham," the captain explained. "And with Ferdinand, of course. But there was no swaying either of them. Rotherham in particular should have known better than to let himself be bamboozled into such a cork-brained venture."

"I trust that you, at least, did not profit from that shabby and totally unprincipled wager," she remarked rather acidly.

"No! Of course not," the captain protested vehemently.

"Not that I would be the least surprised at what gentlemen will sink to when they are bosky," Diana declared with some warmth.

Chatham grinned sheepishly. "To tell you the truth, I lost a pony to old Toby," he confessed. "Rotherham rarely loses a bet, you know. I thought it was a sure thing. And Duvalier was such a Batholomew baby. A real knock-in-the-cradle, if you know what I mean, for all his exquisite airs." He glanced at her apprehensively. "Nobody can explain what happened."

"Well, it is done now," said Diana philosophically. "And there is no undoing it; not if I know anything about how ridiculously pigheaded a gentleman can become where his so-called honour is concerned."

"Oh, but there is."

When Diana looked at him in surprise, the captain wore a self-satisfied smile on his handsome face.

"Do tell," she urged after several minutes had gone by.

"The scheme is a famous one, and it should make everyone happy. All it requires is your consent before we set the wheels in motion."

"My consent?" Diana had a sudden flash of foreboding.

"Yes," Richard continued, so absorbed in his plan to rescue his aunt from her predicament that he failed to notice the dawning apprehension on her face. "Toby and I have devised a plan that will allow you to extract yourself from the protection of old Chris, who's a good enough fellow in his way, but a dashed stickler when it concerns females in his own family.''

''Oh, you have, have you? And no doubt I shall be expected to welcome this unsolicited meddling in my affairs?'' Diana inquired tartly.

''We're only trying to repair the wrong we have all done to you, Diana. Because we are all responsible for this coil you are in. Toby, me, even old Henry. Rotherham's brother-in-law—James Langton—was there too, you know, and I'm sure Lady Langton would kick up a devil of a dust if I were to tell her what her precious husband and brother have got themselves into. Even Chris is no match for Lucinda when she gets into one of her famous rages.''

Diana looked at him in growing agitation. ''How mortifying that so many gentlemen know about the circumstances of my presence here, Dick,'' she lamented. ''Would it not be far better to let the whole thing be forgotten instead of trying to repair what is beyond changing?''

''Oh, no, indeed. You see, Toby and I decided that if a few of us get together . . . only close friends who can be trusted, of course. No sense letting all the loose screws in Town get wind of it.''

''Why bring this whole embarrassing incident up at all?'' Diana wanted to know.

''Because between us we could put up enough blunt to set you up in style. With your looks, Diana, and enough of the ready to throw around on all those fripperies females always seem to need, you will cut a devil of a dash in Town this season.''

''But I am not going to Town,'' she protested uneasily.

''Don't be a peagoose, my dear. Of course you're going to Town. That's the whole point, don't you see?''

''No, I don't see. And what I do see, I don't like the sound of at all.''

The captain looked at her with a pained expression. ''I never took you for such a ninnyhammer,'' he complained. ''What don't you see?''

''I don't see why I am obliged to go to London. What's the point?''

''The point, my dear Diana, is that Toby and I have decided that what you need is a husband who is plump enough in the pocket to give you the kind of life you deserve. Not just anybody, of course.

He'd have to belong to the *ton* and be top-of-the-drawer, you know. No slow tops or mushrooms. Don't you agree?''

Diana had listened to this outrageous proposal with a mixture of astonishment and indignation. Now she pulled her horse to a stop and turned to glare directly at her companion.

"I am not and never was a fortune hunter," she declared heatedly.

"Oh, we know that, Diana. Don't get into a pucker, my dear, but you must admit that it is much more comfortable to have a husband who is well breeched. That's what my Mama is always telling my sisters," he added practically.

"What makes you so sure I even want a husband?"

The captain was amused by this piece of witticism. "All females want husbands." He laughed. "That's one of the ten commandments according to my dear Mama."

"Well, I hate to prove your dear Mama wrong, but it so happens that I, for one, am not in the market for a husband. Now or ever! And I demand that you drop this absurd plan immediately. I don't want to hear another word about it. Do I make myself clear?"

Without waiting for his answer, Diana flicked her reins and sent Perseus plunging off in a reckless gallop down the narrow bridle path.

No sooner had Diana changed out of her riding habit and made her way down to join Captain Chatham in the breakfast-room, than Fortham appeared at the door to deliver a message for Miss Wetherby.

"His lordship requests the favour of your presence in the library immediately after breakfast, miss," he announced in his usual lugubrious tone, his grizzled eyebrows quivering alarmingly.

Somewhat taken aback by this ominous summons delivered in such dramatic tones, Diana tried to calm her apprehension by telling herself that the earl probably wished to assure himself that she was comfortable at the Grange. The ruse did not work, however, and her mind continued to toy with the dreadful possibility that perhaps her imposture had been discovered.

As a result of these unsettling thoughts, she lost her usual hearty appetite and could scarcely swallow one cup of tea and nibble on half a slice of toast. The sight of the captain's plate piled high with sausages, poached eggs, and bacon made her slightly bilious, and she paid scant attention to his bantering conversation before excusing herself and fleeing the room.

Consequently, it was scarcely twenty minutes later that she stood before the earl's library and tapped discreetly on the door.

When she entered, the earl was standing with his back to the door, gazing abstractedly down into the flames of the crackling fire in the ornate marble hearth, one elbow resting on the mantelpiece.

He did not turn immediately and Diana had ample opportunity to admire the width of his broad shoulders encased in a well-cut coat of dark blue superfine worn with buckskin breeches and top boots of a very superior shine. He was, she had to admit, the kind of gentleman expressly designed to give any impressionable young lady a severe case of the vapours. Luckily I am past that stage, she told herself stoutly. This fluttering of her pulse was undoubtedly caused by her fear of discovery rather than admiration for the earl's stalwart qualities.

"Sit down, Miss Wetherby." He had turned and was regarding her with those inscrutable grey eyes.

She felt an unaccountable weakness at the knees and was glad to sink into a leather wing-chair somewhat removed from the hearth.

"You wished to see me, my lord?" she inquired, forcing herself to appear cool and relaxed despite the anxiety she felt.

He did not reply at once but continued to examine her from under a pair of brows that in repose had seemed sculpted, she remembered. Now they were drawn together in a frown.

After two or three minutes of enduring this scrutiny, Diana's sense of humour came to her rescue. She relaxed, settled herself more comfortably in her chair, and her expressive hazel eyes took on an amused gleam.

"You remind me of my brother, Jean-Pierre, when he used to call me into his study to accuse me of instigating something truly nefarious among his precious offspring," she remarked conversationally.

"And of course, you were entirely blameless."

"Well, of course, my lord," she replied brightly. "How can you doubt it?"

"I rather think I would be inclined to agree with your brother."

"How ungenerous of you, my lord." Diana laughed. "Whatever have I done to deserve this reproach?"

"Nothing yet, I trust," the earl replied grimly. He studied her for several moments before continuing in the same formal voice.

"I'll be frank with you, Miss Wetherby. When I made this

wager—reprehensible of me, I'll admit, but what's done is done—I was given to understand, quite definitely in fact, that you were a female of advanced years. In the last stages of decrepitude, if I understood Duvalier correctly.''

Diana began to visualize the whole fabric of her carefully planned impersonation crumbling about her. The earl was about to call her bluff. She rallied enough to make a heated retort.

''That I can well believe, my lord. Ferdinand was ever a loose fish and not above twisting the facts to suit his purpose. There was no love lost between us, but that he would sink to such depths of depravity as to use his own aunt in a drunken wager is hard for even me to accept.''

She paused for a moment before continuing in a voice shaking with barely concealed disgust. ''That a man of your rank and experience should have encouraged this outrageous behaviour is beyond my comprehension. I trust you are proud of the part you played in placing me in this humiliating and intolerable position, my lord.''

During this heated outburst, Diana had risen and walked about the room impatiently. At the end of it, she came to a standstill in front of the object of her tirade and glared at him witheringly.

The earl seemed slightly taken aback by this unexpected attack. He gazed bemusedly down into those stormy hazel eyes and felt a glimmer of admiration for this lively lady who seemed to be unawed by his rank and impressive presence.

''I make no excuses for my own behaviour, Miss Wetherby,'' he said stiffly. ''But no one forced your nephew to suggest such ridiculous stakes.''

''You should have refused the wager,'' Diana retorted angrily.

''Indeed?'' His voice became even colder. ''No gentleman worth his mettle refuses a wager—''

''Fiddle!'' Diana broke in rudely. ''Were you so entirely foxed that you gave no thought at all to the consequences of your action? Are you so careless of other people's happiness that you allowed your own inflated sense of honour to override your good judgement? I can hardly think of anything more dishonorable than what you have done to me. And yet you have the unmitigated gall to stand there and talk to me of honour!''

Carried away by the satisfaction of finally being able to speak her mind on a subject that concerned her so nearly, Diana was slow to perceive the earl's face had gone very white and his lips compressed in a thin, dangerous line. When she did notice his agitation, she suddenly realized the gravity of the accusations and emotions she had dared to put into words.

Her first reaction was fear. This was short-lived, however, and was soon replaced by a sense of fatalism. The earl would obviously send her back to Paris anyway, she reasoned stubbornly, trying to meet the blazing grey eyes without flinching. So she might as well get everything off her chest while she had the chance.

"And as for my age, my lord," she declared hotly, "what fault is it of mine that I am not the platter-faced old harridan you would prefer me to be? Can you tell me that? How dare you imply that I do not live up to *your* standards of what a maiden aunt should be!"

She would have continued, but he cut her short.

"Miss Wetherby! Enough!" he cried heatedly, trying to regain control of this outrageous interview which was not proceeding as he had intended at all. "This is not what I wanted to discuss with you."

This pronouncement did not quench her anger. "Why didn't you say so, then?" she inquired shortly.

"You hardly gave me a chance, my dear girl." A reluctant smile momentarily relaxed his harried expression. "Do sit down."

"I am *not* your dear girl," she cut in sharply. "And I would thank you to remember that I am here under your roof through no desire of my own, but as the result of a drunken wager for which you are entirely responsible." She had resumed her pacing, and the earl seemed mesmerized by this whirlwind of feminine indignation he had inadvertently released.

"I expect to be treated with the respect due a lady." Here she tossed her auburn curls as if to emphasize her point and managed—although her head hardly reached the earl's shoulder—to look down an exceedingly well-bred nose at him. "Whatever you may have imagined, I am not—and will not be—one of your notorious light-skirts. You may count on it."

An abrupt crack of laughter brought her to a sudden standstill.

"My dear girl—excuse me—Miss Wetherby," he corrected himself hastily, "you have a lot to learn, particularly in the art of conversing pleasantly with a gentleman, before you can hope to qualify for such a post. Believe me."

Diana looked at the earl in utter amazement.

Before she could gather her wits to deliver a scathing retort to this highly irregular piece of levity, the earl took advantage of the hiatus in their heated exchange to address the matter with which he had intended to confront his guest.

"Sit down, Miss Wetherby. I have something extremely unpleasant to discuss with you."

Still seething about her host's improper remark, Diana returned to her chair and clasped her hands to stop them from trembling. As the earl's words sank in, however, her anger began to dissipate, to be replaced by a sinking feeling in the pit of her stomach.

"As I was saying earlier, I had expected to receive into my household a female of my own aunt's age. It occurred to me that such an addition might well be providential since it would provide companionship for Lady Ephigenia. However, after meeting you, Miss Wetherby . . ." He paused and regarded her speculatively. "I see that I have been sadly misled."

"I take it that I do not qualify as a lady's companion either, my lord?" she inquired witheringly.

"That is beside the point. As I said, after meeting you, it did occur to me that this whole business of the wager might well be an ingenious plot to install a young and attractive female in a situation which would allow her access to some of the most eligible and wealthy men on the Marriage Mart."

Diana was so shocked by the implication of the earl's words that she felt suddenly light-headed as the blood fled from her cheeks leaving them pale and drawn. What had she done to deserve this insult? she wondered. True, she was an impostor of sorts, although there could be no denying that she was and always would be Ferdinand's maiden aunt.

"So now I'm a fortune hunter, my lord? How droll," she added contemptuously in a desperate attempt to regain her shattered composure.

"Perhaps," he replied, regarding her steadily. "And if it is indeed true, as I believe it is, there is nothing droll about it."

"*If* it is true." Diana caught desperately at this straw in the maelstrom which threatened to engulf her. She jumped out of her chair and paced nervously up and down the earl's richly figured Axminster carpet.

"*If* it is true," she repeated indignantly. "And naturally, my lord, you are assuming that it *is* true, without any kind of evidence." She stopped before him and glared up into his face with such genuine indignation that the earl could not resist applauding her spirited performance.

"Well done, my dear Miss Wetherby." He smiled cynically.

"You have surely missed your vocation. That was magnificent!"

"Your accusations are false and highly reprehensible, my lord," she said haughtily, ignoring this lapse into levity. "And you have no excuse for making fun of a defenceless, destitute, aging female. I would remind you that I am six and twenty, and have been at my last prayers for years now. I am what you see before you, nothing more nor less than an unfortunate female destined to be a maiden aunt to my ingrate of a nephew for the remainder of my days. That is if I don't die of mortification first."

Diana became quite carried away with her own eloquence towards the end of this moving speech. Her voice became husky and throbbed thrillingly as the desolate picture she painted took shape in her own mind.

Meanwhile the earl had been observing her with no little amusement and a dawning admiration in his keen eyes. The wench had style and passion. Dashed if she didn't. The unusual huskiness of her voice touched off a response in him that he was not used to feeling for ladies of the *ton*. His tastes usually ran to females of quite another calibre and he felt shaken by the sudden surge of emotion that invaded his thoughts.

Convinced that he detected a glint of tears in Miss Wetherby's hazel eyes, the earl instinctively put an arm about her shoulders and drew her head down on his blue lapel. He prided himself on being an expert in consoling damsels in distress. Consoling a maiden aunt should give him no trouble at all, especially one as delectable as Miss Wetherby.

Momentarily lost in the sweetness of the embrace, Diana buried her face in the earl's coat and breathed in the comforting masculine smells of shaving soap and tobacco. She felt so safe here, so protected. Something deep within her clamoured for this man with an unsuspected yearning.

Suddenly conscious of the terrible impropriety of her posture, reclining cosily in a strange gentleman's arms, she tried to jerk away but found herself a prisoner, crushed relentlessly against the earl's tall frame.

"Release me this instant," she gasped breathlessly.

"Shouldn't that have been: Unhand me, villain?" the earl's lazy voice inquired from somewhere perilously near her left ear. "I seem to recall those lines being spoken recently by one of our illustrious thespians."

Diana made the fatal mistake of allowing a giggle to escape her. Instantly, strong fingers raised her chin, and a mouth, warm and tender, brushed hers tentatively. When she made no move to resist, the earl's lips bore down on hers in a searing kiss that rocked the very foundations of her being.

Instinctively she pressed herself against the hard length of him, oblivious of anything except the surge of pure pleasure his caress brought to her distraught heart.

Suddenly she was thrust aside so violently that she staggered against the mantel. The earl strode to the door and turned towards her, a sardonic look of triumph on his face.

"No evidence?" he said harshly. "I think this licentious behaviour constitutes evidence enough to prove my point, don't you agree, my dear Miss Wetherby?"

Without another word, he left her, closing the door firmly behind him.

# 5 ·····

# An Invitation

DIANA HAD NO clear recollection of how she spent the rest of that dreadful day. All she remembered was the dull ache that filled her heart and the sense of desolation she could not seem to shake off. After the earl had left her, she crept up to her room, flung herself upon her bed, and indulged in a fit of weeping such as she had not had in many a year. Finally, good sense prevailed. She rose and washed her ravaged face with cool rose water. Then she went into her small sitting-room to feed Bijou as she did every morning.

"What a thoroughly rude and obnoxious creature he is, Bijou," she told the parrot as she changed his water and put fresh seed in his blue tin bowl. "Unprincipled and rakish, too." She paused to tickle Bijou on the head which he had extended for her convenience.

"Men like him are not worth crying over, now are they, *cherie*? Why, he deliberately tricked me into letting him kiss me. Leading me to believe he was merely comforting me."

"*Quelle sottise!*" exclaimed the parrot.

"Quite right, my dear. A regular coxcomb, don't you agree?"

"*Mais oui!*" Bijou agreed.

"And an unscrupulous libertine to boot."

"Toot-Toot," was all the reply she got to that as the parrot sidled over to his dish and began to select his favourite seeds.

Diana smiled at her old friend's enthusiasm for his food. "You are lucky to be so carefree, *mon petit*. It is a good philosophy for living a happy life. Eat, drink, and be merry. Gentlemen do it all the time. One must not be so easily overset by adversity. And I'm sure I don't care a fig for what the earl thinks of me. Why should I? After all, he is nothing to me."

Why then did she feel so terribly low in spirits? The memory of that kiss was still so fresh on her lips and, try as she might, she

51

could not quite convince herself that she had not really enjoyed every second of it, brief as it was. Perhaps she did have a propensity towards depravity, she mused. What would it feel like to be the *chère amie* of a man like the Earl of Rotherham? A tremour shook her at the very thought. Does he kiss his mistresses like that every day? she wondered. More than once? And what other pleasures did he offer them that her own body had seemed to cry out for when she had been crushed in his arms only a hour ago?

Shame on you, Diana Wetherby, she told herself crossly. These are no thoughts for a lady. But a little voice deep inside her whispered perversely that it was often dull work being a lady. Especially when one was a maiden aunt lady into the bargain.

Brusquely she pushed these subversive thoughts aside and addressed the more practical problem of how she was going to face the earl next time they met. Because face him she must. It was inconceivable that she could spend the entire period of his visit shut up in her room, much as she would like to. What if he decided to stay for months? The prospect appalled her.

She walked over to her dressing table and glared back at her pale face in the ornate mirror. How ironic that this particular mirror was set in a beautifully carved frame on which chubby, smiling cupids, licentious satyrs, and lively wood nymphs sported in indiscreet abandon. The scene did not amuse her as it usually did. She felt somehow cut off from the freedom and joy the happy-go-lucky mythological creatures obviously shared in that carved woodland glade.

Glancing at the reflection of the fashionable primrose-yellow morning dress she had put on after her morning ride with the captain, she noticed that it revealed her trim figure to distinct advantage and emphasized the dark beauty of her auburn curls. But what use was it to bother to wear clothes that made one look so attractive if one immediately became the object of lewd advances from one's host? she wondered. Suddenly an idea struck her that caused a slow smile to spread over her face.

"I've got it, Bijou," she cried in delight. "What a famous idea. I'll show that conceited, overbearing Bond Street Beau that I am, in fact, the very model of an antiquated maiden aunt."

So saying, she threw open her wardrobe and rummaged through it until she found the dress she was looking for. Holding the offending garment up against her, she smiled triumphantly. "This will surely convince his lordship that my character is beyond reproach and my intentions most innocuous,'' she told Bijou.

*"Bien sûr,"* he replied, spitting out an empty husk onto the floor.

When Lady Ephigenia came looking for Diana later that morning to invite her to drive the tilbury over to Melbury to pay a social call at the vicarage, she found her guest had undergone a curious metamorphosis.

Gone was the elegant young lady in primrose-yellow morning gown. Gone was the elegant twist of auburn curls caught up with a yellow satin ribbon. And gone were the exuberance and laughter she had come to associate with her beloved Diana.

In her place was a sober matron dressed in a long-sleeved, shapeless dove-grey dress completely devoid of any frivolous ornamentation. Her hair was pulled back ruthlessly into a severe bun encased in a net that prevented even one wayward curl from escaping to lend some softness to the severity of the coiffeur.

Lady Ephigenia was thunderstruck.

"What Canterbury trick is this, my love?" she burst out when she had recovered from her surprise. "And where did you get that hideous garment? I hardly dare call it a dress."

Diana rose upon Lady Ephigenia's entrance and advanced sedately to give her hostess a warm embrace and draw her to the damask-covered settee by the window where Bijou sat sunning himself contentedly.

*"Sacrébleu!"* the parrot greeted her affectionately and extended his head to be scratched.

"My feelings exactly!" exclaimed her ladyship. "What maggot has got into your head, dearest? Surely you don't intend to come down in that . . . that Banbury outfit. You look positively dowdy, love. Whatever will the gentlemen think?"

"It signifies little what the gentlemen think, my lady," Diana replied with some asperity. "Or perhaps I should say that it signifies everything," she contradicted herself. "Since they are the ones who tell us females what we can and cannot do."

"My, you are in a pucker, love. And I cannot make head or heels of what you mean. Please enlighten me, my sweet."

"I should tell you, Aunt Effie, that I have come under the suspicion of being a fortune hunter. So if you consort with me, you run the risk of being accused of conspiring with me to obtain an eligible husband. Although why I would want to be leg-shackled to the kind of loose screws I've encountered so far in this country, I cannot imagine. And why anyone could possibly assume I wish to be leg-shackled at all, is beyond me.''

Lady Ephigenia saw that Diana was indeed upset, and she laid a hand on her arm affectionately.

"This sounds like a real bumble-broth to me, dear. Although I cannot quite see who would fault you for wishing to be comfortably settled. Perhaps you are refining too much on it, my love. Gentlemen being what they are, it is so easy to take offense at their careless remarks. So few of them have any sensibility at all, as you well know, dear.''

She glanced at Diana, who seemed to be giving this line of reasoning serious consideration.

"I heartily agree with you, Aunt Effie," she said finally, hesitant to reveal to this kindly woman the whole story of her humiliating interview with the earl that morning. "One cannot depend on gentlemen to have any sense at all or to think of anything except their own convenience and comfort. It's a very happy coincidence that I am not a high-flyer," she added illogically but with feeling, "because I would never have the patience to put up with all their flummery.''

Her ladyship was momentarily taken aback by the audacity of this last statement. It was not like Diana to make such wildly improper pronouncements.

"What an odd thing to say, dear," she said soothingly. "But, don't worry, love. Nobody would ever mistake you for a member of the muslin company.'' She laughed merrily at the very idea. "I do not profess to be an expert on the topic, since I cannot recall ever having met one. But I am sure you are nothing like those unfortunate creatures, my love. No doubt my nephew could set you straight on that score, if it were at all proper of us to apply to him for such information. Which of course it isn't," she added hurriedly.

"So I have been given to understand," Diana mumbled under her breath as she meekly followed Lady Ephigenia down the stairs and out to where Jupiter and the tilbury awaited them.

At the vicarage, where Lady Ephigenia and Miss Wetherby had been invited to partake of a light nuncheon with the vicar and his sister, Diana was well aware that her friends must be wondering at her somber attire. Both were too polite to ask indiscreet questions, however, and Diana spent an entertaining hour after lunch in spirited discussion with the vicar on Miss Burney's most recent novel. Her ladyship and Miss Fenley, neither of whom had as yet read the novel, preferred to compare home-made remedies for migraine headaches to which the latter had been prone since childhood.

Later, during their several stops in the village, people were not so well bred and Diana had to endure a variety of curious stares and exclamations which sorely tried her patience. This unexpected response from the locals made her wonder if perhaps she had been a little drastic in adopting such conspicuously dowdy clothes.

After her first outburst in Diana's sitting-room that morning, Lady Ephigenia had made no further reference to her guest's unappealing choice of dress. Now, as they descended from the tilbury and handed the reins to old Ben, who was waiting for them, she ventured a casual remark.

"I trust you recall that Sir Rudolph is taking tea with us this afternoon, dearest. Your new green silk would be very appropriate, I believe. That colour is so becoming on you. Unless, of course, you prefer the peach sarcenet?" She eyed Diana innocently.

"I had thought this grey very elegant, my lady," replied Diana, keeping a straight face with considerable effort. "More suited to my years and station, don't you agree?"

"No, I don't agree at all," her ladyship burst out. "I think you are being too ridiculous by half, dear. But if you insist on masquerading as a superannuated governess and putting us all to the blush for you, then I will say no more." With this unequivocal pronouncement, Lady Ephigenia entered the house with an exasperated swirl of silken skirts and left Diana to stare after her ruefully.

As a result of Lady Ephigenia's strongly stated disapproval, when Fortham announced later that afternoon that Sir Rudolph had arrived and that her ladyship desired her presence in the Blue Saloon, Diana came down dressed in rather less stringent attire.

Sir Rudolph rose from the settee as she entered and, advancing upon her with a purposeful gleam in his eyes, raised her fingers gallantly to his lips and pressed a rather lengthy kiss upon them.

Exchanging glances with her ladyship over the baronet's unruly ginger curls, Diana was gratified to receive a nod of approval from her hostess.

"My dear Miss Wetherby," Sir Rudolph began, rising to his

full height and obliging Diana—who had never considered herself as anything but tall—to crane her neck in order to meet his cordial smile.

"I have been trying to prevail upon her ladyship to allow me to escort you both over to the ruins of Holywell Abbey, south of Melbury, tomorrow afternoon. If the weather holds, that is. It is one of the few notable historic sites in this part of the country and well worth the ride."

During this speech, he led her to the settee and settled himself beside her, causing the cushions to sag rather alarmingly.

Diana glanced at Lady Ephigenia and saw with some amusement that her ladyship was barely concealing a satisfied smirk.

"If we left early, I could have my cook pack a picnic basket for us." He smiled at Diana with such enthusiasm that she could not but feel an interest in the proposed outing. "And Lady Effie will tell you that I have acquired no small reputation in these parts," he explained, "for the quality of my cook's picnic baskets."

At that point they were interrupted by the arrival of Captain Chatham and Mr. Tottlefield, come to join the ladies for tea. Both these gentlemen, when appraised by Sir Rudolph of his plan to escort the ladies to Holywell Abbey the following afternoon, expressed their eagerness to be included in the party.

"I am convinced you will find the abbey very picturesque," Mr. Tottlefield confided to Diana, settling himself on her other side and balancing his cup of tea precariously on his knee. Then, leaning closer to her, he added in an undertone: "Dick tells me that you don't approve of our plans."

His ruddy face was creased with an anxious frown and his gaze contained an unspoken rebuke at her lack of enthusiasm.

"We thought it would serve the purpose famously. Get you out of Rotherham's hair, put you in the way of getting buckled to some well-breeched fellow, and be a great lark into the bargain." His face lost its anxious look as he talked, and he grinned encouragingly at her.

Diana was sorry to have to dampen his enthusiasm. "I had no idea I was in Lord Rotherham's hair," she told him sweetly. "And as I made it clear to Captain Chatham, I am past the age to be dangling after a husband."

"I thought we were agreed that you would call me Toby." He eyed her accusingly. "And of course you're in Rotherham's hair. It's bad enough that you're related to Dick Chatham; that's as queer a set-out as I've ever heard of. How do you think he's going to explain that to Dick's mother when she hears about it? She'll think it dashed odd that you ain't staying with her in London.''

"I've never met any of the captain's relatives," Diana quietly pointed out. "Why would they care where I stay?" This was the first time she had considered the effect of her presence at Morville Grange on her new relatives. She made a mental note to ask Chatham about his mother's probable reaction.

"Rotherham's got the devil of a reputation with the ladies," explained Toby, "that's why. Hate to be the one to mention it, Diana, but there it is. And then you turn out to be a dashed good-looking female when we all expected some old ape-leader with no teeth left in her head. See what I mean? Something's got to be done, make no mistake, my girl.''

"What must be done about what?" interrupted Sir Rudolph, who had caught the last past of this muted conversation.

Quelling a strong desire to burst into the giggles at Toby's unflattering description of the supposed maiden aunt won in Rotherham's wager, Diana turned to answer the baronet's question.

"Toby here is anxious that there will not be enough to eat for so many of us with only your picnic basket, sir," she invented smoothly. Ignoring the protest from that maligned gentleman, she added: "He suggests that we prepare another basket from the Grange to make sure there is enough to go around."

This controversial suggestion had the effect of producing a good-natured argument between the rotund Tottlefield and the large baronet—both of whom enjoyed the pleasures of a well-stocked table—as to the precise amount of food and drink necessary to satisfy a party of seven on a country jaunt.

Diana was absorbed in playing referee to this joking exchange, when the earl entered the Blue Saloon, interrupting the lively conversation of his guests. After greeting Sir Rudolph cordially, he accepted Lady Ephigenia's offer of a cup of tea and was instantly appraised by the captain of the planned excursion to Holywell Abbey.

"Hope you are free to join us, Rotherham," Sir Rudolph said jovially. "Tottlefield here has committed himself to procuring a second picnic basket from your cook, so there'll be plenty to eat."

A quizzical smile appeared on the earl's lips as his gaze settled on Diana who, after the briefest of nods, had refused to meet his eyes. Her modestly cut, unornamented afternoon gown and primly

arranged coiffeur had not been lost on him. It rather amused him
that he had been able to provoke her to this display of prudery.

"If Miss Wetherby can bear the thought of adding yet another
unattached gentleman to her entourage, I shall certainly join you,"
he remarked innocently.

The implied reference to that morning's confrontation brought
a faint flush to Diana's cheeks. The man was laughing at her, she
thought. Damn his impudence.

Busying herself with refilling Sir Rudolph's cup, she managed
to answer with tolerable coolness without looking up at him. "It
is hardly *my* entourage, my lord. Sir Rudolph was so kind as to
plan this entertainment for all of us." At this point she bestowed
a glowing smile on the baronet, who beamed at her in return.

"And since he has just invited you to join us, my lord, it would
hardly be polite for me to object, now would it? Even if I had
wished to," she added enigmatically.

"Touché, Rotherham," Sir Rudolph declared loudly, rising
from his seat next to Diana. "Now that we're all agreed on that
point, it's time for me to take my leave of these charming ladies."

He proceeded to do so by kissing their hands with such
exaggerated gallantry that Diana blushed and was acutely aware of
the earl's amused eyes on her. She was relieved when the
gentlemen accompanied Sir Rudolph out into the front hall, and
made it possible for her to escape up to her room.

Unfortunately for Miss Wetherby, the day of the excursion to
Holywell Abbey dawned bright and clear. Diana had half hoped
for rain. She was torn between pleasurable anticipation of an
agreeable afternoon spent in the company of no less than five
highly eligible gentlemen and the thought of having to endure
insinuating comments from the earl.

However, by twelve o'clock the sky was still sunny, although a
brisk breeze had arisen from the north. As Diana allowed Molly to
help her into her old green riding habit, she noted that the well-cut
garment, sadly shabby and outmoded as it was, still set off her
youthful form to advantage. She was not sure she regretted this
fact. After all, she told herself, it was only natural to wish to
appear one's best, even if one were practically in one's dotage.

She had ample evidence of this upon entering her ladyship's
sitting-room. Her hostess was wearing a very modish blue habit
cut in elegant yet simple lines and embellished with military

epaulettes in gold braid which gave her a rakish, debonair appearance.

"Next month, without fail," she declared as soon as she set eyes on Diana, "we must spend a week or two in Bath to replenish our wardrobes, my dear. I know I need several new gowns for the coming season that the local modiste is just not fashionable enough to make up for me." She eyed Diana critically. "We will order you a new riding habit, dear. Perhaps a burgundy would be nice."

"This one is quite serviceable still, my lady," Diana replied meekly, not wanting to set her hostess off into another tirade. "It was all the rage in Paris, you know."

"I don't doubt it, love. When it was new. But you will need something much more dashing if you are going to be riding all over the countryside with a bevy of eligible gentlemen."

It was useless for Diana to point out that she had no intention of doing anything of the kind. Lady Ephigenia merely laughed her tinkling laugh and bustled her guest down the stair to the front hall where the gentlemen were awaiting them.

# 6 .....

# The Picnic

By SOME COINCIDENCE she could not quite fathom, Diana found herself being thrown up into the saddle of a restive Perseus by Lord Rotherham. She thanked him civilly and was rewarded by a drawling reminder that she had best look sharp or she would find herself on the ground again.

"I am quite able to handle Perseus, my lord," she replied tartly. "I was instructed by an expert, and have ridden blooded horses all my life." To lend credence to her words, she brought the bay gelding smartly round and moved to join the rest of the party, now mounted and milling about waiting for the signal to start.

"I do not doubt it," he replied, swinging up easily onto his big grey hunter and staying at her side. "But when one gets to be a certain age, my dear girl, as you insist that you have, one must—"

"It seems to me, my lord," she snapped, glaring into his sardonic grey eyes, "that I have informed you once already that I am *not* your dear girl. Why do you insist on provoking me?"

"That's right, you did," he agreed amiably. "However, my experience, which is—even if it is immodest of me to say so— considerable, tells me that females never mean it when they say such things."

"You are sadly mistaken, my lord. But then, perhaps your experience has not been acquired with females of such advanced age as mine," she could not resist adding sweetly, hoping to put him out of countenance.

She was mistaken in thinking that his lordship would be put out by such an incautious sally. On the contrary, he seemed to relish it, for he threw back his dark head and let out a crack of laughter. His voice, when he answered, was almost caressingly soft.

"Are you proposing to remedy what appears to be an appalling lacuna in my education, Miss Wetherby?"

61

Diana almost choked with mortification at being caught so neatly in her own trap. The implications of his suggestion didn't bear thinking about, and for the space of a heartbeat, Diana found it difficult to breathe. Her sense of humour soon came to her rescue, however, and she saw that to be constantly crossing swords with an expert would only make her look ridiculous. After a moment's reflection, she turned to her companion with a rueful smile.

"Touché, my lord. I see I shall have to guard my tongue when you are about." His lordship only smiled, silenced by the unexpected charm of her dimples. Diana took advantage of the pause to turn to the captain on her left and inquire where they were to meet Sir Rudolph.

"We are to meet Potter here at noon. Potter Hall lies to the northeast of Melbury and he is riding over to the Grange to join the party," the captain explained.

"I trust the fellow will remember his picnic basket," Toby remarked, glancing with some satisfaction at his own handiwork, an enormous wicker basket placed carefully in Lady Effie's tilbury. He had personally supervised the cook's selection of cold meats, sundry game pies, pastries, and fruit, and felt confident that the Grange contribution to the picnic would be every bit as appetizing as the basket provided by Sir Rudolph.

The arrival of Sir Rudolph, mounted on a mettlesome roan and accompanied by a gig driven by his groom, provoked a noisy welcome from the younger gentlemen from the Grange. Toby, who had appointed himself in charge of the provisions, supervised the placing of Potter's picnic basket in the tilbury and good-naturedly wagered him a pony that the Grange basket would be emptied first.

When at last the party set forth, in high spirits and with a good deal of joking among the gentlemen, Diana found herself riding between Sir Rudolph and Dick Chatham. Lady Ephigenia, mounted on her spirited little black mare Cassandra, was flanked by her nephew, Rotherham, and Lord Henry Forsdyke, a tall, congenial young man who sported starched cravats of alarming rigidity. Bringing up the rear, Toby rode attendance on the tilbury loaded with picnic gear.

Their passage through Melbury caused no little stir and, as they reached the Blue Boar, Toby's suggestion that they stop off for a quick pint of Dombey's excellent ale brought a rousing response from the captain and Sir Henry. This momentary desertion left

Lady Ephigenia and Diana, who had both refused the offer of refreshment, to ride on in the company of Sir Rudolph and Lord Rotherham.

Diana found Sir Rudolph to be an entertaining host. His ready laughter was infectious, and she was soon enjoying his seemingly endless amusing tales of his trials in raising five young daughters without the benefit of a mother.

"I am surprised you have not remarried, sir," she ventured to comment during a pause in a lively account of his dissatisfaction with a string of governesses who were, according to Sir Rudolph, either much too young and inexperienced or too old and strict for his darlings.

"Well, you have hit the nail on the head, dear lady," he replied. "I cannot say I have not contemplated a second marriage. On the contrary, I would welcome it. But my girls must come first, you see, and it is hard to find a lady whom they all like who is willing to take on the considerable responsibility of raising five children not her own."

"Yes, I see that might be an obstacle," murmured Diana, glad to know exactly how the land lay with Sir Rudolph. One must be desperate or exceedingly fond of children to embark on such a venture, she thought.

"Not that my darlings are anything but angels," Sir Rudolph added with another one of his great belly laughs.

"Oh, I am sure they are, sir," she replied with a smile, thinking that this man had many admirable qualities and if it had not been for the daunting presence of his five offspring, she might well have been tempted to throw her cap at him. As it was, he reminded her forcibly of her own father, whose good-natured camaraderie had made her own childhood so happy.

"I trust you like children, Miss Wetherby?" he asked her suddenly, gazing anxiously down at her from the height of his raw-boned gelding.

"Oh, yes, indeed," she responded calmly. "Although I daresay two or three would be my choice," she added candidly, hoping to divert any notion he might have of making her the mother of his five little angels.

This seemed to give him pause for thought, and they rode in silence which was soon broken by the noisy arrival of the three gentlemen rejoining the party.

* * *

Holywell proved to be a small village similar to Melbury but with some pretensions to historic significance. The abbey lay rather less than a mile to the south and offered an agreeable view from a plateau.

While the picnic baskets were being unloaded and their contents spread on a trestle table thoughtfully provided by the Grange cook, the ladies and gentlemen explored the ruins of the abbey, which were surprisingly well preserved.

The party had broken up into two groups, and Diana was glad to find herself in the company of the three younger gentlemen, who were all in high gig and bent on teasing her about the Abbey Ghost.

"You are surely bamming me, sir," she declared laughingly when the captain brought up the topic. "I don't believe a word of it."

"Oh, but it's true," Lord Henry put in. "Been around for centuries. Quite a tradition in these parts, you know. Appears in all the Guide Books."

"They'll tell you hereabouts that he only walks at twilight on stormy nights," Toby informed her. "But that's not true. When we were all a good deal younger, we rode over here one clear summer night and dang me if we didn't see him. Plain as day."

"How did you know it was a he?" Diana wanted to know.

"That's the story," Chatham explained. "Apparently back in the eleventh century, a monk was murdered in the garden here. Rather horribly, too, if the locals can be believed."

Diana gave a shudder. "Did they ever find out who did it?"

"Oh, yes," Toby replied. "It seems it wasn't to pray this monk came out into the garden every evening. He was trysting with a lass from the village, and one night her two brothers caught the lovers red-handed."

"The story goes that they mutilated him rather badly," Lord Henry added. "Begging your pardon, but the details are too gruesome for a lady's ears."

"He was buried somewhere here in the abbey garden." Toby indicated the wild tangle of briars and bracken surrounding them.

"They say the lass hanged herself the next day," the captain added. "Although I think that's all a hum. Probably married and had a mess of brats, if you ask me."

"How unfeeling of you," objected Diana. "Only think how the poor girl must have suffered to know that her loved one was murdered because of her."

"Fiddle!" exclaimed Lord Henry. "She probably had another sweetheart in the village. Knowing what females are," he added darkly.

"I gather you have been disappointed in love, my lord?" Diana inquired solicitously.

The captain and Toby both burst out laughing.

"When he was fifteen, Henry formed a lasting passion for some female who was visiting the Grange at the time," Toby explained. "Can't even remember her name now."

"Harriet," Lord Henry supplied.

"That's right. Probably some flirt of Rotherham's. He had just come into the title and the females were buzzing around him like flies. Never could understand it." Toby sighed in comic perplexity.

"What couldn't you understand, Toby?" Diana demanded.

"Why Rotherham never got himself hitched. Not for lack of females flinging themselves at him, that I do know."

"He never got over that Standish chit jilting him at the last moment to marry some marquis or other," Lord Henry said. "Huntington his name was, I believe."

"Balderdash!" exclaimed Toby. "She may have been all the crack back then, but I saw her in town a month or two ago. She's a widow now, you know, and has a vile temper. Still a mighty fine looking woman though," he added grudgingly.

"He's developed a phobia against match-making Mamas." Lord Henry laughed. "Saw them behind every tree there for a while."

"Sworn off females, that's for sure," Toby added. "Except the muslin company, of course."

"Dash it, man. Ladies present," the captain exclaimed in dismay.

"Oh, beg your pardon, Miss Wetherby. Can't imagine what I was thinking of." He blushed crimson at this social solecism.

Diana smiled at him and calmly directed the conversation back to the abbey, along whose maze of long, covered hallways they had been strolling throughout this interesting exchange.

Just as she was about to suggest that they return to the picnic table, Lady Ephigenia, on Sir Rudolph's arm, emerged from one of the monastery cells, followed by the earl.

"I declare a halt to these explorations while we repair to the picnic grounds to sample dear Sir Rudolph's feast," her ladyship called out upon catching sight of them. "I am quite famished."

Sir Rudolph, who could not very well abandon Lady Ephigenia, had to watch while Rotherham offered his arm to Diana and escorted her out of the abbey and across the meadow to the picnic table.

She had been intrigued to learn that this insufferably overbearing man had actually been jilted in his youth and might still, even now, be wearing the willow for that capricious beauty of long ago who had spurned him.

How that must have hurt his pride, she thought. No wonder he is so set against matrimony. The notion that the earl might indeed be suffering from a broken heart made her feel more charitable towards him. As a result, the ride back to the Grange later that afternoon transpired without any further unpleasantness between them.

Two days later, this truce was rudely shattered when the vicar arrived at the Grange and requested a private interview with the earl. An immediate result of this meeting was to put the earl out of patience with Miss Wetherby again.

From the moment he first laid eyes on her, Jonathan Fenley had been impressed by Miss Wetherby's sensible view of life. He found her intellect to be superior and her sense of humour refreshing. Over the three months of their acquaintance, he had come to consider her an ideal partner for a man of the cloth. Besides that, his sister, Josephine, approved of his choice.

Naturally he had consulted with Josephine before making such a momentous decision. He was not an imaginative man, therefore it would not have occurred to him to expect a comfortable marriage to be based on anything but mutual regard and compatibility. If Josephine had a different opinion on the matter, she did not say so to her brother.

When he found himself in the earl's presence, however, Mr. Fenley suddenly discovered that his reasons for wishing to wed Miss Wetherby sounded very prosaic indeed.

The earl had received him cordially. They had known each other for a number of years, and Mr. Fenley was, in fact, very distantly related to his lordship on his mother's side of the family. Privately, the earl considered him rather a dull dog but relatively harmless.

As soon as the vicar made it known to his lordship that he had come to request permission to pay his addresses to Miss Wetherby, however, he found himself up against unexpected resistance.

At the end of half an hour, Mr. Fenley had been convinced that such a union would not be at all to his best advantage. How this had occurred he could not very well explain to his sister upon his return to the vicarage. But it became evident to him, the more he reconstructed the interview, that, without actually saying so, the earl had neatly nipped his matrimonial aspirations in the bud.

Mr. Fenley took this contretemps philosophically. Not being of an emotional disposition, he was able to continue his frequent visits to the Grange without discomfort. He was also able to engage in his literary discussions with Miss Wetherby and Lady Ephigenia, although with the advent of the earl's sporting friends, these enjoyable tête-à-têtes became less frequent.

One morning, a week after his abortive interview with Rotherham, Mr. Fenley was seated in the morning-room at the Grange regaling Lady Ephigenia and Diana with a lively account of his reaction to *Childe Harold's Pilgrimage,* two cantos of which had recently appeared and caused much comment in polite circles.

This agreeable discussion was interrupted by the arrival of Sir Rudolph Potter, whose well-known contempt for anything faintly resembling poetry effectively put a damper on that topic. He had stopped by the Grange for the express purpose of inviting Miss Wetherby and her ladyship to drive out with him behind a new team of bays he had recently acquired in Bath.

Lady Ephigenia excused herself on the pretext of having household matters to see to. Diana gave her hostess a reproachful glance which was studiously ignored. She knew for a fact that her ladyship's excuse was merely a ploy to throw her in the way of receiving an offer from the assiduous Sir Rudolph, who had singled her out for marked attention since the excursion to Holywell Abbey.

Diana accepted the invitation gracefully. Actually, she was glad of the chance to speak to Sir Rudolph privately. She had a proposal she wished to put before him.

Her latest letter from Aunt Sophy had arrived that morning and had revealed, for the first time since their separation, how deeply that lady missed the company of her dear niece. Diana had suddenly realized how selfishly she had taken for granted that her aunt would benefit from the imposture she had been persuaded to accept. As it turned out, Aunt Sophy was miserable in London and had, in this last letter, earnestly begged her niece to devise a plan to bring them together again. Diana felt that Sir Rudolph might just provide her with the means to do so.

Coming downstairs after fetching her bonnet and gloves, Diana encountered the earl emerging from the library in the company of Mr. Massey, his estate agent. After greeting Sir Rudolph and learning of their errand, Lord Rotherham looked at Diana quizzically.

"I trust you do not intend to allow Miss Wetherby to handle your team, Potter," he remarked. "She is liable to put you in the ditch, you know."

"That is unkind of you, sir," Diana expostulated. "I have, after all, driven your greys, my lord. I am sure Sir Rudolph has more confidence in my skill with the reins than you seem to. Isn't that so, sir?"

"Driven his lordship's greys?" Sir Rudolph repeated in amazement. "You must indeed be a splendid whip, my dear Miss Wetherby. I can scare credit it."

"Neither can I," drawled the earl, eyeing her with grim amusement. "But Jeremy tells me that it is indeed so. I wish you the best of luck, my dear."

Ignoring this last remark, unsure whether it referred to the horses or to Sir Rudolph, Diana allowed Sir Rudolph to hand her into his curricle.

Eager to put her plan for Aunt Sophy's removal from London into motion, she lost no time in directing the conversation to Sir Rudolph's daughters. This was not at all difficult to do since the baronet was always ready to recount the latest antics of his darlings.

"Is Miss Green dealing any better with Angela and Lucy?" she wanted to know. Miss Green, the latest governess, had been unable to win the approval of the two eldest girls, who were nine and ten years old. Diana had been informed of this unfortunate impasse two days ago during an afternoon ride with Sir Rudolph in the Grange Park.

Sir Rudolph threw her a harried glance as he guided the four mettlesome bays through the heavy iron gates.

"No, Miss Wetherby. Not at all. In fact, the ungrateful wretch packed her bags yesterday and took the Mail-Coach back to London. I have requested a replacement, of course, but the agency assured me that it might be several weeks before they could find someone suitable." He sighed gustily at the prospect and looked so dejected that Diana had to repress a smile.

"In that case, sir, I may be able to assist you."

Sir Rudolph looked at her in surprise, a hopeful gleam slowly dawning in his blue eyes.

"What I mean," she hurried on, anxious to avoid any misunderstanding of her intentions, "is that I may be able to put you in the way of obtaining some relief until you are able to find a replacement for Miss Green. That is, if you do not object to such an arrangement," she added with a smile.

"My dear lady, how can I possibly object to any suggestion of yours?" he replied with such candor that Diana felt a momentary pang of conscience at the ease with which he had taken her bait. "Please tell me what you have in mind."

Satisfied with the initial success of her plan, Diana explained to Sir Rudolph that her Aunt Sophy, desirous of spending some time with her niece, but reluctant to impose upon the Morvilles, whom she did not know, had asked her to recommend a respectable inn in the neighbourhood where a lady of quality but straightened circumstances might be welcome.

Sir Rudolph blinked once or twice as he listened to this hastily invented Banbury tale; but if he thought it odd, he was too polite to say so.

"My dear Miss Wetherby," he said when she had finished. "You are most kind to put forward such an admirable suggestion, but I could not think of imposing on your aunt." He hesitated, and Diana held her breath.

"However, it would give me great pleasure to extend an invitation to your aunt to stay with us as long as she is visiting you, my dear. She would be most welcome, I assure you. On the condition, of course, that you will also be a frequent visitor at Potter Hall." He looked pleased with himself at having devised this clever arrangement.

"Oh, you are most generous, sir, and I thank you kindly. But I am sure my aunt would never consider such an arrangement unless she were allowed to take responsibility for the girls. At least for part of the time."

Sir Rudolph looked dubious.

"Aunt Sophy is very good with children, sir. You need have no fear of that. Unfortunately she never married herself, but she dotes on my brother's five daughters and has helped raise them. She would enjoy your daughters, sir, I am sure of it."

"Well, if it will make you happy, my dear Miss Wetherby," the baronet capitulated. "I will send over a written invitation tomorrow which you may send on to your aunt with my compliments."

Well pleased with her morning's work, Diana returned from her drive with Sir Rudolph very much in charity with the world. Not even a caustic remark from the earl, whom she encountered on the stair, regarding when he might expect to wish her happy, had the power to destroy her happiness.

# 7 .....

# Aunt Sophy

AUNT SOPHY'S RESPONSE to Sir Rudolph's invitation, forwarded by her niece on a Monday morning, was immediate. By the following Friday she arrived at Potter Hall in the private travelling chaise Sir Rudolph had insisted upon sending to London for her convenience.

Her reunion with Diana, who had ridden over to Potter Hall that morning in anticipation of her aunt's arrival, was both joyous and tearful. The sight of her aunt's slim figure, elegantly though somewhat soberly dressed in a travelling gown of dark green sarcenet with a lace collar, a brown velvet pelisse, and a smart hat embellished with a modest ostrich feather which curled charmingly around her heart-shaped face, aroused an overwhelming nostalgia in Diana's heart.

"Aunt Sophy!" she cried out joyously, running forward to fling her arms around her diminutive aunt in an unladylike show of strong emotion. "You have no idea how glad I am to see you, love."

"So I see, my dear," Sophy answered laughingly, extracting herself with some difficulty from her niece's impulsive grasp. "But please don't strangle me, Diana. I am monstrously glad to see you, too, love, but a little of this enthusiasm goes a long way. Now, aren't you going to introduce me to this gentleman who must be my kind host?"

Sir Rudolph Potter, who had followed Diana out of the house as the visitor's chaise drew up before the front door, now stood observing the happy reunion of the two ladies, his kindly face beaming with pleasure.

There was no mistaking their close relationship. Although Miss Sophia Wetherby had recently celebrated her fortieth birthday, her small figure was still attractively lithe and youthful. The scattering of faint lines around her mouth and eyes gave some hint of her advanced years, but the fact that they were obviously caused by a natural inclination to laugh at the oddities of the world around her made all but the most critical observer disregard them after five minutes in her company. She shared with her niece the clear complexion and auburn hair of the Wetherbys, but her eyes were more green than hazel and her stature less regal than Diana's.

"My dear Miss Wetherby," Sir Rudolph began, advancing towards his diminutive guest with a fascinated expression on his face. "Welcome to Potter Hall." He took Sophia's proffered hand gingerly, as if it were made of porcelain, and raised it gallantly to his lips.

"It is indeed a pleasure for me to entertain two such lovely ladies at the same time. I am privileged, ma'am. Welcome to my humble house," he added, offering an arm to both ladies and escorting them into the hall where the baronet's housekeeper waited to show the guest up to the apartments prepared for her.

"I declare, it is monstrous good of you to invite me, Sir Rudolph," Sophy confided some time later, with her light-hearted laugh, when they joined their host in the drawing-room for tea. "I had quite grown to dislike London. The noise and the constant bustle give me the migraine, and the number of conceited, toplofty dandies, encroaching mushrooms, and simpering chits one encounters at almost every social event quite put me out of patience with town life, let me assure you."

"I couldn't agree with you more, Miss Wetherby," Sir Rudolph replied wholeheartedly. "I have always considered the pleasures of London vastly overrated, ma'am. For myself, I prefer the simple life of the country and go up to Town as infrequently as possible."

By the time they had finished tea and the excellent lemon tarts for which Sir Rudolph's cook was justly famous, any doubts that Diana might have had about her Aunt Sophy's ability to make herself agreeable to her host had evaporated.

She observed that Sir Rudolph had become quite enthralled with her aunt's scintillating laughter and entertaining chatter. She watched with amusement at the ease with which Aunt Sophy encouraged the baronet to describe, in some detail, a hunting party he had attended recently in the north.

Sir Rudolph was in his element. Bluff and country bred as he was, he loved nothing better than a lively conversation on one of the topics dear to his heart: his darling daughters, his horses, his dogs, hunting, and eating. In Miss Sophia Wetherby, he found a perfect audience.

Diana was particularly relieved when her aunt's first encounter with her host's daughters went off without a hitch. Sophy had insisted on being taken up to the schoolroom where the girls were having their tea under the halfhearted supervision of one of the housemaids. Having been warned by her niece that Angela and Lucy, the two eldest, were the ringleaders of the group, Aunt Sophy poured all her charm onto these shy, suspicious little girls.

"Are you the new governess?" Angela wanted to know immediately.

"Oh, no, dear," Sophy answered with a tinkling laugh. "Governesses are so dull, don't you think? I always thought so when I was young. They never let one have any fun at all, and I love fun, don't you?"

Five pairs of eyes stared at her in disbelief.

"That's why I'm here, my dears. I've come to the country to have some fun, and I hope you will be able to help me. I'm sure you must know a hundred different amusing things to do. Will you do that for me?"

The twins, six-year-old Sally and Selena, were the first to capitulate, loudly assuring their visitor that the best time could be had fishing for tadpoles in the pond behind the house. Angela wanted to know precisely what kind of fun this strange female had in mind, while Lucy giggled shyly at the idea of a grown-up lady being interested in climbing apple trees. Baby Jane, a toddler of four, generously offered the jolly lady a lick of a very sticky raspberry lollipop.

It could not be supposed that the arrival in the neighbourhood of such a vivacious and cultured lady as Miss Sophia Wetherby could go long unnoticed. If nothing else, Diana's frequent presence at Potter Hall would have aroused unwelcome speculation had not the two ladies appeared in Melbury one afternoon the following week driving Sir Rudolph's phaeton and accompanied by all five of his daughters.

The local gossips immediately assumed that the visitor must be a relative of Sir Rudolph's, particularly since the five little girls addressed her as Aunt Sophy and treated her with obvious affection. They also showed an unusual tendency to pay attention to her, something no mere governess had ever managed to achieve.

When it was discovered that the visitor was another Miss Wetherby, some eyebrows were raised. Since Sir Rudolph was well liked in the neighbourhood, however, his explanation that Miss Sophia Wetherby, the younger Miss Wetherby's aunt, had been so kind as to agree to come down from London to be an informal companion and chaperone to his little angels until such time as a suitable governess could be found, was generally accepted.

Lady Ephigenia, upon being made privy to a slightly more accurate version of this story, immediately accused Diana of not taking her ladyship into her confidence sooner.

"My dear child," she cried, when learning of the odd arrangement. "We would have been delighted to put your aunt up at the Grange if only you had told me of her dislike for London. I can see her point entirely. I dislike Town life myself, and rarely can Rotherham persuade me to play hostess for him at Morville House on Cavendish Square."

Diana was overcome by this kindness. "I have trespassed on your generosity too much already, Aunt Effie," she murmured. "I could not wish to draw your nephew's displeasure by foisting another maiden aunt off on him."

"Stubble it!" exclaimed Bijou, who had increased his vocabulary of English slang thanks to the amused efforts of the earl's sporting guests.

Her ladyship looked at him with disapproval, then turned to Diana. "What twaddle you do talk, my love. I thought you knew me better than that. And what could Rotherham possibly find objectionable in us inviting your aunt to stay at the Grange? Heavens above, the house is more than half empty as it is. It's not as if we would have to turn anyone out, you know." She laughed at the idea, her crimped curls quivering as she shook her head incredulously.

"But the expense . . ." Diana began, hesitant to tell her ladyship exactly what the earl might well find objectionable about another single Wetherby lady moving into his house.

"Balderdash!" Bijou squawked, jumping up and down on his perch vigorously.

"There you have it," agreed her ladyship. "My sentiments exactly. You can have no notion just how plump in the pocket Rotherham is, dear, or you wouldn't say anything so nonsensical. It can be of no consequence to him at all how many maiden aunts you bring into the house."

When Diana demurred, her ladyship caught her in an affectionate hug and said: "Don't be a peagoose, love. I can't say I feel entirely easy with the idea of your aunt, even if she is an old Tabby like me, staying at Potter Hall as a guest. There is something not quite proper about such an arrangement."

The immediate outcome of this conversation was that Diana drove her hostess over to Potter Hall that afternoon to call upon Miss Sophia Wetherby.

Unfortunately, at least according to Diana's estimation, they did not go alone. As they were being handed up into the tilbury by old Ben, the earl came round from the stables mounted on his big grey hunter, Ajax, and offered to accompany the ladies. Since Diana could not think of any good excuse to exclude him, she was obliged to accept his offer, which she did with such chilly civility that Lady Ephigenia, catching her nephew's eye, raised her eyebrow at his amused expression.

The party was received with great cordiality by Sir Rudolph himself, having just returned from overseeing the installation of a new roof on a tenant's cottage. He was, as always, in high good humour, and escorted his guests into the drawing-room, calling out to a footman to send in refreshments.

"You will be wanting to see your aunt, no doubt, Miss Wetherby," he exclaimed when the party was seated and served tea with a selection of freshly baked pastries. "She is down in the orchard with the girls having a picnic. She is a most charming creature, your aunt, Miss Wetherby. The girls already adore her. Perhaps you would like to join them?" he added when Diana looked somewhat crestfallen. "It's only a short walk."

So it was that after the tea things had been cleared away, the ladies from the Grange accepted Sir Rudolph's invitation to stroll through the back gardens down towards the orchards. There they found an extensive vegetable plot and the now famous tadpole pond—presently occupied by several fat ducks.

They discovered Miss Sophia Wetherby, dressed in a charming sprigged muslin gown of pale lilac, a parasol of the same shade propped against the trunk at her side, holding court under a huge apple tree. She was surrounded by five dishevelled but happy-looking little girls, four half-grown puppies, their pink tongues lolling out from too much exertion, numerous lambs and goats, and a mother cat with six newborn kittens in a box at her feet.

The innocent charm of this pastoral scene seemed to affect Sir Rudolph mightily for he turned to Diana and whispered loudly:

"My dear Miss Wetherby, I cannot thank you enough for making me known to your aunt. She is an extraordinary woman, so cultured and knowledgeable about so many things. The girls are enchanted with her, and I can already see the effects of her influence on them. I do not know how I shall manage without her."

Diana blushed at these effusive compliments and dared not meet the earl's eyes, for he would surely throw her one of those cynically amused glances she dreaded.

Lady Ephigenia, on the other hand, was immediately charmed by the well-bred demeanour of the diminutive Miss Sophia Wetherby. When Sir Rudolph offered an arm to each of the two ladies, they strolled back to the house together very much in charity with one another.

Diana was left to bring up the rear with the earl.

"I see I must congratulate you, Miss Wetherby," he said in a half-teasing voice as soon as they were alone. "For once I must agree with Sir Rudolph's choice of words. A charming creature she is indeed."

"Thank you, my lord," Diana murmured coolly. "You are most kind."

"Not at all, I assure you, my dear . . . that is, Miss Wetherby," he corrected himself quickly with an engaging smile.

Diana devoutly wished he would not smile at her just so, for it did strange things to her composure. Resolutely, she set herself to maintain a correct degree of civility without encouraging the dangerous levity his lordship seemed in the mood to pursue.

"I should warn you, however, Miss Wetherby, that Sir Rudolph appears to be dangerously dazzled by your aunt's charm. Do you think it was quite wise of you to introduce them? If you don't have a care, she will cut you out, and that would never do, now, would it?"

"And I should warn *you*, my lord," she exclaimed angrily, momentarily forgetting her resolve to be cool and civil, "that I will not tolerate any disparaging remarks from you or anyone else concerning my aunt. Is that understood?" She had come to a stop and was glaring up at him, hazel eyes flashing. "And as for insinuating that she is throwing out lures to Sir Rudolph, the idea is preposterous! Only a Johnny-flat would be so idiotish as to imagine that Aunt Sophy could not have married any man she wanted any time these twenty years."

"Then why didn't she, I wonder?" the earl inquired gently. "It goes against the grain to see such a charmer without the protection of a husband, let me tell you."

"That is hardly your concern, my lord," Diana said stiffly. Then, realizing that she had been rather rude to her host, she added in a softer tone, "It is no secret that Aunt Sophy's fiancé was killed in a hunting accident just two months before they were to have married. A true love match, it was too," she added with a faint sigh which was not lost on her companion. "I was only a schoolgirl at the time, of course, but it is my belief that dear Sophy never recovered from the shock. She has never shown any desire to accept another offer, and she has received many of them as you can well imagine," she added defiantly.

The earl, who had been regarding Miss Wetherby closely during this outburst of confidence, seemed to be much taken by the changing expressions on her face as she recounted this tale of love and tragedy.

When she paused, he took her hand, placed it on his arm, and resumed their walk towards the house. "I can sympathize with her, my dear. Something of a similar nature happened to me when I was a callow youth who believed in love and all that flummery. Soon found out that it was a bag of moonshine, of course."

He broke off abruptly, wondering how on earth he had come to mention to a relative stranger an event which he had sworn, ten years ago, to put behind him forever. He glanced down at Miss Wetherby, who was looking up at him with a gleam of compassion in those expressive hazel eyes.

"Your aunt's story almost restores my faith in your sex," he drawled in a deliberately nonchalant tone, watching with amusement as the compassion in her eyes turned to mock incredulity.

"Almost?" she quizzed him. "Surely you are too harsh, my lord?"

"Nothing of the sort. Your aunt's case is one in a million, I would wager. Unless of course you . . . Dare I venture to ask if you have also been languishing with a broken heart all these years?"

Diana glanced quickly up at him but could detect no hint of mockery in his eyes. "Oh, no. Nothing so romantic, I'm afraid. It's just that life was so much fun while my father was alive. He was so gay and carefree. Perhaps a trifle too improvident some would say." She sighed. "But it's no use repining on that now. The thing is he brought happiness to all who knew him. The house was always filled with his officers and friends, and yes, I did receive a number of offers, but I suppose you could call me improvident, too, for I didn't give much thought to the future." She paused, a faraway look in her eyes.

"And then he was killed," she said in a low voice. "And that gay world was closed to us forever. There was nothing left after all the bills had been paid. Nothing. So we had to live with that odious half brother of mine. And then . . . Well, you know what happened then, and I can't imagine why I am prosing on and on, boring you with these sad stories, my lord. Please forgive me."

The earl looked at her searchingly for a moment, then said in a curiously diffident voice: "Not at all, my dear Miss Wetherby. Nothing of the kind, I assure you. However, if it is the gay Town life you hanker after, it is just as well that you did not accept an offer from the vicar. Dull chap if ever I saw one."

Diana looked at him in amazement, the pleasant mood of companionship which had developed between them suddenly evaporating. "Mr. Fenley?" she said. "I have never received an offer from Mr. Fenley, my lord."

"Yes, I know," was the curt reply. "I told him to hedge off."

"You *what?*" Diana's voice took on a distinct note of challenge. "Am I to understand that Mr. Fenley approached *you?* And that you had the unmitigated gall to assume that you could speak for me in this matter? That is the outside of enough," she fumed.

"Did you in fact wish to marry the vicar?"

"No, of course I didn't. That is to say," she hastily corrected herself, "I may well have wished to consider the possibility. But that is not the point."

"Oh, forgive me for being so obtuse," drawled the earl provokingly. "I quite thought it was the whole point."

"Well, it isn't," Diana exclaimed irrationally, fast losing the last shreds of her patience. "And I fail to see, my lord, how it could possibly concern you who makes me an offer. Or what gives you the right to intervene in my affairs."

"Obviously you have not given your present circumstances any serious thought, my dear Miss Wetherby," his lordship replied, in what Diana could only regard as an odiously officious and condescending manner. "If you had, it would be plain to you that the unenviable task of protecting you from any breath of scandal has fallen upon me. Therefore, I must insist that you refrain from jaunting about the countryside inciting the local swains to approach me with ineligible offers."

He looked down at her to gage the effects of these deliberately provocative words and was rewarded by the clear indication that he had left Miss Wetherby speechless.

He smiled mendaciously. "I suggest you do not allow Sir Rudolph to see you with your mouth at half cock, my dear. Not at all the thing. And if I were you, I would not let it get about that I was on the catch for a husband," he added, apparently ignoring the expression of wrath that had suffused Diana's normally placid countenance.

"Nothing scares off a man more effectively than the suspicion that he is the object of some enterprising female's matrimonial urge, you know," he continued, paying no heed to the muffled gasp of indignation from his companion. "If you are so set on getting riveted, I will ask Lady Ephigenia to look around for someone who would be quite unexceptional. Naturally, you will not expect her to produce someone of the first stare. Not for a lady of your advanced age, as you yourself have pointed out to me. But no doubt we can—"

But Miss Wetherby, who had been struck speechless by the conceit and gross impropriety of the earl's casual attitude towards her future, suddenly regained her voice. It had become increasingly evident to her as she listened to him that her host had every intention of palming her off on some country squire. His objection to Mr. Fenley she read unequivocally as a distaste for having her wed any relation of his, however distant that might be. Well, he would soon find out that she was not to be disposed of so easily.

"I suppose Sir Rudolph is one of these ineligible local swains you refer to, my lord?" she inquired in a dangerously calm voice, withdrawing her hand from his arm with more abruptness than was strictly necessary.

"Ah! So it's a title you fancy, is it?" He seemed to be repressing a smile. "I dare say that might be arranged. But put Sir Rudolph out of your pretty head, my dear. My money is on your aunt there."

"You are insufferable, sir," she retorted hotly. "Must you reduce everything to the level of a wager? First you make me the victim of your gambling addiction, and now you have the gall to suggest that my dear aunt Sophy . . ." Words failed her. She felt her throat constrict and turned away from her tormentor and walked quickly towards the house before he could see the glint of tears in her eyes.

# 8 ·····

# Arabella

BY THE TIME she rejoined her aunt and Lady Ephigenia in the drawing-room, Diana had regained a tolerable composure. Her discovery that the earl meant to arrange her future to suit himself had both shaken her peace of mind and destroyed the harmony she had hoped was beginning to develop between them. He was, after all, she decided as she hugged her aunt affectionately and took her leave of Sir Rudolph, every bit as obnoxious and unfeeling as she had expected him to be.

Her mood was withdrawn during the drive home, and she took little part in Lady Ephigenia's chatter which included a good deal of enthusiastic praise for Miss Sophia Wetherby, with whom she had immediately struck a firm bond of friendship.

What the earl thought of the elder Miss Wetherby was not so easily discernible. He seemed to agree with his aunt that the visitor was indeed elegant, well-bred, and blessed with extraordinary beauty and a pleasant personality. In fact, he said all that was polite, but Diana was at a loss to know his real feelings.

Later that evening, as Diana was dressing for dinner, her ladyship came into her bed-chamber and with her characteristic straightforwardness broached the topic again.

"What happened this afternoon to put you so out of curl, my love?" she inquired solicitously. "Has that pesky nephew of mine said something to annoy you again?"

When Diana assured her that nothing at all was the matter, she merely uttered one of her tinkling laughs. "You can't bamboozle me, love. I couldn't help but notice that you looked more than a trifle put out after your tête-à-tête with Rotherham in Sir Rudolph's orchard. I know he can be monstrously disobliging when he chooses, but he is not naturally unkind. Perhaps he was teasing you again about finding a husband. Was that it?''

"As a matter of fact, yes, it was," Diana replied rather belligerently. "He had the gall to suggest that Aunt Sophy will cut me out with Sir Rudolph. At least that is what he was odious enough to tell me. Which is absurd. That is, it is absurd to think that Sir Rudolph had any intention . . . that is, he has never said a word to me about it; and even if he had, which he hasn't, and even if I had wished him to, which I can assure you I didn't . . . Well, what I mean is that the whole thing is a Banbury tale Lord Rotherham has made up to provoke me," she finished lamely.

Midway through this confused and somewhat illogical explanation, Lady Ephigenia threw up her hands in exasperation. "Enough, my dear, enough!" she exclaimed when the tirade had come to an end. "Let us consider this for a moment." She made herself comfortable on the settee and scratched Bijou's yellow head which he stretched out for her attention.

"If you do not wish for an offer from Sir Rudolph," she said after a moment of deep thought, "I cannot imagine why you should get into such a pet over Rotherham's remarks, dear."

"He insinuated that Aunt Sophy was throwing out *lures* to Sir Rudolph," she exclaimed bitterly. "As if she would do anything quite so vulgar. And then he told me he had given poor Mr. Fenley a set-down because he asked permission to address me. Of all the odiously pretentious and overbearing things to do," she fumed, recalling the earl's calm announcement of this piece of meddling.

"Well, just think, dear. I told you myself that I didn't think the poor vicar would suit you. So perhaps it is all for the best."

"How can you say so, Lady Effie?" Diana exploded. "Don't you think I should have been consulted in the matter?"

"Perhaps Rotherham was a bit high-handed, love. But then he often is, although he means well, you know."

"No, I don't know," Diana said mulishly. "And what gives him the right to tell me, in that condescending way of his, that he will ask *you* to look around for someone unexceptional. His very words, Lady Effie! Now if that isn't enough to try anyone's patience, I don't know what is."

"Yes, I can quite see that he was most provoking, dear. But why did you never tell me that you had a wish to be married? I understood that you were quite set against it."

"I was. I mean, I am," Diana cried exasperatedly. "But he had the effrontery to point out that I could not, at my age, expect to attract someone of the first stare. Can you credit it?''

''I admit that is doing it rather too brown, my dear. What maggoty notion could have got into his head, I wonder?'' She paused for a moment to regard the flushed countenance of her companion speculatively, as a novel idea suddenly occurred to her. What if her guest was not quite so disgusted with her host as her protestations seemed to indicate? The notion appealed enormously to her ladyship's sense of intrigue.

''Although, to be fair, love, I've heard you say exactly the same thing at least a dozen times yourself,'' she added gently, wondering what else had been said in that interview in the orchard that Diana was not telling her.

''Yes, of course I have,'' Diana admitted, brushing out her auburn curls with vicious strokes. ''But it's one thing for me to say it and quite another for that odiously toplofty coxcomb to say so in that supercilious tone he uses when he wishes to be particularly unpleasant. As if he meant it, too,'' she added in a strangled voice.

''Well, you can hardly blame him, dearest. I told you how it would be if you insisted on wearing those dowdy gowns. It's true you haven't offended us with that grey monstrosity again, but you seem to take pains to appear—well, positively mousy, my love.'' She eyed her guest with some amusement. ''What are you wearing tonight, for example? Not that dull brown chintz again, I trust?''

''Well, no. Actually I had not planned to wear anything at all, my lady,'' replied Diana, two dimples appearing mischievously in her cheeks.

This sally was met with a tinkle of shocked laughter. ''Now that will surely catch the gentlemen's attention, but it is not something I can countenance, dear. Definitely not good *ton,*'' she exclaimed with mock severity.

''What I meant was that I have worked myself into such a state that I can feel a headache coming on, so I should perhaps not go down to dinner at all tonight.''

''Nonsense, love,'' exclaimed Lady Ephigenia with some spirit. ''Put on that stunning yellow silk we had made up for you last month, and you will feel much better about everything. There's nothing like a pretty dress to make a woman feel more the thing.''

Between bullying and cajoling, Lady Ephigenia managed to coax her guest to step into the yellow silk and to allow her ladyship's dresser to arrange her hair in a new style. The results were highly gratifying, but as she accompanied Diana down to join the gentlemen in the drawing-room, Lady Ephigenia's mind was occupied with romantic speculations about the unusually perverse antagonism between Rotherham and the stubborn Miss Wetherby.

Several days after the incident in the orchard, Diana was returning from an afternoon ride through the Home Park in the company of Captain Chatham, Toby, and Lord Henry Forsdyke, during which the three gentlemen had attempted in vain to convince Miss Wetherby of the advantages to be derived from a season spent in Town.

"Just imagine," Toby insisted, "you will cut such a dash at all the balls, routs, masquerades, drums, and other parties that you are sure to take the shine out of everyone. Since the elder Miss Rogers got riveted to Lord Barnsbury last month, you'll have no real competition either."

"That Rogers chit was a Diamond of the First Water," Forsdyke explained, in response to Diana's raised eyebrows. "Dick here threw out a few lures in that direction, but I heard she was set on having nothing less than a marquis."

"That's why you kept your distance, no doubt." Chatham laughed. "You did the right thing, let me tell you. Too toplofty by half she was. Puffed up beyond anything. Barnsbury is welcome to her, I say."

"If this is any example of how gentlemen discuss innocent females behind our backs, then I want no part of it." Diana laughed. "I wish you would all stop teasing me to go to London. I have no desire to do so, you know."

"Well, so you've told us a hundred times, m'dear," protested Toby. "But it just ain't reasonable. What have you got against matrimony anyway?"

"I have nothing *against* it actually," Diana replied. "I just like my independence too much to relinquish it without a struggle."

"Now that's the biggest Banbury tale I've heard in a long while," chided Chatham. "My mother, who is the greatest authority on the subject, will tell you that all females ever dream of is a handsome Buck, full of brass, who will sweep them off their feet. At least that is what my sisters are forever prattling on about," he added disgustedly.

"I am sure Lady Chatham did not express herself in quite those terms, Dick," Diana said reprovingly. "And there is a vast difference between dreams and reality, let me tell you."

"If you insist on being so perverse, m'dear, I can see that we will have to marry you ourselves." Toby had spoken in jest but no sooner had he said it than his face brightened into a wide smile. "Why, that's just the thing!" he exclaimed happily, as the others stared at him in amazement. "Why didn't I think of it before?"

"That is the most atrocious piece of nonsense I've ever heard," Diana burst out, a faint blush suffusing her cheeks.

"Why not?" Toby asked innocently. "We're all of us about as eligible as you can get, you know. Good families, Pink-of-the-*Ton*, up to snuff on every rig in Town, invited to all the best houses. Not as plump in the pocket as Rotherham, of course, but we are none of us paupers by a long stretch. Of course, Dick is a second son, but that don't signify. He had a fortune from his godfather ten years ago. So there can be no objection there—"

"Stop it this instant," Miss Wetherby interrupted between chokes of laughter. Her momentary discomfort at Toby's suggestion had been overcome by her sense of humour. "You are being absurd, Toby. And besides, I couldn't marry all of you, now could I?"

"No, that would raise the devil of a dust," Chatham agreed pensively. "But dash it, Diana, Toby's right. We all feel somewhat responsible for your awkward situation, so it's only right that we should help to get you out of it. Wouldn't you agree, Forsdyke?"

The latter looked a little startled at the turn the conversation had taken, but he rallied nobly. "No doubt about it. Happy to be of service to you, Miss Wetherby. Any way I can."

"That settles it," Toby declared happily. "It's not every day a female receives a joint offer from three eligible suitors, m'dear. So tell us, which one will you have?"

"You are being ridiculous, all of you," exclaimed that harried lady. She was torn between amusement and annoyance at Toby's effrontery. She knew him to be a careless and perpetual tease, but this foolishness was the outside of enough.

"No, but seriously, m'dear. Let's say if you were to choose among us," Toby insisted, "which one would it be?"

"I like you all. As *friends*," Diana stated categorically. "Now do stop this teasing, Toby. It is not at all proper. And besides," she added, unable to resist the opportunity of giving them all a well-deserved set-down, "why should I be less puffed up than Miss Rogers and settle for less than a marquis? Can you tell me that?"

"Because I don't know any marquis who's hanging out for a wife," Toby pointed out reasonably. "Except old Gatesbury, of course, and he ain't got a feather to fly with, besides being sixty if he's a day."

"That won't do at all," said Lord Forsdyke in a shocked voice. "Can't let you throw yourself away on that ancient fuddlecap, Miss Wetherby. Not up to scratch, if you know what I mean. Very bad *ton*."

"I can see we will have to roll the dice to see who is going to be the lucky man," Toby cried gleefully.

Miss Wetherby took instant and violent exception to this suggestion. "I forbid you to do anything of the kind," she snapped. "I have already been the victim of one game of chance; surely you do not mean to insult me yet again by making me the prize of a dice game?" Her tone was so aggrieved that the three gentlemen ceased their bickering and apologized profusely for being so insensitive.

The rest of the ride transpired without further mention of the subject of matrimony, and Diana had quite put it out of her mind by the time the riding party returned to the Grange.

There they were met by the startling news that Lady Chatham and her daughter Arabella had arrived unexpectedly for a short visit before proceeding to Bath, where her ladyship intended to spend a fortnight drinking the waters.

When Diana descended to the drawing-room that evening before dinner, she found the visitors there before her. Lady Chatham, a rather large female swathed in purple silk and wearing a turban consisting of purple satin and several curling ostrich feathers dyed to match, sat chatting with her hostess on the yellow brocade settee. As Diana approached them, she was conscious of being closely scrutinized and appraised by the visitor and was glad she had taken particular pains with her appearance that evening.

Lady Chatham's sharp eyes took in the distinctive elegance of Miss Wetherby's pale green silk gown which revealed a tall, slender figure, and the simple yet attractive arrangement of her auburn curls. She accepted Diana's curtsy with a slight inclination of her head, and pronounced her—in loud undertones to Lady Ephigenia—to be very proper indeed.

"Arabella, my love, come and meet your cousin," she called imperiously to her daughter who was standing at the pianoforte regaling her brother with the latest on-dits from Town.

Arabella came over promptly and embraced Diana warmly. She was as unassuming as she was lovely. "You will be Cousin Diana," she announced with a gay smile. "Dick has already told me that you are a complete hand and a famous whip who can handle even Rotherham's greys." The last was said with such awe that Diana had to smile.

"What is that?" interrupted Lady Chatham loudly. "Rotherham let you take the reins in his curricle? He must be getting soft in the head. Never have I known him to let a female touch his precious horses before."

"I must confess I did it without his consent," Diana explained. "And he was none too pleased when he found out, I can assure you."

"That I can well believe," the viscountess said in a reproving tone. "Such temerity is to be deplored in a well-bred female."

Lady Ephigenia caught Diana's eye and gave a small shrug. "Diana has more than ordinary skill with a team," she said stoutly. "I would trust her with anything we have in the stables, including those puffed-up greys."

"Are you by any chance referring to *my* greys, my dear Aunt," cut in a drawling voice, and everyone turned to see the earl saunter into the room. He was dressed in pale yellow satin knee-breeches and a tightly-fitting coat of the same hue which showed off his broad shoulders to advantage. His cravat, tied in a creation much envied by the younger set, fell in precise folds over his frilled shirt of finest cambric, and in his hand he carried an exquisite Sèvres snuffbox.

After a cursory glance in the earl's direction, Diana turned back to listen to a remark from the captain, who stood by her side. She heard little of what he said, however, for the sight of Rotherham in all his elegance had upset her tranquillity more than she would have liked. Reluctantly she admitted to herself that her host was one of the best looking men she had ever seen. Even the dashing officers in her father's regiment would have paled beside him. It was unfortunate that beneath that deceptively handsome exterior lay a cold-blooded, obnoxious coxcomb, who had managed, in the few short weeks he had been at the Grange, to disturb her peace of mind more than she cared to admit.

"Christopher!" Arabella shrieked, throwing herself at the earl in reckless abandon. "How wonderful to see you again. You look very top-of-the-trees as usual."

"I beg of you, Arabella, do not use those vulgar cant expressions, dear.'' The words were sharp, but there was a satisfied glint in her ladyship's eyes as she watched the affectionate reception accorded by the earl to her lovely daughter.

Diana noticed her ladyship's expression and wondered if Lady Chatham proposed to succeed where all other matchmaking mothers had failed in catching the elusive earl as a son-in-law. She saw no indication that the earl held Miss Chatham in anything but a brotherly regard, but nevertheless she found the notion of a match between them singularly disagreeable.

During the following week she had ample opportunity to observe Arabella's behaviour and was unaccountably relieved to find that the young heiress treated all the gentlemen in the household as extensions of her brother Richard, whom she adored. She had known them all since childhood and stood on easy terms with them, particularly with Toby, who encouraged her in every mad caper she chose to undertake.

Rotherham, who was accorded no more attention than any of the other gentlemen, looked upon his young visitor with what appeared to Diana to be unusual tolerance. He took her driving in his curricle, although he refused to allow her to handle his greys, and he mounted her on a neat little white mare brought expressly from one of his other estates for her enjoyment.

But Miss Chatham's presence made itself felt most noticeably in the evenings which had, before her arrival, been fairly sober. Now that was all changed. No longer were Lady Ephigenia and Miss Wetherby allowed to while away the evening at a game of whist with the gentlemen. Rarely an evening went by without some form of lively entertainment devised by that enterprising young lady. If it was not a musical evening during which she would persuade Lady Ephigenia to play the pianoforte or beg Diana to sing some of the many French arias and folk songs she knew, in her clear soprano, Arabella would ask her hostess to have the carpets rolled back so they could get up a set of country dances.

Two or three times a week, the Grange party was invited to dine at other houses in the neighbourhood, and since the arrival of the earl, Lady Ephigenia had expanded the number of guests she included in her traditional Wednesday evenings of dinner and cards.

Diana enjoyed the increased social activity and especially looked forward to meeting Aunt Sophy at many of the functions she attended. The neighbourhood had grown to accept the odd circumstances of having a Miss Wetherby in residence with two of the most highly regarded families in the district, and it was only straightlaced puritans like Mrs. Robinson who refused to include Miss Sophia Wetherby in any invitation addressed to Sir Rudolph Potter.

"I think it will all work out for the best," mused Lady Ephigenia one morning as Diana came into her sitting-room to join her in an early cup of chocolate as was her custom.

When Diana looked at her with raised eyebrows, her ladyship confided that she had every confidence that they would have wedding bells before the summer was out.

"I'm talking about your aunt, love," she added, seeing the startled look on Diana's face. "She is a sensible woman, my dear, and I don't doubt that she will make Sir Rudolph an excellent wife."

"She has refused better offers than any he could make her," Diana felt obliged to say. "I rather think my aunt is a confirmed spinster like me."

"If Bijou were here, he would undoubtedly say rubbish! I am the only confirmed spinster around here, dear. You mark my words."

For once, Diana felt disinclined to argue the point. For days she had been sorely tempted to tell her beloved hostess about the multiple offers she herself had received recently from the captain and his two cohorts. She knew her ladyship had as lively a sense of humour as her own. More than anyone else except perhaps Aunt Sophy, her ladyship would enjoy the irony of that unusual occurrence.

The temptation to tell all was simply too much for her to resist when Lady Ephigenia asked her out of the blue if she was disappointed at Sir Rudolph's desertion.

"You would not suit, of course," her ladyship pointed out tactfully. "No more than you would with poor Mr. Fenley. But it is rather lowering to be cut out—as my nephew put it—by a female nearly twice one's age, my love."

"Oh, Sir Rudolph is still attentive enough." She laughed. "I believe the poor man is dithering between us, Lady Effie. If he could have us both, I'm sure he would. I could listen to his endless hunting stories and Aunt Sophy could bring up his daughters."

"So you have not received an offer, then?"

"Not from Sir Rudolph," Diana responded with a gleam of

unholy merriment in her hazel eyes which caused her ladyship to regard her with sudden interest.

"I gather from your expression, my love, that you *have* received one from another gentleman and I hope you do not mean to keep me in suspense. Tell me at once, you tiresome girl."

Diana paused for effect, then confided in a studiously casual voice: "Actually I've received three."

"Three?" her ladyship gasped in astonishment, her cup of chocolate quite forgotten on the breakfast tray. "From whom?"

"From Lord Forsdyke, Mr. Tottlefield, and Captain Chatham," she replied with a straight face. "All of whom were kind enough to assure me they were eminently eligible."

Lady Ephigenia was struck speechless by this information but managed to ask apprehensively, "And which one have you accepted, dear?"

"Why, none of them," Diana answered airily. "You see, it was rather difficult to decide, since they all asked me at once."

"They *what?*" her ladyship gasped incredulously.

"Yes, I know what you must be thinking. I did feel it was rather irregular at the time. However, I told them I would settle for nothing less than a marquis. Like the redoubtable Miss Rogers, you know. I felt I could do no less."

"You did what? And who is this Miss Rogers? I declare, my dear, you've put me all in a twitter."

"Miss Rogers is—and I have this from those who have been at her feet last season and know from whence they speak—is a Diamond of the First Water; a Nonpareil in other words. My informant assures me that she was riveted to the Marquis of Barnsbury last month and is now quite out of the running and should present no competition whatsoever if I wished to take the Town by storm this season."

"Will you stop bamboozling me and explain exactly what is going on here," her ladyship burst out in injured tones. "What has Miss Rogers got to do with anything? And whatever inspired those three jackstraws to offer for you all at once? I can believe it of Toby, but Dick and Henry are usually more up to snuff than to do anything so havey-cavey."

"Well, it's a long story, Lady Effie. One I have wanted to tell you since I first arrived at the Grange, for it was obvious to me then that you had no knowledge at all of the real reason I am here."

"Whatever can you mean, love?" was her ladyship's perplexed reply.

So Diana told her, as briefly and succinctly as she could, about the infamous wager, leaving out only her own imposture which she did not quite feel at liberty to reveal.

"So you see, ma'am," she concluded after the sordid tale was told and her ladyship had not yet recovered from the severe shock her nerves had sustained, "the gentlemen feel guilty for getting me into this fix. That is why they feel honour-bound to restore my reputation. And as you have said yourself so often, a respectable marriage does wonders for any female's reputation, however tarnished."

# 9 .....
# The Ball

THE IMMEDIATE OUTCOME of Miss Wetherby's confession to Lady
Ephigenia, which brought her ladyship many sleepless nights, was
to precipitate an acute attack of soul-searching. It was not often
that her ladyship, so open and straightforward in her own dealings
with everybody, had cause to ponder the advisability of her
actions. In this case, her quandary lay in the circumstance of her
very favourite nephew having comported himself in a reprehensible and highly improper manner unworthy of a gentleman, and
totally unacceptable in a Morville. It is not to be thought that her
ladyship did not endeavour to find mitigating circumstances to the
affair. She did indeed, but to no avail. Any way she looked at it,
Rotherham appeared as the villain. Unaccustomed as she was to
prevarication, she felt personally affronted, as a Morville herself,
by the ugliness of her nephew's wager. She saw it clearly as her
duty to demand that Rotherham repair the wrong he had committed.

Lady Ephigenia did not deceive herself into thinking for a
moment that his lordship would take kindly to her interference in
his affairs. And she was right. But once she had seen her duty
clear, Lady Ephigenia did not hesitate. So it was that one morning,
a sennight after Diana's confession, her ladyship bearded the earl
in the library after breakfast and laid the whole matter before him.

"So you think I should offer for the wench?" he said shortly,
after a considerable pause during which he wore a path on the
Axminster carpet between his desk and the window.

"There is no need to be flippant," his aunt replied sternly.
"Miss Wetherby's father may have been only a second son, but
her mother was a Devanaugh and granddaughter to the old Duke
of Wexley. And the Devanaughs can trace their family back to the

Norman Conquest, you know, which is more than the Morvilles can boast of.''

He stood with his back to her, looking out on the formal rose gardens that were beginning to show the first buds of spring. It occurred to her ladyship that her nephew, although clearly put out by her knowledge of the affair, had taken her intervention rather mildly and had not bitten her nose off as she had half feared he would.

''You have not answered my question.'' He had turned and was regarding her with cool, unreadable grey eyes.

Lady Ephigenia returned his gaze unflinchingly. ''It seems to me that you cannot expect to discharge your obligation to Miss Wetherby by marrying her off to some country squire of no account; which is what she has informed me is your intention. I, for one, will not countenance any such ramshackle alliance, Rotherham. You may rely on it.''

''It was not my intention to do so, ma'am. I hope you know me better than that.''

''And so I should hope, my dear boy. But neither can you abdicate your responsibility just because three of your friends seem ready and willing to undertake it. Diana assures me she has received offers from all three of them. My understanding is that she has refused them all, of course.''

The earl's lip curled slightly. ''Of course,'' he echoed cynically. ''Now doesn't it seem to you highly unlikely, Aunt, that a female of Miss Wetherby's age and situation would not jump at the chance to form such an eligible alliance? Forsdyke should have been especially attractive because of the title. I find it hard to believe. Sounds very havey-cavey to me.''

''I can't help what you believe, Rotherham,'' her ladyship retorted. ''The fact is, my dear boy, I like Diana excessively. I am generally a fair judge of character, and I refuse to accept that she is guilty of anything besides a natural frustration at being placed, through no fault of her own, in an intolerable situation.''

The earl looked skeptical. ''I would like to believe you, Aunt, but can you tell me why Miss Wetherby turned down a chance at escaping from her dilemma through an eligible marriage? It doesn't sound reasonable to me.''

Lady Ephigenia gave a snort of humourless laughter. ''If someone told you to your face that an offer was being made only to assuage a feeling of guilt, what would *your* answer be?'' she demanded without mincing matters.

Having no ready answer to such a question, the earl turned again to stare out the window, although it was doubtful he noticed the roses in their formal rows.

"So, you would have me wed, Aunt?" he murmured softly as if to himself. "I don't relish the idea, of course, but if you really feel the Morville honour is at stake, I shall gladly throw myself into the breach, so to speak." He turned as he spoke and a whimsical smile played on his lips as he regarded his aunt affectionately.

"Try not to be absurd, Rotherham," she said tartly. "This is not a laughing matter. And besides," she said sententiously, after a moment's pause, "it's high time you settled down and produced an heir."

"Oh, but I have an heir, my dear Aunt. My cousin Hugo lives in daily expectation of something unpleasant happening to me, as you well know. I would hate to cut his pretensions off so unexpectedly."

"Nonsense," her ladyship snapped with exasperation. "Hugo Morville is a loose screw, there is no other word for it. And I, for one, hope I may never live to see him master of Morville Grange."

Seeing his most cherished relative so obviously rattled caused the earl to relent enough to offer her a glass of ratafia. Her ladyship impatiently rejected this offer, declaring ratafia a drink only fit for the weak spirited. Instead, she ordered her nephew to pour her a glass of his best sherry, which succeeded so well in soothing her ruffled nerves that when they parted shortly thereafter, she was able to pronounce herself well pleased with the interview.

"I am glad you have seen where your duty lies, my dear boy. Your father would have been proud of you," she observed as she left the library, leaving her nephew to stare after her with a perplexed frown.

Even if the earl had any intention of acting immediately on his aunt's advice, he could hardly have found the opportunity to do so. The Grange was suddenly thrown into a veritable whirlwind of activity when, in either a weak or inattentive moment, the earl agreed to Arabella's insistence that it was only proper for him to give a ball to ensure that her stay at the Grange would be something out of the ordinary.

Arabella was instantly thrown into transports at his acquiescence, and could talk of nothing else but which of her various gowns would be most suitable for the occasion and the numerous shopping trips which must be taken into Melbury. She even prevailed upon her host to escort her and Lady Chatham on an extended journey further afield to Sherborne, some ten miles to the north, where, she claimed, a larger selection of slippers, silk stockings, ribbons, and other fripperies was available.

The bulk of the innumerable details involved in such an undertaking as a formal gathering for upwards of twenty to thirty couples naturally fell to Lady Ephigenia and Miss Wetherby. Lady Chatham condescended to give her advice on how such affairs were managed in her own London establishment, but since her taste rarely appealed to either of the Grange ladies, her voice went mainly unheeded. Her strongly worded attempts to determine which of the local gentry should be honoured by an invitation to dinner and which should only be too glad to be invited to the ball also fell on deaf ears. Lady Ephigenia privately informed Diana that, having lived in the neighbourhood a good deal longer than Maria Chatham, she was well able to decide for herself who should dine at the Grange.

On the evening of the ball, Arabella burst into Miss Wetherby's dressing-room in a flurry of excitement to see what her dear cousin Diana had chosen to wear that evening. She surveyed her friend critically and declared that the pale orange Italian taffeta with low-cut bodice trimmed with ivory lace was exactly right for the occasion.

"That colour makes you look very dashing indeed, Cousin," she said approvingly. "You were quite right to select it rather than that Nile green silk which I thought not quite the thing for a grand ball."

"This is hardly a grand ball," Diana corrected her gently. "I am sure Lady Ephigenia had nothing like that in mind. Remember that we are in the country, dear. And country assemblies must necessarily lack some of the brilliance of the London gatherings."

"Oh, fiddle," Arabella exclaimed. "Of course it will be a grand ball. You must know that it will be my first, Cousin. Mama has refused to let me attend anything but the most insipid of the London evening entertainments because I have not yet had my come-out. She was even a little reluctant to let me attend this ball, but Christopher persuaded her that there was no harm in a family affair with only close friends in attendance. I adore that man, Diana, and if I were a little older, I would marry him."

"Would you indeed, you minx? Well, you should know that a well-bred young lady is never so vulgar as to express a preference for a particular gentleman so openly. It is not at all the thing, you know. Gentlemen prefer to make their own choices, and if they suspect you are setting your cap for them, they will hedge off. Believe me, dear.''

Arabella dissolved into unladylike giggles. "But how else is a gentleman to know you like him above all others, silly? I never could understand how that happens, and Mama is so disobliging. All she will say is that I will know when the time comes. It all sounds very tame to me.''

"Your Mama is very wise, dear. And she is absolutely right. Do you think those garnets are quite the thing with your white figured silk?'' Diana remarked to change the subject. "I quite expected your Mama to recommend the pearls.''

"Oh, she did. But I like the garnets. My grandmother Chatham left them to me in her will, and I have never worn them.'' She paused for a moment, watching as Lady Ephigenia's dresser arranged Diana's auburn curls into an elaborate knot on top of her head and allowed several long ringlets to hang down over her bosom.

Then she added in a deceptively nonchalant voice: "Don't you like them, Cousin?''

"Oh, yes. They are very prettily cut. But there is something so elegant and impeccable about a good set of pearls. I'm wearing mine, as you see. They were my dear Mama's, and I treasure them.''

She said no more, having learned through the experience of ten days in Arabella's company that where the young and impulsive heiress could not be pushed, she could often be gently led. So it was with considerable gratification that Diana noticed, as the two young ladies descended together to the drawing-room, that the offensive garnets had been discarded in favour of a really beautiful pearl necklet and eardrops.

Diana had deliberately chosen to enter the drawing-room in the company of the beautiful Arabella, thinking to escape unwelcome attention as all eyes must necessarily be drawn—or so she thought—to the younger lady's fairer and more fashionable good looks. In this she was only partially correct. Little did she realize that her darker, warmer colouring and orange taffeta displayed to advantage beside Arabella's pale, golden loveliness. While it was true that most of the company was drawn to the blond beauty, at

least one pair of eyes dwelt with unexpected pleasure on Miss
Wetherby's graceful form.

Glancing casually around the room as they made their entrance,
Diana could not help but intercept Rotherham's quizzical eyes
upon her. Feigning unconcern, she pulled her spangled gauze
shawl more closely around her bare shoulders and made her way
to a high-backed chair close to where her hostess and Lady
Chatham were recalling the more lurid family scandals of the
expected dinner guests.

These soon began to arrive, and Miss Wetherby had little time
to be self-conscious in the bustle of greeting the newcomers as
they were announced by Fortham in his inimitably antique voice.
By the time the drawing-room clock marked five minutes to six, all
the dinner guests were assembled except Lady Eliza Standish, who
was chronically late for every event she attended.

Lady Ephigenia was debating whether to have dinner set back
a quarter of an hour when the doors were thrown open once again
to admit a majestic lady of uncertain age in a flowing ball dress in
the latest French fashion of narrow, form-revealing, green silk.
Lady Standish was a practised hand at making an entry, and this
one stopped all conversation in the room as heads turned in her
direction.

Visibly gratified by the effect of her appearance, she sauntered
into the room and approached her hostess with regal condescension. She was tall for a female, and the exotic green creation set on
top of her unnaturally yellow curls made her appear gigantic. She
towered over the tiny Lady Ephigenia and acknowledged Lady
Chatham and Miss Wetherby with a cordial nod of her green
headdress which already showed unmistakable signs of disinte-
gration.

Catching Arabella's eye as she came up to salute her ladyship,
with whom the heiress had been a great favourite before Lady
Chatham decided that Town life suited her better than country
boredom, Diana was forced to turn aside to hide a smile. This was
a mistake, for she almost collided with the earl who had come up
behind her to greet the last of his dinner guests.

Flustered at his proximity, she stepped back too suddenly and
was only prevented from falling into Lady Chatham's ample lap
by the earl's strong arm steadying her.

"Sorry to have startled you," he murmured as she regained her
balance and withdrew from his grasp. "May I say that you are in
excellent looks this evening, Miss Wetherby."

His words were warmly flattering, but Diana noticed that his eyes regarded her with cool deliberation. "Dare I hope that you will save the first waltz for me, Miss Wetherby?" he added, with a faint smile. "You do waltz, I gather?"

"Having been out for years, my lord, as you well know, I certainly do," she replied rather tartly. "But allow me to point out that there are other ladies present who have a greater claim on your attention than I can boast of, my lord. Lady Standish, I'm sure, would be only too glad to oblige you," she added archly, unable to resist the opportunity to administer a mild set-down.

His dark brows rose questioningly. "You presume to tell me who I can waltz with, Miss Wetherby?" But Diana was saved from having to reply to this rebuke by Fortham who at that moment opened the doors to announce that dinner was served.

When Diana looked back on that magical evening, she could not help thinking that it was just as well she did not know the turmoil and distress that was in store for her. Blissfully ignorant of the gathering storm, Diana was able to enjoy herself more than she had since she had attended the gay balls and routs given by her Mama in Paris before her father's death.

She had gone into dinner on the arm of Toby Tottlefield and, given the seating arrangements at the dinner table, which adhered strictly to protocol, Diana had been seated halfway down the long table and limited to conversing with Toby and Lord Forsdyke on her other side. But since she could hardly have chosen more congenial table companions, the conversation did not drag, and by the time the company repaired to the ballroom on the second floor, Diana was assured of at least two eager partners.

"Dashed good turnout," Toby commented as he and Forsdyke accompanied Diana and Arabella up the wide staircase to where the musicians had already struck up a country dance.

"For a country ball, it's not too bad," agreed Lord Forsdyke amiably.

"How can you be so paltry, Henry," Arabella scolded him laughingly. "As I told Cousin Diana, it's a truly grand affair. Lady Morville brought in musicians from Bath and I hear they're all the crack. I can't wait to dance. Hurry up, Toby, or have you forgotten that you are leading me out in the first set?"

Tottlefield looked down at her glowing face with fond affection and thought privately, not for the first time, that Miss Chatham was as delightful and unassuming a companion as any man could ask for. Pity that old dragon of a mother was doubtless already scheming on a title for her darling. Rarely did it occur to Toby to regret that he was not possessed of a title in his own right. As only heir to his childless uncle, the fourth Earl of Ridgeway, Toby was assured of one day coming into the earldom, but since he had, at the age of thirty-one, a considerable fortune of his own, inherited from his father, it was not in his nature to wish an untimely end to his favourite uncle. Now, however, as he gazed on Arabella's irrepressible loveliness, he found himself, for the first time in his life, envying his good friend and crony Henry Forsdyke, who commanded both a respectable title and a considerable fortune to go with it.

As they took their places in the set that was forming, Toby could not help noticing that Miss Wetherby was attracting quite as much attention as his own partner.

"Your cousin is in fine fettle tonight," he commented to Arabella as the set came to an end and he escorted her to a seat beside her mother.

"Oh, do you really think so?" the heiress inquired innocently. "I do wish you would tell her so, Toby. The silly goose is so set on playing the maiden aunt that she refuses to see that she is so impossibly elegant. I confess I feel quite squatty beside her."

"You are too harsh on yourself, m'dear," Toby expostulated, his cherubic face registering his profound revulsion at the thought.

"At least admit that I am short, then," Arabella insisted.

"Nothing of the kind, m'dear. You are just the right height, so stop being a peagoose and let me get you a glass of lemonade."

Since he was promised to partner Miss Wetherby in the next dance, a quadrille, he remembered Arabella's words.

"You are in prim twig, this evening, m'dear," he told her as they took their places on the floor. "I swear you are wasting your talents here in the country. If you would only let us frank you to a season in Town, I can guarantee you'd be all the crack. Ten to one you'd nab a duke, or at the very least a marquis before the year was out. Think about it, m'dear."

"I have no wish to 'nab a duke,' as you so elegantly put it, Toby. And I have thought about it, don't think I haven't. But it just won't serve, Toby. So please don't tease me any more about it."

"If ever there was a peagoose, you're it, m'dear. Never saw a female who didn't want to cut a dash at all the *ton* parties. No reason why you shouldn't. This excuse of being at your last prayers is balderdash and you know it. Beats me what your game is. Hate to see you go into a decline, y'know.''

He looked so perplexed that Diana had to laugh. ''I have no game, Toby. And I can't think of anything more enjoyable than being able to dance again, and wear a pretty gown, and have good friends like you, Henry, and Dick. And that's exactly what I am doing. So there's no likelihood of my falling into a decline.''

His merry face brightened at her words, and he said no more on the subject until the set was over and they stood together near one of the French windows which had been thrown open to let in the cool spring air.

''But our offers still stand, y'know,'' he said seriously, the topic obviously still very much on his mind. ''I speak for all of us, of course. If you decide you can accept any of us, that is. We all stand ready to get riveted at a moment's notice. Just say the word, m'dear. Just say the word.''

Diana was touched at this display of loyalty. ''I am lucky indeed to have such a friend as you, Toby,'' she said, a catch in her throat. ''You are kind and generous; a true gentleman. Not like some others I know. If things were different, I would be happy to accept your offer. But, unless I am a poor judge of people, I think your affections lie elsewhere,'' she ventured with a smile. ''And I wish you luck, Toby, I truly do.''

Toby looked at her with a mixture of surprise and apprehension. ''Is it that obvious?'' he asked. ''It's impossible, of course,'' he rushed on before she could reply. ''No sense even thinking about it, so please don't let that influence your decision. Come to think of it, we would deal famously together, m'dear. You're a bruising rider and drive a team of four to an inch. I'll bet you also hunt, don't you?''

''Yes,'' Diana replied dryly. ''But we could hardly spend all our time in the stables, Toby. Be reasonable. You must see it wouldn't serve.''

''I thought you liked horses, m'dear,'' Toby complained in an aggrieved tone.

''And so she does,'' broke in Richard Chatham who had come up in time to hear Toby's remark. ''What's this all about, anyway? Ain't stealing a march on the rest of us, are you, Toby? Mighty unsporting of you. Shall have to call you out if you do it again, I'm warning you.''

"The devil fly away with you, Chatham," answered Toby, his round face regaining some of its habitually merry expression. "Miss Wetherby and I were having a serious conversation, I'll have you know."

"Yes, so I heard. About horses." Dick grinned at his friend. "Just the kind of frippery that would interest a beautiful lady, I'm sure."

"Horses are a serious business, let me tell you—"

"Yes, I'm sure they are. But Diana doesn't want to be jawed to death about them at a ball, you muttonhead. Miss Wetherby," he said, turning to Diana with a mocking bow. "They are about to strike up the first waltz and I believe you are promised to me. Am I not right?"

"No," drawled a voice from behind them. "Miss Wetherby is unequivocally promised to me."

Unable to think up an acceptable excuse at such short notice, Diana was obliged to allow the earl to lead her back onto the floor and place an arm about her slim waist as the musicians struck up one of the season's popular waltzes.

She had rarely allowed herself to indulge in idle fantasies about her host, so it came as somewhat of a shock to rediscover how exciting it felt to be held so close to him that she could detect the faint, pleasant aroma of his shaving lotion. Overcoming her momentary agitation, she glanced up at him through her long lashes and saw that he was gazing down at her with a faint frown.

After several moments of silence, which her partner showed no signs of breaking, Diana's sense of humour inspired her to say, rather daringly, "If you insist on glaring at me in that cross way, my lord, you will have me thinking that you regret asking me to stand up with you."

"Nothing of the kind, my dear Miss Wetherby," he responded smoothly. "You are an excellent dancer, as I expect you already know. And I regret nothing, except perhaps . . ." Here he paused, looking at her with such a strange expression in his eyes that Diana felt her colour rising.

"Except what?" she demanded, more brusquely than she had intended.

"I was going to say except perhaps the improper circumstances which brought you to Morville Grange in the first place, my dear."

"Well, that's water under the bridge, isn't it?" she replied impatiently. "And how many times do I have to tell you—"

"Yes, I know, Miss Wetherby. Forgive me. You are not my dear, as you have told me several times already. Beef-witted of me to forget it. Isn't it?"

"Yes, indeed!" she retorted, her heightened colour giving her rather serious features a vivacity that enhanced her looks and caused her partner to revise, yet again, his original impression of her. "Must I assume that you are in the habit of being so condescending to all the females of your acquaintance, my lord?" she inquired with some asperity.

"Only to those who deserve it," he answered ambiguously.

"I see," she said, not at all sure that she did. "And what have I done to deserve your condescension?"

He was looking down at her with such amusement dancing in his grey eyes that Diana felt he must be teasing her.

"Cannot you guess, Miss Wetherby?" he asked, his lips twitching.

"I am no good at guessing games, my lord; and if you will insist on hoaxing me, I shall have to talk about the weather. Or about the impropriety of your standing up with me for the first waltz, or something of that trivial yet irreproachable nature."

"What a sad bore that would be, I don't doubt," he said mockingly. After a moment of looking at her speculatively, he continued in a softer tone. "You should wear your hair like that more often, Miss Wetherby. It makes you look quite beautiful. I can't remember seeing you look less like the maiden aunt you pretend to be."

"That's a back-handed compliment if ever I heard one," Diana replied with mixed emotions. "I had hoped that by now you would have accepted my single status as permanent. You had only to ask my Aunt Sophy if you doubted my word," she added, indicating with a slight gesture Miss Sophia Wetherby who, at that precise moment, twirled past them, a vision in pale green silk, in the arms of a beaming Sir Rudolph Potter.

"From what I have been able to see of your Aunt Sophia," he replied with a short laugh, his eyes following the waltzing couple, "a woman is never too old for romance."

"That may be true, my lord, at least in theory. For females have very vivid imaginations, you must know." She glanced up at him with laughter in her eyes. "But in practice it is exceedingly rare for an elderly female to find the man of her dreams. I can only be glad that Aunt Sophy seems to have done so," she added with a hint of wistfulness in her voice that did not escape her partner.

''I gather that you have yet to encounter this paragon,'' he remarked with a hint of sarcasm.

''You can laugh all you want, my lord,'' she said with some asperity. ''But at least I am not cynical about the opposite sex, which you seem to be. I fail to see that this attitude can bring you any satisfaction at all.''

''Whereas your stoicism does?''

''Certainly,'' she replied firmly. As the music ended at that moment Diana was saved from having to explain the precise nature of the satisfaction she derived from her stoic acceptance of her single state, something which she felt entirely incapable of doing the more she thought about it.

The earl relinquished her to Sir Rudolph who appeared at her side to claim the next dance, and Diana was neither surprised nor offended that the entire set was spent talking about the many charms and accomplishments of Miss Sophia Wetherby.

''Devilishly fine woman, your aunt, m'dear,'' the baronet began enthusiastically. ''Hope you won't take it amiss if I say so, Miss Diana.''

''No. Why should I?'' Diana asked innocently. ''It so happens I agree with you. I have known my aunt far longer than you have, sir, and I am well aware of her admirable qualities.''

''Relieved to hear you say so, m'dear. She has quite endeared herself to us all at Potter Hall. Can't remember when things ran so smoothly. After my poor Agatha died, of course. I can quite see that we lacked the woman's touch. Old Mrs. Teather—the housekeeper, you know—has quite taken to her and between them they intend to refurbish the morning-room. Sent off for samples for new curtains, they have. And banished the dogs, too,'' he added with a laugh. ''I must admit I had fallen into the habit of having them in during the evenings. Not the thing at all, I know.''

Diana smiled at him and reflected that her aunt was lucky indeed to have fixed the interest of such a kind and jovial gallant as Sir Rudolph. She hoped he would not be too devastated if the fiercely independent Miss Sophia Wetherby decided to forego marriage yet again in favour of her single state. Diana was well aware that her aunt would not be tempted either by Sir Rudolph's title or by his tidy fortune. Like Diana herself, Sophia was a romantic, and her niece knew that her heart had remained frozen in the past for twenty years, ever since the death of her dearest Robert. However, she had also noticed a subtle change in Aunt

Sophy's behaviour over the past two or three weeks. If she had not seen it with her own eyes, Diana would not have believed it. Her sophisticated, worldly-wise aunt was becoming positively domestic! Perhaps there was hope for Sir Rudolph after all.

# 10 .....

# Unwelcome Proposal

TWO DAYS AFTER the ball, which had been declared the most successful social event of the year by those local matrons who considered themselves quite up to snuff on such matters, Diana's peace of mind was suddenly shattered.

She had taken Perseus out for an early morning ride and, on a whim, had traversed the Home Wood towards the small artificial lake which the present earl's grandfather, an avid fisherman, had constructed as a breeding pond for his favourite speckled trout. The trout-raising project had long since been abandoned, and the lake was now inhabited by a family of noisy ducks and several fat brown geese.

Diana had had the foresight to provide herself with a bag of old bread crusts from the kitchen and was welcomed with much fanfare by the waterfowl as she dismounted and tied Perseus to a nearby tree. Taking care not to tread on the friendly ducks as they crowded around her feet, she sat down on a conveniently placed bench and began to dispense her largess.

So engrossed was she in seeing that the baby ducklings got their fair share of the bread crumbs that she failed to hear the approach of another rider until he stood beside her bench.

Smiling down into her startled face, Rotherham apologized for having frightened her. "You presented such a charmingly rural picture, Miss Wetherby. I was forcibly reminded of your namesake, that fiercely virgin goddess, and felt myself—for a moment at least—quite the intruder, like that unfortunate Actaeon. I trust you will forgive me and not set my own dogs to tear me limb from limb. I imagine that could get very unsightly."

Remembering that her namesake had been caught bathing in the nude by that unlucky young hunter, Diana could not stop herself from wondering how far the earl had gone in imagining her in that

107

classical situation. Even if he had stopped short of disrobing her in his mind—a possibility she set no store by—the comparison he had suggested was highly improper. So it was with heightened colour that she responded.

"You deserve nothing less, my lord, for putting me to the blush with your unflattering comparisons. I used to agree with your Aunt Effie, who feels sorry for that impertinent young man, but I now see that the punishment quite fits the crime. His excuse that he happened by the goddess's pool accidentally simply won't wash. He richly deserved his fate. I hope you do not mean to take his part, because I warn you, it's a lost cause."

As she talked, conscious of being somewhat flustered by the turn the conversation had taken, Diana concentrated on the hungry ducks who demanded ever more tidbits from her bread bag and avoided more than a glance in the earl's direction.

"In that case, I shall do nothing of the sort," he responded easily, seating himself on the other end of the bench. "Besides, I did not come to pull caps with you, my . . . Miss Wetherby. Quite the opposite in fact. I have come to propose a truce between us. What do you say?"

Diana suddenly found it very hard to breathe. But her initial feeling of elation very soon gave way to anger. This provoking man had the amazing audacity to propose a truce with her after going out of his way to insult her and make fun of her dear Aunt Sophy. He deserved a thundering set-down, but unfortunately she could not think of one that would suit her purpose.

After a few moments of reflection, however, she was able to master this violent impulse and reply in a tolerably civil tone.

"I was unaware that we were at odds, my lord," she said lightly, opening her hazel eyes in a fair imitation of incredulity.

His immediate answer was a crack of laughter.

"You are a complete hand, Miss Wetherby. But you cannot have forgotten that first interview we had several weeks ago during which I took certain liberties with you? I fancied at the time that you were not entirely unresponsive to that kiss."

"You are utterly mistaken," Diana interrupted tartly, her colour deepening. "I was quite paralyzed with fright and indignation, as I recall. I am not accustomed to such insolent treatment from complete strangers."

His reply to this was another crack of laughter.

"You may well laugh, Lord Rotherham, but your behaviour

was abominable," she said stiffly, throwing a piece of bread to a timid duckling who held back from the crush around her feet.

"Well, now that we know each other better, perhaps you can be more comfortable," he murmured, ignoring her caustic remark. "And next time you won't be quite so paralyzed," he added in a lazy, amused drawl.

"There will be no next time, sir," she snapped angrily, staring at him in stunned amazement. "I can see that you are determined to put me out of countenance. Well, let me tell you that I am not one of your schoolroom misses who can be put in a quake by such scrambling manners."

"You can have no notion how that air of righteous indignation becomes you, Miss Wetherby. It quite takes twenty years off your age."

Diana was hard pressed not to smile at this outrageous remark. "You are quite absurd, my lord. I believe you followed me here today for the express purpose of tormenting me with your queer starts."

"You are mistaken, Miss Wetherby. I followed you here for quite another purpose."

Something in his tone made Diana look round at him in surprise, and the intense expression in his grey eyes caused her heart to leap into her throat. She instantly discarded her intention of asking what that purpose might be and tried to cover her agitation by saying, "If you have come to tease me again about accepting some local squire so that you may be relieved of my presence, allow me to tell you, my lord," she declared in a voice made husky by anger and resentment, "that if events go as I think they might, I will not hesitate to remove myself from your house with all possible speed."

Rotherham watched with interest as Miss Wetherby glared at him, indignation and something he could not quite determine making her eyes flash and her lips quiver invitingly. Perhaps, he thought to himself, his cynicism for once deserting him, following Lady Ephigenia's suggestion of just where his duty as a Morville lay might not be so tiresome after all. The revelation that the execution of his duty might, in fact, be unexpectedly pleasurable amused him.

He regarded her angry profile for several moments before saying in a mollifying voice, "Did it never occur to you that I might have no desire to be relieved of your presence? And that quite the opposite might be true?"

Diana laughed shortly. "Now I know you are trying to bamboozle me, my lord. Do you really expect me to believe such a Canterbury Tale? You must have a very poor opinion of my intelligence if you do. Which is no surprise to me, of course. You impress me as one of those persons too full by half of his own consequence."

"I thought we had agreed on a truce, Miss Wetherby, and here you are insulting me again."

"If I have insulted you, which I seriously doubt, then I beg your pardon. But I don't recall agreeing to any truce."

"Enough of this equivocation, my dear," he said impatiently and with a swift movement moved closer to Diana and took one of her hands in his. "Aren't you in the least interested in my purpose for being here this morning, my love? You disappoint me."

Taken by surprise at this sudden turn of events, and distracted by the term of endearment he had used, Diana did not even have the presence of mind to withdraw her hand, but could only stare at him blankly.

"What? Paralyzed again, my dear? You must learn to overcome this tendency to fall into a trance when a gentleman makes you an offer, Miss Wetherby. Dashed unsettling, I can tell you. Rather puts one off, too."

This unexpected pronouncement had the effect of jolting Diana out of her shock. She snatched her hand out of his grasp, jumped up, and turned on him in a white fury.

"You are despicable, sir. How dare you mock me? Is nothing safe from your cynicism? Must everything be a source of amusement?" Her voice trembled with suppressed emotion and her face had gone very pale.

The earl had also risen and now grasped her by the shoulders in a vice-like grip. His expression was thunderous and his lips were set in a thin line. "You are being deliberately perverse if you think this is a joke, Diana. Before you interrupted me with your tirade of abuse, I was about to make you an offer of marriage. I can think of nothing more serious than that, can you?"

"Then someone put you up to it. Am I right?" Diana blurted out before she could stop herself. "Or perhaps it was another wager. Is that it? Why else would you do such a thing?" This horrible possibility, which had only just occurred to her but which sounded, in her distraught state, to be highly probable, caused angry tears to start in her eyes.

"Don't be a little fool," he retorted, thoroughly incensed at the turn his good intentions had taken and more than a little guilty at how close to the truth Miss Wetherby's accusation had come. "I know you don't think very highly of my behaviour, but surely you cannot believe I would be such a villain as to trifle with you in such a way?"

He tried to draw her into his arms as he spoke, but Diana resisted with all her force. Rotherham had always considered himself to be well up to snuff in pleasing members of the opposite sex; at least he had never received any complaints from the many females who had caught his eye and with whom he had, over the years, conducted various degrees of flirtations. With Miss Wetherby, however, he had to admit that he had made a hobble of the whole affair. Instead of sinking gracefully into his arms as a female of any sensibility at all would have done immediately with only the slightest encouragement from him, here she was fighting like a silly widgeon. He couldn't understand it at all and finally released her so suddenly that Diana almost fell into the pond.

Regaining her equilibrium with an effort, Diana was not so successful in regaining her composure. Impatiently she brushed the tears from her face and stood, staring out unseeingly across the water, wrestling with emotions that threatened to overwhelm her, and trying to suppress the sobs that rose unbidden in her throat.

There was an uncomfortable silence, broken only by the disappointed quacking of the ducks who still milled about Diana's feet in hopes of wheedling a few last crumbs out of her bread bag.

Rotherham was the first to speak, addressing himself to Diana's rigid back when she showed no signs of turning around.

"I take it that you are not yet ready to receive my addresses, Miss Wetherby," he said in a cool, formal voice. "I can assure you that I am entirely serious, however, in spite of what you seem to believe. Perhaps after a period of reflection you will be less inclined to fly into a pucker at the idea of a union between us. I can only hope so, because I shall not take no for an answer."

Diana did not trust herself to reply. Too many conflicting emotions ran riot in her breast. On one hand she was utterly transported that the Earl of Rotherham, no less, had made her an offer of marriage. Her head reeled at the enormity of this conquest, for she finally admitted to herself that, in one sense, he came close to being the man of her dreams. On the other hand, her heart could not accept the idea of a loveless marriage, and this was what he had offered her. No word of love or even ordinary affection had passed his lips. He was obviously callous to the extreme, and however much he denied it, Diana knew he must have been put up to the idea either by Lady Ephigenia or by his military friends.

Nothing, she told herself fiercely, nothing on this earth could persuade her to accept any man under those humiliating conditions. And especially not any man who had the unmitigated gall to tell her he would not take no for an answer. It would be a bitter triumph, of course, but she would show him just who would have the last word in this encounter.

This resolution made her feel somewhat recovered, and she turned to tell him not to waste any more of her time with unwelcome addresses, but he was gone. She saw him riding off into the wood and stood gazing after him long after he had disappeared from view before she remounted Perseus and rode slowly back to the house.

# 11 .....

# Lady From the Past

IT WAS SEVERAL days before Diana could bring herself to speak to her host with any semblance of composure. She had even abandoned her early morning rides to avoid the possibility of running into him on the grounds. Instead she now rode out every afternoon in the company of Lady Ephigenia and Arabella. Where Arabella went, Toby was more often than not in attendance, and where Toby went, his military friends would also go unless they were out shooting rabbits or pigeons with the earl's gamekeeper.

Thus it was quite a cavalcade that rode through Melbury one afternoon a week later. The party from the Grange had been invited to take tea with Lady Eliza Standish, who lived two miles on the south side of the village.

Lady Ephigenia and Lady Chatham were driving Jupiter in the tilbury, but Diana and Arabella had chosen the more rigorous exercise of riding with the gentlemen. Arabella was engaged in showing off the paces of the little mare Lord Rotherham had provided for her use, whom she insisted on calling Buttercup in defiance of the predominance of classical monikers sported by the horses in the Grange stables.

Toby and Lord Henry Forsdyke formed an admiring clique to this equestrian display, while Diana rode with Captain Chatham.

"I think you should know, Cousin," he said after a comfortable pause, "that Rotherham has taken us to task for, as he put it, playing fast and loose with your affections, m'dear." He laughed at this clear example of what he considered his friend's quirkish notions. "A blistering set-down he gave us, I can tell you. Taken some freakish bee in his bonnet about it, for some reason."

Diana stared at him in disbelief. "What right has he to set rules for the behaviour of others?" she demanded with such warmth that Chatham glanced at her curiously.

"It is his house, you know, coz," he replied with a grin. "Never known him to cut up so thick over such a trifle, though. Lord knows he should have thanked us for being willing to—" He stopped, glanced at her with an embarrassed expression on his face, and laughed ruefully at what he had come close to blurting out without thinking.

"Willing to take me off his hands, I presume you meant to say, Cousin?" Diana completed his sentence with a wry laugh.

"Nothing of the kind, coz," he protested. "Anyway, I told him he could save his breath, because you wouldn't have any of us. On account of having your heart set on a marquis, of course. He seemed to think that was amusing."

"Oh, he did, did he?" retorted Diana with spirit. "It would serve him right if I did accept one of you. That would teach him not to pry into other people's affairs. Wouldn't you agree, Cousin?"

Although he couldn't for the life of him see how such an event would teach Rotherham anything, Chatham agreed amiably.

"I fancy that Toby is out of the running, however," Diana continued. "He seems to have formed a strong *tendre* for Arabella, or haven't you noticed?"

"Oh, Toby has always had a *tendre* for Arabella, even when she was a schoolroom chit forever getting into one scrape or another. They deal famously together, although I rather fancy the little minx regards him more in the light of a brother than a suitor. She's too young by far to be fixing her interest anyway, and Mama can be counted on to make a push to hitch her to some title or other."

"So poor Toby won't stand a chance?"

"Not unless that uncle of his sticks his spoon in the wall," Dick replied bluntly. "Which he ain't likely to do. Healthy as a horse he is. And Toby wouldn't want that either. Dashed fond of his uncle, he is."

The rest of the ride passed in companionable chatter between the young people, but her cousin's words had given Diana serious pause for thought. She was at a loss to understand the earl's motive for warning his friends to desist from their attentions to her. The only explanation that made any sense was the one he himself had given her: that he would not take no for an answer. The more she thought about it, the more determined Diana became to resist such high-handed impertinence.

As it turned out, the information she received during that

afternoon's visit to Lady Standish seemed to Diana to preclude the necessity of her exerting herself to put up any resistance at all.

One of the very first things that imposing lady did, once her visitors were comfortably seated in her spacious drawing-room overlooking a formal flower garden at the back of the house, was to announce the imminent visit of her beautiful niece, Chloe.

This unexpected news created quite a stir among the gentlemen, none of whom seemed capable of mentioning the Incomparable Lady Chloe Huntington without prefixing the adjective "beautiful" before her name. This common quirk of speech gave Diana to understand that they considered Lady Chloe no ordinary Beauty but rather an indisputable Non-Pareil among the fairer sex.

Lady Chatham gave it as her considered opinion that the Beauty would find country life sadly stale after her London successes.

"I myself find it intolerably dull," her ladyship claimed sonorously. "There is something about the bucolic existence that sadly deflates the spirit and inhibits good manners. I distinctly remember that when my dear Chatham was still with us, Chatham House was constantly filled with talk of the stable. I am sorry to say that both my eldest born and Richard take after their father in that respect. It is no wonder that I refuse to stay there anymore and have chosen to remove permanently to London where life is more bearable."

"Oh, Mama, you know that Alexander will want to take up residence at Chatham House when he comes home from Spain."

"If he ever does, my dear," Lady Chatham cut in sharply. "For the life of me I cannot understand why the head of the family should choose to fritter away his days on the Continent when he should be looking after his interests here in England."

"Well, now that Chloe has put off her black gloves," Arabella remarked with all the frankness of her seventeen years, "perhaps Alex will come home again, Mama. I hope you remembered to tell him that Lord Huntington broke his neck last year. That should have made poor Alex feel more the thing."

This ingenious speech was met with shocked silence by the elder ladies present and with ill-concealed amusement by the gentlemen. Diana, to whom this information regarding Viscount Chatham's previous attachment to Lady Chloe was news indeed, wondered just what his role had been in the ill-fated engagement of the Beauty to the Earl of Rotherham ten years ago.

"Arabella!" Lady Chatham remonstrated in awful tones. "Pray

watch what you say. It is unbecoming in a young lady to be so forward.''

"Dash it, she's right, Mama," her brother remarked carelessly. "Everybody knows that Alex made a dashed cake of himself over Chloe, and that she only accepted Rotherham because he had more blunt.''

"Oblige me by not using that vulgar language in my presence, Richard," the viscountess said in arctic accents. "And I think you owe Lady Standish an apology. She is, after all, Chloe's aunt.''

"I do beg your pardon, Lady Standish," Dick hastened to say. "But you know better than anyone how it was with the Incomparable.''

"Yes," sighed that lady. "A more self-willed chit I have yet to meet. I was intensely mortified, I can tell you, when she cast poor Rotherham aside as soon as the marquis came up to scratch. Which none of us thought he would, you know.''

"Yes," Toby put in candidly. "The bets were running against him in all the clubs. And I confess I lost a pony on it. Never thought Huntington could be so taken in, myself. And then to go and break his neck in that way is beyond anything foolish.''

"Lord!" exclaimed Forsdyke impulsively. "Do you suppose the Incomparable means to throw her handkerchief at Rotherham again?''

"Wouldn't put it past her," responded Toby gloomily. "But I have a monkey that says he don't take the bait this time. He can't be that daft in the head.''

It was lucky for Toby that his hostess was engaged in relating the latest London adventure of her wayward niece and did not hear this unflattering exchange. Diana had heard it, however, and it was with a heavy heart that she rode back to the Grange, hard put to contribute anything but the barest civilities toward the merry chatter of her friends, most of which was based on speculation about the earl's reaction when he found out that his former love would soon be in the immediate vicinity.

It so happened that none of them witnessed Rotherham's reaction to this piece of news since by the time they all gathered for dinner that evening, he was already in possession of the information. When Toby ventured to quiz him on this sudden reappearance of the Incomparable Lady Chloe, all he got in response was a cool stare that made him wish he had not broached the subject.

* * *

If the earl showed no perceptible enthusiasm over the prospect of the Beauty's arrival, at least he was not backward in observing the common civilities of the occasion. A week later, he willingly accepted Lady Ephigenia's invitation to escort the ladies over to Standish House to pay a morning call on Lady Standish and the young widow.

Diana had tried to cry off from this expedition, not feeling up to meeting this Nonpareil, but her ladyship would not hear of it.

"Nonsense, my dear," she said briskly, correctly surmising the reason for her guest's reluctance. "She won't eat you. And besides, learning to deal with Chloe is an adventure in itself, and you are bound to run into her sooner or later. So my advice is to take your fences head-on, my love. And if it's any consolation to you, remember that she is four years older than you."

"That may well be," responded Diana glumly. "But she has the whole world at her feet, Lady Effie."

"Ah! but you can be quite sure that she has never received three matrimonial offers simultaneously from three different gentlemen, my love. Not that you would want to puff that up at all. But do, I pray you, let it set your mind at rest that the grand Lady Chloe, though undoubtedly an accredited Beauty in her youth, must by now be showing signs of wear. At least one must hope that this is the case," she added with a mischievous smile, quite spoiling the effect of her bracing speech.

Although no one from the Grange had been privy to the earl's reaction to the news of Lady Chloe's arrival, they all witnessed his encounter with the lady in the Blue drawing-room at Standish House that spring morning at eleven o'clock. And they were all disappointed.

Arabella, who had secretly hoped for a romantic, perhaps even tearful, scene of reunion between the lovers of long ago, was perhaps the most disappointed, for nothing could have been less romantic than the formal bow the earl executed to both ladies, accompanied by the most prosaic commonplaces. She considered this to be insensitive to the highest degree and lost no time in telling him so when she got a chance.

Blissfully unaware of Arabella's sentiments, her mother watched the couple with hawklike attention, ready to read into the slightest inflection of the earl's voice a dreaded renewal of his earlier infatuation with the Beauty. Although Lady Chloe's welcoming smile was warmer than she considered strictly necessary, the viscountess was somewhat mollified by Rotherham's cold formality.

The three other gentlemen present thought he acted just as he ought and were perhaps rather more relieved than disappointed at the prospect of avoiding a repetition of the painful episode of Rotherham's aborted engagement to the Beauty so many years ago. His aunt, on the other hand, was more skeptical of her nephew's cool civility. Perhaps because she knew him better than anyone, she entertained an uncomfortable suspicion that this cool formality he presented to the company was a trifle overdone.

Diana, who had not really known what to expect but had naturally anticipated the worst, was pleasantly surprised and relieved that the earl seemed to show such little inclination to remain at the Beauty's side after he had made his bow. The fact that he came over to sit with her and Lady Ephigenia on the long blue settee and made himself useful fetching their teacups and passing round plates of cucumber sandwiches could not fail to gratify her, although the speculating glance thrown in their direction by the Beauty did not make her feel as comfortable as she would have liked.

For her part, Lady Chloe was no fool. Having been brought up in the belief that no other female could come close to her in looks or accomplishments, she immediately saw her erstwhile suitor's cool behaviour as a sign of pique. What other reason could he possibly have, she reasoned, for choosing the company of an aging spinster—pretty enough in her small way of course, but no match for her own scintillating looks—when he might have basked in the presence of the Beauty herself. She decided at once that he must be brought to heel.

The first course of action was naturally to detach the earl from Miss Wetherby's side and capture the centre of attention for herself. This she achieved by the simple method of sweetly ordering her dear Christopher to give up his seat on the settee so that she could renew her long-standing acquaintance with Lady Ephigenia and establish a new one with dear Miss Wetherby, whose friendship, she assured everyone who cared to listen, she desired above anything else.

Diana was not taken in for a moment by these diversionary tactics. She returned the marchioness's dazzling smile and murmured that she, too, had looked forward anxiously to making her ladyship's acquaintance. The proximity of the Beauty allowed Diana to examine her presumed rival at leisure as Lady Chloe chattered animatedly with Lady Ephigenia, mostly about her own exploits in London during the last season.

The first thing Diana's critical gaze discovered was that the startling impression of Lady Chloe's youthful beauty had been an illusion. Those large green eyes were indeed magnificent, but Diana soon noticed that they had an unnaturally bright and restless glitter to them. The perfect, heart-shaped face was marred by tiny, insistent lines around the eyes and mouth which suggested that their owner was rather older than she tried to appear. At rest, Lady Chloe's small mouth was beautifully shaped, but it was rarely relaxed and more often than not showed a lamentable tendency to curl up at the right corner in a moue of impatience or disdain.

Diana had to admit, however, that in spite of these minor and, to the uncritical eye, virtually invisible blemishes, Lady Chloe Huntington cut a very dashing figure indeed. Her extremely fashionable afternoon gown of green silk taffeta, with tiny rows of pearl buttons at the cuffs and a flounce of Brussels lace at the low-cut neckline, showed off her slim, girlish figure to advantage, and her tawny gold ringlets, gathered in carefully controlled exuberance around her lovely face, formed a magnificent halo around her delicate head, giving her an appearance of fragility and luminosity which most women would have given their eyeteeth to possess.

The prospect of competing with such a heavenly vision was so absurd that Diana thought it best to admit defeat at the outset and remove herself from the vicinity of the Beauty in whose presence she felt eclipsed. So taking advantage of Lady Chloe's absorption in her conversation with Lady Ephigenia, Diana rose and made her way to the tea-table, ostensibly to refill her cup, but actually to join the more congenial group gathered around Arabella and Toby.

"The Beauty too much for you, m'dear?" Toby inquired with the total lack of tact which often embarrassed his friends. "Can't say I blame you," he added, when Arabella giggled and Diana looked guilty. "She always had that effect on me. Too dashed beautiful for her own good, I'd say. Makes one mighty uncomfortable. Too managing by half is our dear Chloe."

Diana was inclined to agree with him.

Lady Chloe Standish had always felt—and nine years of marriage to a doting husband considerably her senior had done little to shake this conviction—that every single one of her whims should be instantly gratified. Her favourite expression, when faced with even a hint of opposition, was invariably "I refuse to take no for an answer," delivered in her clear, faintly condescending voice and accompanied by a brief but dazzling smile, nicely calculated to settle the matter without further ado.

Miss Wetherby discovered very early in their relationship that Lady Chloe meant exactly what she said and was not, as might naturally be assumed, merely indulging in conventional pleasantries. Short of actually being rude to her, which Diana stoically refrained from doing out of consideration for Lady Ephigenia, there was no way to avoid being caught up in the round of frenzied activities the Beauty held to be de rigueur for an acceptable rural existence.

"I see no reason why we should all die of ennui just because we happen to live so removed from London," she declared with characteristic vigour one afternoon soon after her arrival, as she sat drinking tea at the Grange with Lady Ephigenia and her guests.

Diana started to protest that, far from dying of boredom, she found life at Morville Grange a refreshing change after the bustle and noise of Paris, when she caught Lady Ephigenia's amused glance and resigned herself to being told, in tones that brooked no argument, that it was unforgivably gauche to confess a preference for country living above the excitement of a season in Town, unless the former was spiced with a liberal sprinkling of assemblies, routs, alfresco parties, musical soirées, informal dinner and card parties, or driving excursions guaranteed to relieve the tedium of pastoral isolation.

Without realizing quite how it happened, Diana found herself included in an alarming number of schemes which, as she complained wryly to Lady Ephigenia on their weekly trip to the Melbury lending library the next morning, would leave her little or no time to read anything but the bare headlines of the *Morning Post* at the breakfast table every morning.

"If you disliked it so much, you had only to explain your preference for reading to Lady Chloe," replied her ladyship, a mischievous twinkle in her blue eyes. "I am convinced dear Chloe would have understood perfectly."

Diana glanced at her in amusement. "You are roasting me again, Lady Effie. From what I have seen of Lady Chloe, that is the last thing in the world she would understand. You will be telling me next that she sews her own gowns and never learned to waltz."

Lady Ephigenia made no reply to this witticism beyond a gurgle of laughter, for round the bend ahead of them swept a sporting curricle drawn by four familiar grey horses. Diana's heart gave a leap of joy as she recognized the earl's team, but this was quickly followed by a sinking feeling when she saw that Lady Chloe was sitting in the carriage beside him, her face positively radiant with pleasure.

Expecting the curricle to sweep past them, Diana drew Jupiter well into the side of the lane to allow the earl plenty of room to pass. She was surprised when he drew rein and came to a standstill next to the tilbury.

"Good morning, ladies," trilled Lady Chloe, obviously well pleased with her morning's sport. "I have prevailed upon Rotherham to bring me over to the Grange to visit you, and I find you tooling about the countryside," she said teasingly. "What a lucky thing we met, because I have conceived of a famous scheme which I want to share with you immediately."

"I trust it is not one of your hoydenish starts, Chloe," Lady Ephigenia inquired with some severity.

"Oh, no, Lady Effie. No such thing." The Beauty laughed indulgently. "It's just that I have sent up to London for my curricle and, since I have heard that Miss Wetherby is such a famous whip, I wish to challenge her to a friendly race. I can conceive of nothing more diverting, can you?"

Since this ingenious remark seemed to be directed at her, Diana overcame a strong desire to tell her ladyship that she could think of several vastly more diverting occupations than setting herself up against the Incomparable, and answered reasonably: "I am afraid you have been sadly misinformed, Lady Chloe. I doubt I could provide your ladyship with a worthwhile challenge. And besides, I no longer have a team of my own, so you will have to excuse me," she added with as much finality as she could muster in her voice.

"Nonsense!" exclaimed the Beauty, gaily disregarding Diana's obvious reluctance to endorse the scheme. "Rotherham will lend you his greys, I am sure," she added, throwing a captivating smile at her companion.

"Well, I am sure he will do nothing of the sort," Diana interjected. "I have it on good authority that no mere female drives those greys. So we will have to think of something else to amuse ourselves."

"How can you say so, Miss Wetherby," drawled the earl in

obvious amusement, "when you know very well you have already driven them?"

"You have?" asked the startled Beauty. She had been quite ready to tease Rotherham into relaxing his well-known ban on females handling his cattle, but was more than a little miffed at the discovery that the spinsterish Miss Wetherby had already enjoyed that privilege. A privilege, furthermore, that she herself had never been able to boast of.

Diana threw an accusing look at the earl, but he only grinned at her. The last thing she wanted was to start an open feud with Lady Chloe or to provoke her into a disagreeable scene which, if Diana was to believe the stories told by Toby and his cronies, the Incomparable would not hesitate to conjure up if crossed in the smallest degree.

"It was only during an emergency," she explained, wishing to set Lady Chloe's mind at rest. "Scarcely a mile, I would say," she added. "And the team was hardly fresh."

"You do yourself an injustice, Miss Wetherby," the earl interposed, an enigmatic smile on his lean face. "Jeremy tells me that you handled them in bang-up style. I would be happy to let you drive them again."

Both Diana and the Beauty seemed to be struck speechless by this generous offer. Lady Ephigenia, however, looked from the two ladies, both obviously put out by this turn of events, to her nephew, and wondered what deep game he was playing.

# 12 .....
# The Race

DIANA SOON DISCOVERED that the earl's offer of his curricle for her race with Lady Chloe had one serious drawback. He insisted on driving her out every morning to show her the paces of his famous greys. Her first inkling of this arrangement came that evening after dinner when the gentlemen had left their port to join the ladies in the drawing-room upstairs.

"What a complete hand you are, Diana," Toby exclaimed, entering the room in his usual high spirits and flinging himself into a chair beside Diana. "How did you convince Rotherham to let you drive his greys? I have been trying to do so for months, and all I get for my pains is a dashed set-down. What's your secret, m'dear?"

Diana glanced at her host and found his familiar sardonic smile unnerving. "I have no secret, Toby," she replied, wishing that were true. "His lordship was kind enough to offer his greys when Lady Chloe mentioned her desire to set up the race. Naturally I could not oblige her, not having a team of my own."

"I wouldn't mind betting that our Chloe was thrown into one of her pets when she heard Rotherham offer you his greys, Miss Wetherby," Lord Henry Forsdyke remarked with a laugh.

"Well, she didn't," Diana pointed out. "Because it was her idea in the first place."

"What? That Christopher lend you the greys?" Toby asked in surprise.

"Of course, you totty-head. Isn't that what we're talking about," cut in Forsdyke impatiently.

"Well, of all the jingle-brained things to do," Toby said disgustedly. "Trust Chloe to suggest something that bird-witted when she knows Rotherham don't let females tool his cattle."

"He did this time," Forsdyke remarked cryptically.

"That's just it," Toby exclaimed. "She couldn't have known he would, could she? Did she, Rotherham?" he added, addressing himself to the earl who had been helping Arabella set up her music at the pianoforte.

"Not unless she read my mind," Rotherham answered laconically.

"Well, I doubt she did that. Which means to say that our Incomparable Chloe was playing off one of her May games and caught cold at it," Toby concluded, evidently deriving much satisfaction from the thought.

"I daresay she was only hoaxing Miss Wetherby and had no intention at all of racing," Forsdyke suggested.

"Oh, no," exclaimed Diana. "Lady Chloe seemed quite set on it. But if you think she did not mean it, I would be happy to withdraw."

"Certainly not!" cried Toby loudly. "I have backed you to win, m'dear. And how can I lose if you are to be tutored by one of the most prestigious members of the Four-in-Hand Club? Don't be a peagoose. Do you wish to spoil all our fun?"

Diana stared at him, an uncomfortable suspicion taking root in her mind. "And who is this peerless tutor?" she inquired with dangerous sweetness.

"Oh, he must be talking about Rotherham." Arabella laughed. "You must know that he is considered one of the top whips in England, Diana. He even beat the Regent once, and now Prinny won't race with him anymore. Isn't that true?" She threw a saucy look at Rotherham.

Controlling a strong desire to box his lordship's ears, Diana stared him straight in the eye. "If you had such misgivings about my ability to handle your team," she said coolly, "you should never have offered them, my lord. And since you did offer them, I can only assume that you trust me not to run them off the road. So I see no need for tutors."

"I have every confidence in your driving ability, Miss Wetherby, but if you wish to win a race with a strange team, you ought to be glad of the few hints I can give you," his lordship responded smoothly.

"Of course she is," cried Arabella excitedly, then turned to Rotherham with a wheedling note in her voice. "And please say I may go with you. I have a strong desire to learn how to drive a team of four."

"No you may not, puss," his lordship said dryly. "Now sit down and sing for us, you naughty minx."

So it was that the following morning Miss Wetherby was taken up at the front steps by the Earl of Rotherham in his racing curricle and began her instruction on how to loop the reins and flick the long whip with precision. Such was her concentration on these niceties of driving etiquette that she was able to avoid the necessity of making civil conversation with his lordship.

At the end of an hour, however, the earl took over the reins, drew his team to a walk, and turned to his companion with a gleam of amusement in his grey eyes.

"You have the lightest hands I have ever seen on a female," he said conversationally. "Tomorrow we will drive over the course so you may familiarize yourself with it."

"I see absolutely no need for you to accompany me on these practice runs, my lord. I had best take Jeremy up behind me which is how the race will be run, after all. Why did you not bring him today?"

"You know very well why I did not bring him, Miss Wetherby. I wish to be private with you, that's why. And I am forced into these machinations because you have deliberately been avoiding me."

Diana's colour rose at the truth of this statement, but she answered coolly enough. "I have been doing nothing of the sort, my lord. And as for being private with me, why, you have only to summon me into the library in order to abuse me with your false accusations and unwanted attentions. I wonder that you have not again resorted to that high-handed strategy."

The earl gave a crack of laughter. "That kiss still rankles, does it, m'dear?"

"Not at all," Diana replied stiffly. "I always try to put unpleasant incidents behind me. And that was certainly one of the worst I have been subjected to recently," she added with considerable satisfaction at the opportunity to give his lordship the set-down he so richly deserved.

Although Miss Wetherby continued to maintain that these morning excursions in Lord Rotherham's curricle were entirely unnecessary, she soon began to look forward to them with increasing pleasure. His lordship was excellent company, and

Diana's cool reserve was soon replaced by an easy intimacy reminiscent of her days in Paris.

During these blissful mornings in his company, entertained by amusing stories of his exploits in the army, Diana was tempted to believe that a future with him might be very enjoyable indeed, even if he did not love her as she had always dreamed of being loved. In the afternoons and evenings, however, she was forced to observe him being equally or even more attentive to the entertainment of other females. In particular, Diana was frustrated by the earl's attentions to the Incomparable, who seemed to be a permanent fixture in the Grange party.

If the Beauty resented the mornings Diana spent in Rotherham's company, she was far too clever to show it. Instead she concentrated on monopolizing his attention at every other opportunity. Diana's patience was sorely tried by the unrelenting flirtation Lady Chloe carried on, not only with the earl, but with every other available gentleman, including the vicar, poor Mr. Fenley, who was unmistakably dazzled by her charm.

Time and again, Diana told herself that she should simply cry off from the seemingly endless round of entertainment instigated by the Incomparable. But somehow she could never find the resolution to do so, and deprive herself of the exquisite agony of watching her host dance attendance on Lady Chloe.

You do look blue-deviled, my love," Aunt Sophy told her one afternoon as the two ladies sat drinking tea in Diana's small sitting-room. "And I can well imagine why. It's that dazzling widow Huntington, isn't it, love? I, for one, will be glad when she goes back to London."

"It doesn't look as if she ever will," murmured Diana so mournfully that Sophy had to laugh.

"Well, you only have yourself to blame, dear," she said in a valiant attempt to console her niece. She had driven over to the Grange to share a particular piece of happy news with Diana, but she had found her niece in such low spirits that she was reluctant to mention it.

"You had only to accept Rotherham's offer of marriage, my love, and he would not now be dangling after that widow."

"He's not dangling after her," Diana replied crossly. "And Rotherham did not make me an offer, Aunt, he only said he was going to. Which is not quite the same thing, you must admit. And anyway, I made it quite clear to him that I would not accept him even if he did, so that's an end to it.''

"There's no need to fly into a passion, my love," Sophy said soothingly. "I do think it is a pity, however, that you did not give a little serious consideration to the advantages of such an alliance. Just think, dearest, how wonderful it would be to have you established as Countess of Rotherham, and so close to Potter Hall. How comfortable we could be!''

Diana regarded her aunt with amazement. "Is this my own Aunt Sophia Wetherby I hear talking?'' she exclaimed in horrified tones. "The very same woman who was forever telling me that one can be very comfortable indeed without a loveless marriage to a despotic husband? I cannot credit it, Aunt. Tell me you are roasting me.''

A rosy blush suffused her aunt's cheeks, and Diana stared at her for a full minute before she guessed the reason for Sophia's confusion.

"Ah!'' she said in a melodramatic voice. "I see it all now. You have betrayed the cause of maiden aunts and fallen a victim to the blandishments of the enemy. Sir Rudolph has beguiled you with his wealth and title. Aunt Sophy, how could you?'' she wailed, tears of merriment springing into her eyes.

"Oh, tell me you don't dislike the idea too much, dearest,'' begged poor Sophia, not at all certain whether her niece was serious or not.

"Of course I don't dislike it, you ninny,'' cried Diana, embracing her diminutive aunt impulsively and squeezing her in a bear hug. "How can you even ask such a nonsensical question, dear? I am very happy for you and wish you the most wonderful marriage of all time. When is it to be?''

"Well, that's what I came to talk to you about, my dear. You see, Sir Rudolph wants to tie the knot as soon as possible, so we have set the date for next Saturday, and Reverend Fenley has promised to marry us.''

"Surely you will need a special licence, won't you?''

"Yes, dear. Sir Rudolph has already approached the Bishop in Bath for one, and he would like to take me to London for a few days afterwards. But the thing is, I hate to leave the girls with only the servants to care for them. Now if you would consent to stay with them, dear, I would be so much easier. Do you think you could?'' She looked so anxious that Diana hugged her tightly again.

"Of course I will, my dearest Aunt. But don't forget that the curricle race will be held on Saturday afternoon. I was counting on you to cheer me on, but I can quite understand that you will have other things on your mind," she added with a teasing look which caused another blush to colour her aunt's cheeks.

Although both Sir Rudolph and his betrothed had agreed that a small, quiet wedding would suit them best, as soon as word of the bridal got out, the ceremony acquired all the importance of a major social event. The bride, attended by her niece and her five young stepdaughters, was given away by no lesser a personage than the Earl of Rotherham himself, who was happy to oblige his friend and neighbour, Sir Rudolph Potter. Lady Ephigenia had insisted upon holding what she termed a small wedding breakfast in Morville Grange, which turned out to be quite a crush as she had, in a burst of enthusiasm, sent invitations to everyone in the neighbourhood, including all Sir Rudolph's tenants.

A note of humour was introduced when the bride's bouquet of white roses and blue forget-me-nots tied with a white satin ribbon was cast into the air by the new Lady Sophia Potter. She had deliberately sought out her niece among the group surrounding the carriage which was to bear the newlyweds to London. But in her excitement she tossed the posy too high for Diana's reach and it sailed over her head to be grasped by none other than the earl, standing directly behind her, who automatically raised his hand to capture it.

The crowd burst into a roar of laughter at this feat, and the earl was immediately subjected to any number of good-natured, teasing comments from his friends and guests.

Diana, who had turned around in time to witness this incident, also had to laugh at the surprise registered on the earl's face.

"Shame on you, my lord," she chided gaily. "Don't you know that only females are supposed to catch a bride's bouquet? Now you have deprived some poor girl of the romantic fantasy of imminent wedding bells for herself." She was rewarded by an answering smile, but before the earl could speak, an unmistakable, lilting voice intruded on their ears.

"You are absolutely right, Miss Wetherby," trilled the Incomparable, who had been standing close enough to witness the exchange. "It is monstrous of you, Rotherham, to dash our tender hopes so callously," she added with such seductive insinuation in her voice that Diana felt distinctly de trop. "You must, I insist upon it, present the posy to a lady who, in your estimation, is most likely to find a handsome husband in the near future.''

As she spoke, Lady Chloe had tucked her hand confidently into Rotherham's arm and now smiled up at him with such an open invitation in her half-closed eyes that Diana turned away in acute embarrassment and misery.

Before she had time to escape into the crowd, however, she felt a hand on her arm and turned to find the earl looking down at her as though he had read her thoughts.

"From what I know of your aunt, Miss Wetherby, I wouldn't hesitate to say she meant the bouquet for you. So here it is, with my compliments.''

His eyes contained a tenderness and shared amusement Diana had never thought to see in them. Resolutely, she tore her gaze from his face and wished her heart would cease doing unconscionable things in her breast. With considerable effort, she maintained a semblance of composure as he thrust the posy into her nerveless fingers.

She managed a small smile of thanks but when she glanced at Lady Chloe, she saw that the colour had drained from the Beauty's lovely face. A tight, pinched look appeared briefly around her petulant mouth, and an expression of intense hatred flashed into her green eyes as they met Diana's hazel ones. The expression was gone in an instant, however, and the Beauty smiled her most condescending smile and said sweetly: "Congratulations, my dear Miss Wetherby. I do trust you will not be too disappointed. Men are such fickle creatures, as you probably know.''

Diana banished these cutting words from her mind in the bustle and tearful farewells of her aunt's departure. She had little time to feel sorry for herself, however, since preparations for the curricle race later that day got under way almost immediately.

The race was to be run entirely on the Grange estate. The agreed-upon course ran from the starting point in front of the main house, across the huge Park, along a twisting lane through the Home Wood, a straight mile-long stretch beside the east boundary line, then along a winding road that separated the south meadow from the tenant cottages, back along the west boundary line, cutting across behind the stables to the Home Wood again, and finally back to the front entrance of the house.

This course had been calculated at slightly more than six miles in length and should take, according to Toby's considered opinion, no more than twenty-five minutes to complete.

"That is if Rotherham's sixteen-mile-an-hour tits live up to their reputation and Miss Wetherby don't overturn them," Toby added provokingly, as Diana took her seat in the sporting vehicle which had been brought round from the stables by a tight-lipped Jeremy. His lordship's groom had made no secret of his disapproval of any sporting event in which females played a part. "Too flighty by 'alf," was his dour prediction, although he had so far overcome his prejudice as to compliment Miss Wetherby the day before on her ability to feather her corners in bang-up style.

"But style ain't speed," he had felt it incumbent upon him to warn Diana more than once. "And her ladyship is a neck-or-nothing whip. More speed than style in those bits of blood of hers, if you ask me. Prime cattle they are, too, but she'll fret them into a lather before they've gone a mile. Too nervous by 'alf she is. And mind you, miss, her ladyship is out to win this gig. Even if it kills her," he added darkly. "Don't like to lose, that gentry-mort. And don't you forget it, miss."

These admonitions were muttered in a running undertone after Jeremy took his place behind her. The greys, who were beginning to fidget in their well-bred way, were held by two stable lads in readiness for the signal to cast off.

Lady Chloe was already seated in her curricle and, as Jeremy had predicted, was fretting her team into a lather of excitement. The four good-looking bays had been driven over to the Grange the day before to allow the Beauty to try out their paces on the course and had remained overnight.

Diana cast an experienced eye over the rival team with some apprehension. She had to agree with Jeremy that the animals, Welsh-bred, with broad chests and strongly muscled haunches, were built for speed.

"Remember what I told you," the earl reminded her, handing her up the long whip. "Do not, under any circumstances, spring them until you get past the cottages. They will want to bolt, because they ain't used to eating dust, but keep them steady and well in hand. Pass on the west boundary if you must, but I strongly suggest waiting until you get behind the stables. That will be your last chance to do so safely. By then Chloe will have become careless; but don't count on an easy victory, my dear girl."

Diana glared at him in response to this last remark, as he knew she would. "And good luck!" he added, smiling up at her scowling face until she relented and returned his smile, too excited to be angry with him.

There was time for no more talk as Toby, who had taken upon himself the role of starter, shouted at the two ladies to draw level and be on their mark.

All too soon for Diana the signal was given and, again as predicted by Jeremy, the Beauty urged her team forward at a furious gallop. The greys surged after her with such force that Diana was hard put to it to hold them steady as she had been instructed. Fearing she had already lost control of them, she tightened her hold on the reins and, with a vast feeling of relief, felt them respond to her touch.

"Steady, girl, steady," she heard Jeremy yell from behind her, but she had mastered her momentary panic and had the well-behaved team under iron control.

She had lost some ground at the outset and was unable to make it up on the winding lane through the wood. However, when she swept into the long east boundary line and saw Lady Chloe far ahead of her, she let her horses out a little at a time until she had reduced the distance between the two vehicles considerably.

Several minutes later, she saw the Beauty turn into the winding road with hardly a check in her speed. For a horrifying moment, her curricle swayed dangerously, and Diana thought it would overturn. When this did not happen, she heard Jeremy muttering, "Cow-handed, cow-handed," in disgusted tones.

Diana checked her team slightly and swept safely round the same bend without mishap. Ahead of her, Lady Chloe seemed to be springing her horses, for the distance between the vehicles opened up rapidly.

"Hold 'em, hold 'em," Jeremy shouted as Diana was debating whether to risk giving her own team their heads. Obedient to this command, Diana kept her team steady as they clattered past the cottages, in front of which the earl's tenants and their families had gathered to enjoy the sport.

Five minutes later, when she turned her racing team expertly into the long stretch of lane along the west boundary, she was surprised to see that her rival team was not as far ahead of her as she had imagined.

"Winded 'em already, she has," muttered Jeremy. "Now's the time to start pressing her. Let 'em out a bit, miss. Let 'em out."

Diana was only too glad to obey. Her restive horses, seemingly as fresh as when they started, responded to her signal eagerly by shooting ahead in a spurt of speed that rapidly closed the gap between the two vehicles.

Diana saw Lady Chloe's groom glance once over his shoulder and heard him shout something that was lost in the rush of wind. His mistress began to use her whip freely, and her team responded valiantly with a surge of extra speed. This did not last, however, for the team was tiring from the breakneck pace they had been asked to maintain.

The greys drew inexorably closer until Diana could catch the rank smell of sweat from the lathered team ahead of her. She considered the possibility of passing as the two teams, now so close that the greys seemed to be breathing down her ladyship's groom's neck, approached a wider stretch in the lane.

"Wait, lass," Jeremy shouted as if reading her mind. Obediently, Diana checked the greys slightly to allow her ladyship room to make the turn into the stable lane safely. Diana noticed in surprise that Lady Chloe deliberately kept her team in the centre of the widening lane. If she had wanted to pass at that point, she would have had to drive to an inch to avoid scraping the wheels of the other vehicle.

"Foul!" muttered Jeremy harshly. "She ain't goin' to let us pass, lass. I told you she don't like to lose, she don't. You're goin' to have to do some fancy driving to pass on the stable lane."

He fell silent and Diana felt a knot of apprehension forming in the pit of her stomach as she watched her ladyship's team turn into the stable lane. This part of the course had been chosen to allow the party from the house to watch part of the race from the drawing-room on the second floor. Diana could imagine that the whole household must be staring down at them that very moment.

Putting this thought from her mind, she turned her own team into the lane and let them out enough to catch up to the rival team now making heavy going of it, still firmly in the centre of the lane.

As the lane widened behind the stables, Diana knew she would have to make her move now or lose the race.

"Get ready, lass," Jeremy muttered from behind her. "When I give the word, let 'em go, and the devil take the hindmost."

Diana saw it coming before Jeremy opened his mouth. The lane ahead made a wide sweep into the stable-yard before continuing to the east boundary line, and Diana knew that this had to be the place to pass.

Later she could not recall hearing Jeremy yell, but she knew that he must have done so at exactly the same instant she sprang the greys and felt the exhilaration of their strong response as they swept up on the other curricle and inexorably inched past her ladyship's labouring team.

She did recall a glimpse of the Beauty's pale face and the sound of the lash on the backs of her bays. Her own leaders were in the clear and her wheelers drawing parallel to her rival's leaders; she was almost home free.

Suddenly she felt a jolt, and heard Jeremy utter a stream of oaths as her horses reared and screamed in panic.

The curricle lurched, and she felt herself flung violently out of the vehicle. As she fought against the blackness that enveloped her senses, she murmured disjointedly: "Jeremy, the greys, the greys, the . . ."

# 13 ·····

# Ferdinand

As DIANA SLOWLY regained her senses, her first sensation was of
being cradled in a cocoon of warmth. The smell of lavender water
assailed her nostrils, and she felt a welcome coolness being
applied tenderly to her aching head.

She sighed and snuggled closer into the warm embrace.
Gradually she became aware of sounds and muted voices around
her, and then she realized with a shock that from the warmth of her
pillow emanated the unmistakable scent of a man's shaving soap.

Her eyes flew open, and she found herself gazing up into two
pools of grey in the depths of which flickered a bewildering
mixture of emotions. Diana closed her eyes again quickly, feeling
extremely dizzy. She must be dreaming, she thought. Or she could
have died and gone to heaven. Although she did not feel dead, her
heart seemed to be beating with quite extraordinary strength, and
she could have sworn that she had felt warm breath on her cheek.

She was about to let the sweet warmth of that breath lull her into
oblivion again when she suddenly remembered, with terrible
clarity, the events leading up to the accident.

With a little cry of fear, she struggled to sit up, fighting quite
ineffectually against the strong arms which held her down. "The
greys," she murmured weakly. "The greys. Oh, please see to the
greys, Jeremy."

"Damn the greys," a lazy voice said next to her ear. "You must
not worry your pretty head over four overpriced, overfed, tiresome
beasts. I insist upon it, my dear girl."

She looked up to find the earl smiling at her, an ironic twist on
his well-shaped lips which, Diana felt, were far too close for
comfort.

"You can't mean it," she said breathlessly, quite unable to
believe that Rotherham was actually talking about his famous

**135**

team. "Oh, please say they are not hurt. They behaved so well; I cannot believe this happened. We were going to win." This speech was punctuated by anguished sobs which, try as she might, Diana was unable to control.

The earl only smiled and brushed a kiss on her damp cheek. Allowing his eyes to drop to her neckline, he raised an eyebrow in a very rakish manner. "You had best cover yourself, my dear, or I shall be tempted into what you would probably call outrageous behaviour. A man can resist only so much, you know."

At his teasing words, Diana suddenly became aware that she was in her own bed, in her diaphanous silk nightgown, with her auburn curls falling riotously about her shoulders. During her struggles to sit up, the bedclothes had slipped down and she realized with horror that her thin nightgown left very little to the imagination.

"Oh!" she gasped, hurriedly sliding back under the covers, which she drew protectively up under her chin. "What are you doing sitting on my bed?" she demanded, her face flushed with embarrassment at the novelty of a man in her bedroom.

"I carried you upstairs, my dear, almost two hours ago. And although I was not allowed the pleasure of undressing you, I think I deserve a little consideration for my pains, don't you?"

"No, I certainly do not," Diana retorted, taking refuge in anger. "And do you mean to tell me that I have been unconscious for two hours, my lord? I can scarcely credit it."

"Well, it's true. The doctor has come and gone and says that you took a bad fall, but no bones are broken. Only some severe bruises which will keep you very sore for at least a week."

"What happened to cause the accident? I don't remember anything except the noise of the horses. Is Jeremy all right?"

"Yes, luckily he escaped without a scratch."

"But what happened?" she insisted.

He looked at her for a moment without saying anything. "I think the less said about this incident the better it will be for everyone involved," he said finally. "The race was cancelled, so you didn't lose and nobody won. Toby is somewhat upset, of course, but that's to be expected. We are all rather relieved that you are still alive. You were really springing those horses, my dear." His eyes held a gleam of fond admiration which made her heart leap. "Nicest piece of driving I've seen in a long time."

Resolutely, she brushed this praise aside. There was something she needed to know. "Yes, but what really happened? Can't you tell me?'' She had an uncomfortable suspicion that Lady Chloe had somehow had a hand in the disaster, but she wanted to hear the explanation from the earl himself.

''No. I'd rather not,'' he replied shortly.

''Was it my fault, then?'' she wanted to know.

''No.'' His eyes became hooded as he gazed at her speculatively. ''You are sure you remember nothing at all?''

''Only a terrible jolt and the horses screaming. Then a blackness. And Jeremy cursing, of course.'' She smiled slightly at the recollection. ''I don't recall what he said, but I could tell he was in a rage about something.''

His face relaxed and he smiled at her. ''Perhaps it's just as well you remember so little. The doctor says you should try not to think of it. You sustained quite a shock, you know. Not just the physical bruises, but also the mental anguish.'' He reached out and brushed a stray curl from her brow, the gentleness of his touch sending a tremour through her bruised body.

''So try to rest for now, my dear. I'll send Lady Ephigenia in to sit with you for a while.'' He got up abruptly and moved to the door, turning to look at her over his shoulder. ''Promise me you won't think any more on this unfortunate incident.''

She nodded silently, but her heart was heavy. What was he trying to keep from her? Diana had a hazy suspicion she could not quite banish from her mind that Lady Chloe was somehow involved in the accident. She shook herself impatiently. That was impossible. But what if there was some truth in it? a little voice persistently nagged at her.

Diana stubbornly shied away from this uncomfortable thought. In the end, however, her dislike for prevarication forced her to admit that if it were indeed true that the Beauty had in some way contributed to her accident, then the earl's insistence on keeping the affair secret took on a less flattering light. If that were the case, his concern could not be for her own recovery so much as to protect the reputation of her incomparable rival.

This conclusion so lowered her spirits that Miss Wetherby had to call upon all her strength of character to put it out of her mind and fall into an uneasy sleep.

By the time Sir Rudolph and Lady Sophia Potter arrived back from their honeymoon a week later, Diana was feeling much recovered physically. Spiritually she was feeling blue-devilled. She had had no further opportunity for private conversation with the earl, and nobody else seemed willing to talk about the accident.

"No need to bother your pretty head about it," Toby told her forcefully one evening after dinner as he and Dick Chatham sat with Diana on the yellow brocade settee at the far end of the drawing-room. "Could have happened to anyone. The Beauty was always cow-handed, anyway," he added rather disconnectedly. "Right, Dick?"

"Neck or nothing," replied that worthy disgustedly. "No real style at all, of course, but always game for a lark. That's our Chloe."

"I still don't understand how it happened," Diana complained, a note of exasperation in her voice. "And everybody was watching us from this very window." She gestured towards the long French windows that overlooked the back gardens and stables.

"That's where you're wrong, m'dear," said Toby. "Both curricles were behind the main stable building when it happened."

"We knew something was wrong when we heard the horses screaming. I can tell you that it was one mad scramble to get down there," Dick remarked.

"When I got there, Rotherham was already bringing you back to the house, m'dear. Pale as death you were. Gave us all a bad start. I for one thought you had put your spoon in the wall, m'dear. Dashed glad I was wrong, though. Never could stand funerals."

"Toby!" exclaimed Arabella, who had come up in time to hear the last remarks. "Don't be so tactless. Diana is safe and sound, so don't upset her with your stories."

Toby mumbled an apology before allowing Arabella to drag him off to turn her music for her at the pianoforte.

Exasperated, she turned to Chatham. "Why will nobody talk to me about the accident, Dick? Surely you can do so. In fact, as your aunt, I demand that you do so," she added with mock severity and a beguiling smile. "Tell me what the deep, dark secret is."

He laughed at her rather self-consciously. "There's no secret, coz. If you must know—and promise me you will not discuss it with anyone—our precious Chloe played off another of her famous Banbury tricks. She was always manipulative, even as a child. And when she don't get her own way"—he looked at Diana with a crooked smile—"well, there's the devil to pay, m'dear, and no mistake. You'd think she would have outgrown such peevishness, but she ain't."

So I was right, Diana thought. Lady Chloe *was* involved. After a moment, she demanded to know if this was the reason Lady Chloe had not visited the Grange since the race.

"Well, with Chloe you never know. She went off to Bath in a big flurry the very next day. Something about a promised visit to her mother-in-law. But that's a whisker if ever I heard one. Chloe was always at daggers-drawn with old Lady Huntington. Out of sight—out of mind, that's Chloe. When she comes back, she will act as though nothing had happened."

"That's what Lord Rotherham seems to want to do, too," Diana said in a low voice.

He glanced at her searchingly before replying. "Well, don't tease yourself on that account, coz. Very likely Rotherham is *epris* with the Incomparable. We were afraid this might happen, but I gave him more sense than to let that little schemer make a cake out of him again. It wouldn't surprise me if he's had a *tendre* for her all these years. Devilish cutup he was when she hedged off to marry Huntington."

These words confirmed Diana's worst suspicions, and she fell into such a fit of the dismals that when Rotherham came over to beg her to sing a French ballad for them, she answered curtly that she had the headache and intended to retire early.

She slept badly, and her spirits were still low the following morning when she sent round to the stables to have Perseus saddled. An overwhelming need for her aunt's comforting advice had made her decide to impose upon the new Lady Potter, who had returned from her London honeymoon the previous afternoon.

Half an hour later, installed in Lady Potter's private sitting-room which had been refurbished in pink satin and was now filled with spring sunshine streaming in through the open windows, Diana felt at peace for the first time in days.

After greeting her beloved aunt effusively, Diana poured out an emotional account of all her woes. Starting with the offer she had almost received from Rotherham by the duck pond, the accident in the curricle race, and her own suspicions about the real cause of the disaster, she concluded with her conversation with Chatham the previous evening which seemed to confirm her worst fears.

Lady Potter sat on the pink brocade settee beside her niece during this recital, murmuring soothingly and pouring fresh cups of tea at appropriate intervals.

"You are obviously in love with him, my child," she said at last, handing Diana her cup.

"No!" Diana replied adamantly. "I hate him."

"Just so, my love." Her aunt nodded sagely. "I saw it coming, but I must confess that it is perverse of him to appear to dangle after this Huntington wench on one hand while making you offers of marriage on the other. Most perverse."

"He did not precisely make the offer, Aunt. But he said that I needed a period of reflection to see the advantages of marriage with him. Which of course is pure pompous flummery." She snorted in disgust. "And then when Lady Chloe appeared on the scene, I could see he must have been amusing himself at my expense. You saw for yourself how beautiful she is. It is ridiculous to think he could prefer me. Even if I wanted him to, which of course I don't," she added perversely.

Lady Potter only nodded. "Yes, my dear, you are certainly in love with him. We must consider what is to be done."

Diana laughed rather shakily. "Oh, there is nothing to be done, dearest. I shall remain what I have always been. An ape-leader. An old maiden aunt who will dote on my five new stepnieces and teach them French and watercolours."

The prospect was so daunting that she burst into an unexpected fit of tears and had to be cuddled and cosseted by Lady Potter before she regained her composure.

When she was comfortable again, Diana begged her aunt to recount her experiences in London and the parties she had attended.

Lady Potter clapped a hand to her brow. "I had forgotten all about it, my love, but I have the most dreadful news to impart to you."

Startled by this outburst, Diana stared at her aunt apprehensively. "What can you possibly mean, Aunt?" she whispered nervously.

"Don't be such a goose, dear. It's nothing to become alarmed about, really it isn't. I was exaggerating a trifle. The thing is that while I was in Town I ran into a dear relative of ours, my love. He was most obsequious when he discovered I am now Lady Potter and most insistent that I disclose your whereabouts, dear."

"It's not Ferdinand is it?" And when Lady Potter nodded grimly, she cried, "Oh, it can't be. You didn't tell him where I am, did you? What can he possibly want with me do you think?"

"I didn't say a word, dear. But of course, he can find out easily enough. All he'd have to do is inquire in the clubs or follow us back to Dorset. I rather think he did the latter, for I think I caught a glimpse of him at one of the posting houses. But I could have been mistaken, dear, so pray don't tease yourself. After all, there's nothing he can do to you now."

Lady Potter's good-natured though misguided advice did little to console Diana the following afternoon when Fortham scratched at her sitting-room door to inform her that a *vicomte* Duvalier had arrived and was asking for her.

"A young gentleman from Paris, miss," the butler clarified in tones which clearly conveyed his disapproval of yet another foreigner appearing at the Grange. "I have put him in the Yellow Saloon, miss."

"Thank you, Fortham. I shall come down directly," Diana replied with more composure than she felt.

As soon as the butler had gone, she ran along the hall and tapped at Lady Ephigenia's door. She found her hostess being fitted for a new afternoon gown of exquisite lavender silk with a double row of pearl buttons from neckline to waist.

"What's all the excitement about, dear?" inquired her ladyship, recognizing at a glance that something momentous was in the wind.

"I need your support downstairs, Lady Effie," explained Diana with some agitation. "In the Yellow Saloon. Please do not desert me."

"Who is it, love?"

"That dreadful nephew of mine from Paris," she replied, disregarding the interested expressions of her ladyship's dresser and the local dressmaker. "Ferdinand Duvalier. But I see you are busy. So never mind. I will ask Arabella to accompany me."

"Arabella is out riding with Tottlefield and Chatham," her ladyship said dryly. "But don't worry, child. I shall be down directly."

When Miss Wetherby entered the Yellow Saloon ten minutes later, she was greeted with exaggerated civility by her young French nephew. Having become accustomed, during her months at the Grange, to dealing with gentlemen of large stature and casual elegance, she regarded Ferdinand with a critical eye. His medium height and slim build seemed to her rather puny, and his delicately-moulded features and graceful carriage struck her as too effeminate by half.

What offended her the most, however, was his choice of clothes quite unsuited to afternoon calls in the country. Tearing her eyes away, with considerable difficulty, from a bright green waistcoat, heavily embroidered with gold thread, Diana advanced into the room and reluctantly gave him her hand.

"My dear, dear Diana," he murmured suavely, bowing low to plant a kiss tenderly on her fingers. "Can it be, *cherie*, that you are not entirely *ravissante de me voir*?" He raised an ornate quizzing-glass to one eye and regarded her intently.

"Don't try to bamboozle me, Ferdinand," Diana replied shortly. "What are you doing here? And what do you want?"

He assumed an expression of injured innocence. "But my very dear aunt, what makes you think I want anything? I find myself in the district, and could not but make a small side trip to ascertain how my dear friend Rotherham is treating you, *cherie*. What could be more natural?" He smiled at her with such blandness that Diana was sorely tempted to box his ears.

"Aunt Sophia tells me you accosted her in London. I suppose you made it your business to follow her into Dorset? You always were a busybody, Ferdinand. But you must realize that she is now completely beyond your reach. You can torment her no longer, thank goodness."

Ferdinand observed her with an amused gleam in his eyes. "So she was at pains to inform me, my dear." He observed her closely. "I gather that you have not been so fortunate, *cherie*. If indeed one may call marriage to such as Sir Rudolph Potter a fortunate event."

He laughed lightly when Diana bristled with anger at this remark. "Do not, I beg of you, my dear, play the innocent with me." He raised his quizzing-glass again and spent several minutes examining Diana from head to foot.

"I see that you have been well provided for, *cherie*. That gown is in the first style of elegance, and your hair is most charmingly arranged. By a professional I would wager. I am pleasantly surprised, I confess."

Diana's crushing retort was interrupted by Fortham who brought in a tray of refreshments and took his time arranging the glasses and sherry on the gate-legged table before the hearth.

As soon as the butler had gone, Ferdinand helped himself to the sherry and regarded his aunt speculatively.

"You have done exceedingly well for yourself, *cherie*, that I will grant you. However, I do find it a trifle odd that you are installed in Rotherham's household in place of our dear Sophia. My understanding of the wager with Rotherham was that Sophia would be his pensioner, my love, not you." He raised an eyebrow inquiringly.

"Aunt Sophy is now married," Diana replied shortly. "She is obviously living at Potter Hall."

"Yes, that is entirely understandable. Where else would she live?" Ferdinand said pleasantly, apparently enjoying himself. "But you see, my dear, I was informed at the Blue Boar Inn in Melbury that she never was a guest at Morville Grange. But you were." He smiled unpleasantly, and Diana was reminded forcibly of a cat playing with a mouse.

"I confess I found that very curious, *cherie*. And then it did occur to me that perhaps there had been some little mistake, *n'est-ce pas?*" He paused for effect and regarded her complacently. "Then I told myself that if such a mistake had been made, it most certainly had been done deliberately. Wouldn't you agree, my dear?"

"What nonsense are you saying?" Diana cried desperately, suddenly realizing where this conversation was leading. "And if you think you can barge in here and make trouble for us, you are quite mistaken, believe me. I am a guest in this house, and I have only to complain to Lady Morville and she will have you thrown out."

"Perhaps," her visitor agreed. "And then again, perhaps not. Especially if I were to explain that I am related to Captain Richard Chatham, who is, I have been informed, also a guest of *mon cher ami* Rotherham."

"The Earl of Rotherham is no friend of yours," Diana retorted contemptuously. "Quite above your touch, nephew. And besides, he doesn't consort with totty-headed April squires with puffed-up illusions of their own consequence."

As the *vicomte* listened to this impassioned speech, he regarded Miss Wetherby intently and a slow, knowing smile began to form on his rather thin lips.

"Aha!" he exclaimed softly when she finished. "So that is how the wind blows, my dear," he said smugly. "Our darling Diana has a *tendre* for Rotherham. How very unfortunate. Can you have forgotten, *cherie*, that you are already promised to M'sieur Cardeau?"

"Nonsense," snapped Diana. "I am not promised to anyone, and you know it, Ferdinand. So don't tease me with that."

"I beg to differ, *cherie*. My father has made all the arrangements, and it only wants your sweet presence for the marriage to become *un fait acompli*. I have been sent to bring you home, dear aunt, and I advise you not to give me any trouble." he grinned at her in triumph.

"You always were an odious creature, Ferdinand. I shall ring for Fortham to show you out. I am quite tired of listening to you rattle on." She moved determinedly towards the bell pull.

"I wouldn't if I were you, my dear." The menace in his voice was unmistakable. "I doubt your precious Rotherham would be amused to discover that the maiden aunt he has been harbouring these past months is an impostor. Wouldn't you agree, my dear?"

# 14 · · · · ·
# Toby Takes Over

Diana was saved from having to respond to this thinly veiled threat by the appearance of Lady Ephigenia, who burst into the Yellow Saloon in a flurry of sea-green silk and apologies for having kept Diana and her guest waiting so long.

She caught sight of Diana's distraught expression over the *vicomte*'s pomaded head as he bowed low over her hand and immediately determined to put an end to this unwelcome visit as soon as civility permitted. So adept was she at this enviable social skill that within less than ten minutes of her arrival, the *vicomte* found himself delivering his *congés* to the ladies without having obtained the least encouragement to repeat his visit.

"I am very sorry to have to say anything so disobliging, my love," her ladyship remarked emphatically as soon as the door closed behind the visitor. "But your nephew seems to me to be nothing but a Bond Street fribble. That waistcoat may be all the crack in Paris, but it certainly will not do for a sojourn in the English countryside. It is the kind of sartorial atrocity that gives me the migraine, dear. Luckily we were able to get rid of him before I was quite overcome."

Diana could not help smiling at her ladyship's whimsical remarks, but her face sobered as she recalled Ferdinand's threat to expose her as an impostor.

Lady Ephigenia, who had been observing her closely, drew Diana down beside her on the yellow brocade settee and said invitingly, "I can see that you are really put out by this simpering jackstraw, my love. There is bound to be a story here that you have not told me." She smiled encouragingly at Diana, whose anxious expression clearly confirmed the truth of this statement.

"You know you can trust me, dear. So be a good girl and tell me what this *vicomte* fellow did or said that put you in such a pucker.''

This was all the encouragement Diana needed, for she was more than willing to unburden herself to her dear friend.

"You must promise not to tell the earl," she began hesitantly. "You see it concerns him and that silly wager he made with Ferdinand last winter."

"Of course I won't say a word if you do not wish it, my love. But you must not continue under this misapprehension that Rotherham is some sort of an ogre. He may seem so at times, I'll admit''—she laughed—"but he is really quite sensible and understanding. For a man, that is," she hastened to add with a chuckle. "You can trust him to do the right thing, dear."

"Oh, I am well aware of that," murmured Diana, remembering the painful scene at the duck pond when Rotherham had obviously tried to do what he thought was right by making her an offer. "But you see, this is precisely the kind of coil a gentleman is least likely to condone. I am sure that you will understand perfectly when I confess that it was not I who was wagered in that game but my Aunt Sophia. She was so unwell when we reached London that I insisted on taking her place."

"That is entirely as it should be," exclaimed her ladyship, much intrigued by the romantic tale unfolding around her.

"I thought that it would not matter to the earl which maiden aunt he got. And I really am, after all, Ferdinand's aunt."

"Quite so, dear," murmured her ladyship, hiding a smile.

"But don't you see, Lady Effie," cried Diana, close to tears. "I have been living here under false pretenses all this time. And now the earl is going to make me an offer because he is convinced he has wronged me, or some such fustian nonsense." She looked so miserable that Lady Ephigenia clasped one of her hands affectionately.

"So Rotherham made you an offer, my love? Why, that's splendid. It will answer very nicely."

"Well, not exactly. I was able to stop him in time. But it is all very awkward because he said he would ask me again. And now Ferdinand is threatening to reveal the truth unless I go back to Paris with him to marry old M'sieur Cardeau, who is a miserable squeeze-crab with absolutely no sense of humour." By the time she reached this point, her future looked so bleak that Diana could not prevent two large tears from rolling down her pale cheeks.

Her ladyship blinked. This was a coil indeed, but she gamely pulled herself together and managed to say bracingly: "Come, come, child. This sounds like a hum to me. There is no way the *vicomte* can force you to go back to Paris. So calm yourself, my love."

"Yes, I know," whispered Diana brokenly. "But he will tell Rotherham that I am not the maiden aunt he thought I was. And he will think I have tricked him into making me an offer, which is exactly what he accused me of wanting to do. Oh, I can't bear it," she cried.

Lady Ephigenia blinked again as she tried to make some sense out of this confusing tale.

"Come, my dear," she said finally. "Pull yourself together. Things cannot be as bad as you seem to think they are. Rotherham is no fool. And as for your contemptible nephew, we will merely refuse to see him if he calls again. And if Lady Potter does the same, I see no reason why he should remain in the vicinity for more than a few days."

She was wrong, of course. Two subsequent attempts by the *vicomte* to call on the ladies at the Grange were met with the information, delivered by Fortham in his most supercilious manner, that Lady Ephigenia and Miss Wetherby were not at home. The first indication they received that the *vicomte* Duvalier had not simply disappeared because they refused to see him came one afternoon, two days later, when Arabella danced into the Blue drawing-room where the two ladies sat drinking tea with Lady Chatham.

"You will never guess whom I met just now at Lady Standish's," she cried, after greeting all three ladies affectionately. She looked pointedly at Diana and the latter sensed that disaster was about to strike again.

"You never told me your nephew, the *vicomte* Duvalier, was staying in Melbury, Diana," she said accusingly. "He was sitting with Lady Standish and Chloe, amusing them with stories about his adventures in Paris. And oh, how charming he is, Mama. You never saw such elegance. I swear he quite put Toby in the shade."

Toby, who had followed her into the room, together with Dick Chatham, took exception to this, remarking that the *vicomte* was too dandified for his taste.

"Silver-embroidered waistcoat," he said digustedly.

"And the palest yellow unmentionables." Arabella giggled. "I swear it is just the shade I have been looking for, Mama. For that new evening gown you promised me. The *vicomte* invited me to drive out in his curricle tomorrow morning. Do say I can go.''

During her young friend's chatter, Diana cast an anxious look at Captain Chatham, to whom she had confided her desire to avoid Ferdinand's company because she had no wish to return to Paris for a distasteful, arranged marriage to a man thirty years her senior.

Chatham immediately came over to her side. ''Is this true, Dick?'' she queried. ''Has Ferdinand actually insinuated himself into Lady Standish's good graces?''

''He's just the kind of smooth charmer that ladies seem to dote on, Diana,'' he answered with a grin. ''Greeted me as bold as brass and inquired most civilly after you, m'dear. Seems to be living in Lady Standish's pocket. Quite taken with him, she is. And Chloe, of course, is delighted to have a young buck dancing attendance on her. Just the kind of flummery she thrives on.''

Diana frowned with annoyance. ''He does have a certain insidious charm, I'll have to admit. But I would hate to see Arabella drawn into his toils, Dick. She is such an innocent. I thought that if we refused to see him, he would go away. But I should have known he would worm his way into my life again one way or another.''

''You are refining too much on all this, m'dear,'' Chatham remarked lightly. ''True, he is somewhat of an impudent puppy and cockscomb, but I doubt he can do as much harm as you seem to think. Short of abducting you, he cannot force you to return to Paris. If it will make you any easier, I will undertake to keep an eye on him for you.''

With this, Diana had to be content. But her uneasiness grew as, with increasing frequency, she encountered her French cousin, nattily attired in a seemingly endless array of extravagant waistcoats, at every social event she attended in the neighbourhood. He was invariably attending the Incomparable Lady Chloe and charming all the ladies present with his polished address.

She was particularly incensed when she discovered that Dick Chatham had relaxed his promise to keep an eye on the *vicomte*, preferring instead to take his gun out after pigeons in the Home Wood with Toby and Lord Henry Forsdyke. As a result, Arabella had taken to riding out in the afternoons with Ferdinand, loosely chaperoned by Lady Chloe.

Diana came upon them one afternoon on her way back from Melbury and was startled to see the degree of intimacy which had already sprung up between her nephew and the young heiress. Lady Chloe, who had resumed her easy intimacy with Diana after her return from Bath without showing—as Chatham had predicted— the least remorse over the curricle accident, seemed to be highly amused by the *vicomte*'s marked attentions to Miss Chatham.

"Such a handsome young couple. Wouldn't you agree, Miss Wetherby?" she asked gaily, bringing her high-spirited chestnut mare into step beside Diana's bay gelding. "Dear Ferdinand has that marvellous Gaelic charm and wit that cannot help but please. I predict they will make a match of it before the season even gets underway."

"Arabella is not out yet," Diana felt obliged to point out. "And I doubt Lady Chatham would want her to marry so young. She is a considerable heiress, you know, and might look as high as she chooses for a husband. A young man who has not yet reached his majority and is still dependent on his father can hardly be considered an eligible *parti*."

"Are you hinting that our darling Ferdinand might be a fortune-hunter, my dear Miss Wetherby?" Lady Chloe's tinkling laughter had an unpleasant ring to it. "Well, I won't argue with you about that. For who should know of these things better than you?" she added innocently, a malicious little smile hovering on her beautiful lips.

Diana bit back an angry retort and kept her opinion to herself. Privately she considered that her nephew was quite capable of marrying to improve his fortunes. His father provided him with a generous allowance, as Diana well knew, but the thought of Arabella's fortune might be too great a temptation for Ferdinand to resist, given his predilection for extravagance.

Determined to discover the seriousness of the heiress's new flirt, Diana slipped into Arabella's bed-chamber that evening, after she had dressed for dinner, in time to help her young friend arrange her hair in delicate ringlets around her heart-shaped face.

From Arabella's artless chatter, Diana was able to deduce that the heiress found the *vicomte*'s attentions flattering mainly because she considered him to be a very Tulip of Fashion, complete to a shade in every way.

"He treats me like a real lady," she confessed innocently. "Not like my brother and his friends who treat me as if I were still in the schoolroom."

"Well, dear, you are not out yet, you know. And until you are, you should not be encouraging gentlemen, however attractive, to dangle after you.''

"Oh, no!'' Arabella looked shocked at this novel idea. "He is not dangling after me, Diana. At least, I don't think he is.'' She gazed at Miss Wetherby in alarm.

"Well, then he is certainly flirting with you, which is far, far more reprehensible, let me tell you,'' Diana said reprovingly.

Arabella's face cleared at this, and she replied with a gurgle of laughter: "There is nothing wrong with a little harmless flirting, Diana. My brother is always telling me so. Besides, Toby and Lord Henry are always flirting with me,'' she added saucily. "Even Rotherham calls me his favourite little puss, you know. You have heard him do so, surely.''

Diana, who had certainly heard the earl refer to his young guest in such brotherly terms, regarded her young friend ruefully. How was she to explain to this innocent miss that there was a vast difference between the playful demonstrations of affection indulged in by long-time friends and the insinuating flattery from an acquaintance of barely a fortnight's standing. Clearly it would do no good to warn Arabella that it was not quite the thing to be forever hanging on a gentleman's sleeve or to treat her new admirer as she was used to treating her brother's intimates. She could easily imagine the laughing response such an admonition would provoke, accompanied no doubt by a request that Diana cease being such a silly goose. Given Arabella's trusting disposition, there was little likelihood of any such warning being heeded. The thought disturbed her more than she cared to admit, even to herself, and she decided it was time to seek Toby's advice.

It was not until late the following afternoon, however, that she was able to persuade Toby to take a turn with her in the shrubbery where she hoped they would not be disturbed.

"What has put you in such a pucker, m'dear?'' Toby inquired as soon as they were alone. "It's not like you to get hipped over a bagatelle.''

"I am worried about Arabella, Toby.''

"So am I, m'dear,'' he interrupted shortly. "But she has told me not to pinch at her, which I feel it is my duty to do when she will insist on throwing herself at that French fribble. Forgive me for being so frank, m'dear, but that nephew of yours is exactly the kind of rackety Town fop who can dazzle a chit like that into doing something foolish.''

"Oh, I agree with you, entirely," Diana replied, thankful that Toby had at least noticed the encroachment of a rival in the affections of his *bien aimée*. "But what I do not understand, Toby—and forgive me if I am too blunt—is why you have retired from the lists, so to speak, and left that cockscomb the run of the field."

Toby gave a short laugh. "Surely you do not expect me to compete with that Tulip of Fashion, m'dear," he said with a tinge of bitterness in his usually jovial voice. "For I assure you, I will do no such thing. I refuse to get myself up to look like a dashed Park Saunterer just to impress some bird-witted chit who hasn't enough sense to recognize a curst jackstraw when she sees one. And when she tells me for the fifth time that this overdressed, French toad-eater quite puts me in the shade, m'dear, what can I do but wash my hands of the silly goose?"

Diana realized with a shock that Toby had been deeply wounded and set herself at once to assuage his male ego and convince him that Arabella needed his support if she were to avoid falling into a serious scrape as a result of her innocence.

Toby remained dubious, however. "Dash it, Diana, she's right," he exclaimed. "I'm hardly the romantic figure a chit of her age expects to come riding up to carry her off." He looked down wistfully at his abundantly filled waistcoat. "Too many late night suppers and bottles of port," he grumbled. "Never thought I would live to regret the day. But can't say I blame her. The truth is, m'dear, I just don't have the kind of youthful figure anymore that appeals to a chit of seventeen. Now when I was twenty . . ." He trailed off in a profound sigh which would have been amusing had it not been so heartfelt.

"If you would stop moaning about what is past, you would see that you have several advantages over my nephew," Diana said impatiently.

"No use bamming me, m'dear," Toby cut in pessimistically. "Not at all kind of you, you know."

"Nonsense," was her quick retort. "You have the distinct advantage of being a man of considerable substance. And I don't mean in wealth alone. Only think, Toby, you are all the crack on the hunting field, and—"

"If I can find a horse that's up to my weight," he reminded her morosely.

"You have an enviable military record," she continued, ignoring his remark, "and were wounded in the service of your country

when Ferdinand was still in short-coats. You are an excellent
dancer, an accomplished fencer, and—from what Dick has told
me—show to advantage in the ring and have what he calls a
punishing left.''

"Ladies don't care for such things," Toby pointed out deject
edly.

"Well, you are quite wrong there, sir. I am always impressed by
a gentleman's athletic achievements, and Arabella certainly thrives
on such feats. But to top it all, Toby, remember that you drive to
an inch and are a member of the Four-in-Hand Club. Now that is
something my nephew will never achieve however much he may
aspire to such an honour.''

Toby showed signs of cheering up as Diana recited this list of
his masculine attractions. Encouraged, she slipped her hand
through his arm and squeezed it affectionately, gazing up at him
with a dazzling smile.

"And furthermore," she declared seriously, "you are the
kindest, most thoughtful, wonderfully generous man I have ever
met and, if things were different, I would marry you in a minute,
for I love you dearly, Toby.''

Impulsively, she reached up and placed a friendly kiss on his
plump ruddy cheek.

"What a tender scene, to be sure," drawled a cool voice from
behind them, causing Diana to jump back self-consciously and
Toby to yank nervously at an impeccably neat cravat.

They turned to confront the earl who had paused on the grass
pathway to observe them through his quizzing-glass. "Forgive me
for interrupting this intriguing tête-à-tête," he murmured with a
sardonic smile curling his taut lips. "I had thought to have a
private word with Miss Wetherby, but I gather I shall have to wait
my turn.''

He looked meaningfully at Toby, who quailed visibly and
muttered: "Don't go off half cocked, Rotherham. It's not what
you think. At least, not exactly . . . that is . . . Dash it, man,
Diana—that is to say, Miss Wetherby—was merely advising me
on a matter that concerns us both. If you knew the whole, you
wouldn't glare at me in that crusty way. Quite the contrary,
wouldn't you say, m'dear?" he added, glancing appealingly at
Diana.

"I am all ears, my dear fellow," the earl replied with deceptive
civility, for Diana perceived that the fingers holding his quizzing-
glass were white at the knuckles.

"Oh, I can't tell you, old chap," Toby blustered. "You'll have to ask Diana about that. I was just off, anyway. Miss Wetherby." He bowed to Diana and walked swiftly away towards the house.

His departure was followed by a short silence during which Diana mentally reviewed all the excellent qualities she had previously listed as Toby's attractions and discarded the majority of them. His good qualities had—in her estimation—been sadly undercut by his cow-handed handling of this unexpected encounter with Rotherham. Furthermore, his chicken-hearted retreat had left her in the unenviable position of trying to explain away a simple situation to which Toby's blustering had given a severely compromising aura.

"My compliments, Miss Wetherby," Rotherham said stiffly. "I gather from this touching scene that you have contrived to bring Tottlefield up to scratch. I am only surprised you did not set your cap for poor Forsdyke who is a rather better catch, if one believes the gossips at Almack's. They should know these things, of course. It's their business to know, or at least they make it so."

When Diana, struck speechless by this cutting remark, made no reply, his expression hardened into something close to a sneer.

"When am I to wish you happy, my dear?" He raised his quizzing-glass and examined her insultingly as Diana strove to keep her temper in check.

"You are rather too quick to assume the worst, my lord," she replied with as much composure as she could muster. "Or the best, as the case may be," she added capriciously. "For there is no doubt in my mind that Toby will make the best of husbands."

She paused to see the effect of this essentially truthful statement and was so alarmed at the sudden harsh expression which appeared on the earl's face that she added hastily, "For Arabella, that is. As soon as that silly little goose wakes up to the treasure that is hers for the taking. And so I told him, my lord."

"Doing it rather too brown, my dear Miss Wetherby," he replied with a short, mirthless laugh. "I come upon you kissing a gentleman, with obvious pleasure I might add, and you have the effrontery to tell me that you were discussing Arabella. What kind of flat do you take me for?" he said harshly.

"Well, it's true, regardless of what you think. And I was only giving Toby a sisterly kiss because he was feeling so low. There was no harm in it at all."

"I see," he said coldly. "And that is why you were telling him you would marry him because you loved him, I suppose?" He had stepped closer to her as he said this, and Diana was quite appalled at the bleakness she saw in his eyes as he glared down at her. "Am I to assume that is what you are also calling sisterly?"

Diana stared up at him dumbly. Her heart had suddenly become a painful weight in her chest and she felt the urge to burst into tears. She would not give him the satisfaction of knowing how much he had hurt her, however, and lifted her chin stubbornly.

"You are deliberately misunderstanding the whole affair, my lord," she said in a low voice that quivered with suppressed emotion. "Have you so poor an opinion of me to suppose I would try to replace Arabella in Toby's affections? It would be an impossible task, I assure you. A sorry creature indeed you must think me, my lord, if you believe that I would play her such a scurvy trick."

"You have given me little reason to think otherwise," he said bluntly. "This little scene I have just witnessed speaks for itself. I find it hard to believe, in view of this evidence, that any consideration you may profess to have for Miss Chatham would prevent you from snaring a husband as you seem bent on doing." His mouth was a thin line set in a rigid expression of disgust and anger.

"I resent the implication that I am out to *snare* a husband," Diana exclaimed angrily. "As you very well know, I gave you to understand that your own offer would be unwelcome to me not so long ago," she reminded him acidly.

He let out a crack of laughter. "Yes, I remember, only too well." He caught her wrist in a vice-like grip and pulled her against him. "I did not realize at that time that you prefer brotherly kisses, my dear."

"Let me go," Diana hissed, struggling ineffectually in his grasp. "You are hurting me, sir."

"It's time you learned that brotherly kisses are all right in their way, my dear, but they can't hold a candle to the other kind."

Diana made the mistake of looking up at him as his other arm encircled her waist and drew her closer. A slow smile curved his lips as if he were enjoying her distress. The anger in his eyes dissolved and was replaced by a strange intensity Diana could not fathom but which made her heart leap into her throat. Her struggles ceased abruptly and, as if impelled by a will of their own, her lips lifted to receive his kiss.

"That's much, much better, my dear," he murmured against her mouth as his lips took possession of hers, gently at first, then with increasing passion until Diana felt a sweet warmth envelop her as in a dream world.

She came to her senses when she realized that he had broken the spell by raising his head to listen intently to the sound of faint voices coming from the direction of the house.

He glanced down at her and his lips twitched into a smile. "I am glad to see that you agree with me on something, Miss Wetherby," he murmured, still holding her unresisting form against his tall frame. "But I fear we are about to be interrupted, so please allow me to escort you to the house, my dear."

He released her and, placing the nerveless fingers of her hand on his arm, led her down the pathway towards the approaching voices.

"I can tell you one thing, my dear," he said conversationally as they strolled along. When she looked up at him inquiringly, he smiled at her in such a way that two spots of colour appeared on her cheeks.

"You will not, I repeat, not marry Tobias Tottlefield, or anyone else for that matter, unless it is over my dead body. I want you for myself."

As they made their way through the shrubbery towards the house, Diana tried to compose her tumultuous thoughts and calm her beating heart. She paid little heed to the casual conversation the earl was carrying on effortlessly as they walked. She kept hearing those precious words ringing over and over in her ears: *I want you for myself. I want you for myself.*

# 15 ·····

# The Masquerade

THEY HAD NOT gone very far before they came upon Arabella, accompanied by Lady Chloe and the *vicomte* Duvalier. As soon as she saw them, Arabella clapped her hands and called out excitedly, "Diana, my love! Here is Lady Chloe come over to the Grange expressly to invite us all to an impromptu masquerade Lady Standish has devised for tomorrow night." She grasped Diana's arm and skipped along beside her, blissfully unaware of her friend's agitation. "Mama thinks it will be just the thing to liven up our stay."

Lady Chloe, by no means as unobservant as her young friend, saw at once that Diana was unnaturally subdued. A glance at Rotherham told her that something had transpired between them that had put him in one of his freakish moods. As the party turned back towards the house, she managed to fall into step beside Diana, who had detached herself from the earl's arm ostensibly to pluck a rosebud from one of the rosebushes which lined the walk.

"What do you intend to wear to the masquerade, dear Miss Wetherby?" she inquired in her sweetly lilting voice. "I don't mind telling you, since you are a particular friend, that I will go as Cleopatra. I trust you will not betray my little secret, my dear."

Murmuring that she would never dream of doing such a thing, Diana made as if to join the rest of the party, but Lady Chloe detained her.

"A word in your ear, Miss Wetherby," she said with an air of concern that Diana could not help but feel was false. "I am sure you will not mind if I tell you, as one who is your friend, that it is not at all the thing for single ladies to make assignations with gentlemen in the shrubbery." She smiled roguishly at Diana's look of surprise. "Ah! I could not help noticing that Tottlefield came charging out of the bushes as if a bee had stung him. And then I find you clinging to Rotherham's sleeve as if you never intended to let it go.'' She laughed a tinkling laugh as if she had said something profoundly witty. Diana stared at her in stony silence, her mood of euphoric happiness dissipating under this malicious attack.

"La, my dear Miss Wetherby, that will never do, you know,'' she added gaily. "As a woman of fashion who has seen a great deal of the world, I should warn you that no gentleman—and especially no gentleman of Rotherham's rank and address—likes to be bamboozled into making a cake of himself by an inconsequential female who has wormed her way into his household under false pretenses."

Stunned by the bluntness of this speech, Diana forced her frozen lips into the semblance of an innocuous smile. "You are too kind, my lady. Much too kind. And I am sure you are quite right. I shall take your words very much to heart. One cannot—I am sure if you say so—be too careful with inconsequential females. They are everywhere, don't you agree?"

When Diana saw Lady Chloe's moue of impatience at these insipid remarks, she regained her sense of humour and began to enjoy herself. "I shall certainly be on the watch for any who might try to worm their way into the Grange," she added earnestly. "And if they dare to try to bamboozle any of the gentlemen staying there, I shall denounce them immediately. Do you, by any chance, my lady," she inquired in a hushed whisper, "know if any such females are in the neighbourhood?"

"You are being absurd, Miss Wetherby," snapped her ladyship, mutilating a perfectly innocent rosebud with nervous fingers. "I merely meant to impress upon you that gentlemen do not marry inconsequential females. They may flirt with them; they may even go so far as to kiss them." She looked at Diana smugly through her long lashes as she said this. "But they do not offer them matrimony. At most, they may offer them *carte blanche*, which no respectable female would even contemplate, of course. But it is often all an inconsequential female may hope for."

"How tragic," remarked Diana as the two ladies strolled towards the house. "But I am glad that you have enlightened me, Lady Chloe. I have often wondered about all those dashers and high-flyers upon whom gentlemen are said to lavish enormous amounts of money and attention. It all sounded so romantic and enviable I used to think. But of course it can't be, can it, if they are all inconsequential?" She stopped to draw breath and smile simperingly at her companion whose face was set in ill humour.

"Ladies should know nothing of such gentlemanly pursuits,"
Lady Chloe stated haughtily, apparently forgetting that she had
herself introduced the topic.

"Single ladies, to be sure," Diana agreed readily. "But I
imagine it is unexceptional for married ladies, ladies of fashion
such as yourself," she added blithely, "to know of these things. I
have even heard it rumoured, though of course I could be
mistaken, that it is the fashion for some daring married ladies to
become dashers of the first water themselves, especially when
they are leg-shackled to husbands somewhat advanced in years."

She glanced innocently at Lady Chloe as she made this last
remark and was convinced, from the startled look of guilt in her
ladyship's green eyes, that she had scored a direct hit. The thought
was infinitely comforting.

The masquerade was a huge success by local standards.
Although not so elegantly appointed as the Earl of Rotherham's
ball, Lady Standish's masquerade attracted all the young people in
the surrounding area who vied among themselves to obtain
invitations. Since Lady Standish was well known for her infor-
mality and considered to be bang up to the mark by the younger
set, there were few families of any consequence in the neighbourhood who did not receive an invitation.

The result was a sad squeeze as Lady Standish herself proudly
pointed out to Lady Ephigenia, as the party from the Grange
descended from the two carriages which had conveyed its eight
members to Standish House.

"My dear, how enchanting," exclaimed Lady Chatham, indicating the hundreds of coloured lanterns that had been hung about
the garden and around the ornamental fish pond. Her ladyship had
been cajoled by her hostess into coming as a Turkish matron and
her gaudy purple domino was topped by a hideous green turban
surmounted by five enormous peacock feathers.

Arabella, who wore a fetching fairy costume of palest pink, with
pink ribbons of a darker shade trailing from her tiny waist and a
pink mask through which her blue eyes twinkled beguilingly, was
as enchanted as her Mama with the decorations.

"I declare I have never seen anything so grand, Lady Eliza,"
she told her hostess in thrilling accents.

Lady Standish embraced her affectionately. "I see you come
prepared to break every heart in the house, my dear Arabella."
She laughed, very much in spirits at the success of her party. "And

Miss Wetherby, I declare you look equipped to slay all your admirers with your bow,'' she added gaily. ''Between you, there will be no gentlemen left for everybody else.''

Diana, who had chosen to adopt the dress of her namesake, the huntress Diana, wore a simple, white, sleeveless tunic, girded around the waist by a loose leather sash which supported a short dagger in an ornate sheath. Her domino was of a woodland green, as was her loo-mask, and over her shoulder she had slung a quiverful of arrows and a bow she had discovered in the Grange attic.

The four gentlemen had come in their scarlet regimentals, concealed under black dominoes, while Lady Ephigenia had indulged her romantic imagination by appearing as an exotic Eastern princess in a fetching gown of silver studded with sequins and coloured stones.

As the Grange party trod up the red-carpeted stairs to the first floor, they heard the musicians striking up the first country dance of the evening. Arabella, who had promised the first dance to Lord Henry Forsdyke, grasped his arm unceremoniously and hurried him into the ballroom to take their places in the set. Toby claimed Diana's hand and joined another set which was just forming.

''Dashed hot these dominoes, m'dear,'' Toby complained as they went down the set together. ''I shouldn't have listened to Chatham. As a career officer, he's used to dancing in these dashed regimentals, but my uniform seems to have become a little tight since I last wore it on the Continent.''

''You look very dashing, Toby,'' Diana told him with all sincerity. In spite of his tendency to portliness, Toby's height lent him a commanding air which was pleasing to the female eye.

Leading her back to where Lady Ephigenia was sitting chatting with Miss Josephine Fenley and Lady Bagley, the squire's wife, Toby reminded Diana that she was promised to him for the first waltz. When the strains of this dance struck up, however, Toby was nowhere in sight and Diana, having refused several offers from other gentlemen, was about to retire to her seat when Rotherham appeared at her elbow, made her an elegant bow, and said glibly, ''Toby sends his apologies, Miss Wetherby, and asks that you accept me as his substitute for this dance.'' He looked mildly amused at her skeptical expression.

''That's a whisker if ever I heard one,'' Diana remarked acidly. ''You should be ashamed of yourself, browbeating poor Toby as you probably did, just to badger me into dancing with you.''

"How ungenerous of you, my dear. I never badger females into doing anything with me that they don't enjoy wholeheartedly," he murmured gently but with a glint in his eye that told Diana more clearly than any words could have done that he was thinking of the kiss he had given her in the shrubbery the previous afternoon.

Her heart skipped uncomfortably at this reminder of an incident she had tried her best to forget. Yet he was right, she had to admit to herself. She had certainly enjoyed the kiss wholeheartedly. However, Lady Chloe's whispered warnings in the rose garden had had their effect. Her initial euphoria had been replaced by a swarm of doubts that had deprived her of sleep and filled her heart with misgivings. Those precious words, *I want you for myself,* no longer had the power to fill her with joy. Now they seemed to have taken on a more sinister meaning, forcing her to ask herself if she were indeed one of those inconsequential females Lady Chloe had described, destined to live on the fringes of society, fêted, sought after, admired, even kissed and courted, but never accepted by the Polite World.

These dire thoughts and more flooded through her mind as she stood staring up at the man who had caused both the greatest joy and the profoundest misery to engulf her in the past few hours.

Rotherham was startled to see the bleak expression of utter misery in the depths of Miss Wetherby's beautiful hazel eyes before they were veiled by curling dark lashes. Fleetingly he wondered if he had been mistaken in thinking that she was indifferent to a possible alliance with Tottlefield. It was, of course, what he wanted to think. And in spite of his rather blunt accusations in the garden yesterday afternoon, he had not seriously believed that she had set her cap at Toby. She had allowed him to kiss her with quite indecorous enthusiasm, he remembered with a tingle of pleasure. It had never occurred to him to wonder if perhaps Toby had kissed her with equal passion. He had been eager—perhaps too eager, he thought ruefully—to accept her explanation of the intimate scene he had witnessed between her and Tottlefield. Now he did wonder, and the thought brought a deep frown to his lean face.

He recalled that he had been standing staring at Miss Wetherby for quite some time in full view of a battalion of biddies who would like nothing better than to have a new scandal to amuse them. He held out his hand, and Miss Wetherby mechanically placed her small one into it and allowed him to lead her onto the floor.

Thoroughly cast down by her train of thought and inhibited by the earl's sudden frown, Diana made no attempt at polite conversation as they circled the floor, keeping her eyes studiously fixed on the earl's elegant waistcoat. Several attempts on his part to draw her out met with the shortest possible replies uttered in a monotone of civil disinterest.

"If you refuse me the pleasure of one small smile—that's all I ask—people will think that you are out of sorts with me, m'dear," he finally suggested in a voice that held a hint of restrained amusement. "I had not expected you to be overjoyed at having to forego a waltz with Tottlefield, for he is a great hand at waltzing, I admit; but neither did I expect, when I accepted to stand in for him, that you would cut me so devastatingly, Miss Wetherby. I can tell you, I am quite cast down. Therefore, I appeal to your better nature, my dear. Please smile at me."

He did not sound in the least cast down and Diana, her sense of humour intrigued by the pleading tenor of this request, glanced up at him through her lashes and murmured, "I have done nothing of the sort, my lord. You are provoking me, as usual, and I do take exception to that." But she could not repress the tiny smile that twitched her lips.

"That is much better!" he exclaimed with an engaging smile. "You look so adorable when you are provoked, my dear. I cannot help myself."

"There you go again, my lord," Diana said reprovingly. "It is not proper for you to flirt with me, you know. Such frivolous attentions can only be distasteful to a female of my years. If you had any sensibility at all," she continued, aware that she was beginning to sound like the intolerably prosy kind of female she most disliked, "you would desist from making a cake of yourself. And of me," she added as an afterthought.

This remark was greeted by an involuntary crack of laughter that caused several of the younger ladies present to wonder enviously what the goddess in white had said to amuse one of the most eligible gentlemen in the room.

One of these ladies was dressed as Cleopatra, queen of the Nile, in a flowing pale amber tunic, liberally spangled with gold sequins, which clung rather daringly to her slender figure. Her mass of golden curls was crowned by an extravagant diamond and ruby tiara which seemed to reflect every candle in the room as the lady swung her head to gaze speculatively at the earl and his partner. Her green eyes turned suddenly dark with anger when she realized that the goddess in white was none other than that inconsequential female Miss Wetherby.

"It looks as though my dear aunt has made a conquest, my lady," murmured the *vicomte* suavely, correctly reading the moue of annoyance in Lady Chloe's beautiful face. "Though why he would look twice at such an old ape-leader is beyond my comprehension when you are present in the same room, *cherie*," he added glibly, secretly amused at the petulant expression in her ladyship's magnificent green eyes.

"Rotherham always had a quirkish sense of humour," she replied curtly. "But he is making a big mistake if he thinks to outwit me, my dear *vicomte*." The smile which accompanied this remark made Ferdinand glad that he was not in the unfortunate earl's shoes.

"I made a regrettable mistake all those years ago, but I do not intend to repeat it. And with your help, my dear Ferdinand"—she smiled coquettishly up at him—"there will be no fear of that happening, will there now? You help me, *cheri*, and I will help you win an heiress, agreed?"

"Agreed, my lady," Ferdinand replied with a smirk.

It was just as well that Diana was not privileged to hear this exchange. If she had, she might have been less tolerant of her nephew's flowery compliments when she accepted his request for a dance much later in the evening, after the general unmasking of the guests at the stroke of midnight.

Ferdinand was an excellent dancer and had become a favourite among the young ladies in the neighbourhood. Diana was a little surprised when he asked her to stand up with him for a cotillion, but supposed him to be anxious to win her support in his attempt to obtain Arabella's hand. He behaved so creditably, in fact, that she was quite in charity with him by the time the dance ended and he returned her to her seat beside Lady Ephigenia.

A few minutes later, during a lull in the dancing, the *vicomte* returned with Arabella on his arm to beg his aunt to accompany them into the lamp-lit garden since dear Miss Chatham was desirous of taking the air in these romantic surroundings. Pleasantly surprised at his concern for convention, she agreed, and if she wished the invitation had come from quite another gentleman, she was sensible enough to know—she reminded herself wryly— that inconsequential females must take what they can get.

A romantic at heart, Lady Standish had outdone herself in converting her garden into a wonderland of romantic delights.

Gaily coloured lamps guided the strolling couples down winding pathways through the shrubbery and beneath tall chestnuts already in full bud. Elegant tables loaded with refreshments were scattered strategically about under silk canopies. Comfortable chairs were grouped here and yon, and rustic garden benches provided the chance for privacy in secluded arbours.

Arabella was enchanted and Diana had to agree that even in Paris she had never seen anything so inviting.

A lady on each arm, the *vicomte* seemed to be in his element and on his best behaviour. He encouraged Arabella's innocent chatter, listened politely to his aunt's remarks, and entertained them with amusing stories of his first impressions of London society.

Diana was having so pleasant a time and was beginning to think that perhaps love had improved her nephew's selfish disposition when their path took them past one of the secluded arbours. Distracted by movement and a stifled exclamation, they stopped in their tracks and looked into the recess of the private nook.

The lamplight was dim but it was more than sufficient to show the broad back of a gentleman dressed in scarlet regimentals who seemed to be passionately embracing a lady who had clasped her white arms firmly around his neck. This was the scene that met Diana's startled gaze, and if the thought did flash across her mind that there was something familiar about those broad shoulders, she quickly dismissed it as absurd. After all, there were several other gentlemen in regimentals at the masquerade.

As she attempted to turn quietly away, Ferdinand cleared his throat noisily and remarked in a mocking stage whisper, "*Mon dieu!* We seem to be very much *de trop* here, ladies. Let us leave these lovebirds to their pleasant occupation."

The couple broke apart immediately, and the lady, her diamond and ruby tiara catching the twinkling rays of the coloured lamps, peeked around those broad shoulders at the *vicomte*'s party and cried breathlessly, "Ah! Rotherham, my love. We are discovered."

Diana stood as though she were rooted to the ground. She felt suddenly very cold; her heart seemed to have stopped beating, and she found it hard to draw a breath. When the gentleman slowly turned to confront them, she found herself staring straight into the dark, unsmiling face of the Earl of Rotherham.

# 16 ·····
# Point Non Plus

SHE NEVER KNEW exactly how she escaped from that horrible scene. All she remembered was Ferdinand's facetious remarks, Lady Chloe's tinkling laugh, Arabella's frantic tugging on her arm, and Rotherham's eyes, slate grey in the lamplight, staring right through her.

Somehow she avoided him for what was left of the party, and when it came time to go home, she felt relief to be in the same carriage with the other ladies.

She managed to get up to her room without once having to address the earl, although she was painfully aware that his eyes were riveted on her. When she was alone, Diana gave way to her emotions and sobbed out her unhappiness and heartbreak into an unresponsive pillow until she fell into an uneasy sleep.

But before going to bed, she had already made up her mind what must be done. She could no longer stay under the same roof as that despicable man. She would accept her aunt's invitation to join her at Potter Hall, although how she would do so without offending Lady Ephigenia was something she did not immediately know.

Morning brought no slackening of her resolve to abandon the Grange. As she put away the crumpled white tunic she had worn to the masquerade, Diana wondered if she would ever look at it again without remembering that dreadful scene in the arbour, or cease to hear Lady Chloe's triumphant, tinkling laughter, or feel Rotherham's cold stare pierce her heart.

Knowing that Lady Ephigenia would already be up, sipping hot chocolate in her private sitting-room, Diana tiptoed down the silent hall and scratched on her door.

"You are up early, my love," her ladyship commented as soon as Diana was seated beside her in a comfortable armchair. "I

165

suppose you are going out on one of your mad gallops?'' she said with an affectionate smile. ''You wouldn't by any chance happen to be going in the direction of Potter Hall, would you, dear?''

Surprised, Diana said she had indeed planned to visit her aunt but before she could say more, her hostess was begging her to convey an invitation to dear Lady Potter to bring the girls over to see Rotherham's new litter of puppies, an event they had been looking forward to for several weeks.

Diana promised to do so, and then added casually: ''I really came to consult you about that invitation from my aunt to spend a few days with her at Potter Hall, Lady Effie. She insisted again last night, and if you do not find the idea objectionable, I would like to go over today if you would undertake to take care of old Bijou for me. He has become very attached to you, as you well know.'' She laughed, knowing full well that Lady Ephigenia doted on the parrot herself.

Having obtained her ladyship's blessing, Diana left instructions with Molly to have one of her small trunks, which she had packed herself last night, conveyed to Potter Hall in the tilbury, and proceeded to the stables to have Perseus saddled.

She had certain qualms about taking one of Rotherham's horses on this particular mission, but she convinced herself that it would be easy enough to send the horse back to the Grange with the groom who brought her trunk.

Although the hour was still early when she reached Potter Hall, both Sir Rudolph and his lady were in the breakfast-room partaking of a hearty meal of sirloin, ham, eggs, and bacon. They were somewhat surprised but delighted to see Diana and received her with the kind affection they reserved especially for her. Sir Rudolph's deep affection for his diminutive wife was evident in his every word, while Lady Potter herself, Diana had to admit, seemed to grow even more beautiful under the glow of his loving attention.

Diana felt a pang of envy and immediately rebuked herself for this ungenerous attitude. She was genuinely delighted that her dearest Sophy had at long last found the happiness she deserved.

When he had finished his breakfast, Sir Rudolph rose from the table and gave his wife an unselfconscious kiss on her upturned face. ''I'll be taking myself off now, m'love. It's plain as a pikestaff that you two ladies have a deal of talking to do.'' At the surprised expressions that greeted this remark he laughed and added: "About last night's goings on, m'dears. You can't fool me."

As soon as he was safely out of the room, Lady Potter examined her niece's ravaged countenance and calmly remarked: "Come up to my sitting-room, my dear, and you can tell me all about it."

Since the recital of her woes was punctuated by frequent bouts of tears and fits of angry recriminations against a certain gentleman, it was not until almost two hours later that Diana began to feel the relief of having got the whole ugly incident off her chest.

After bathing her tear-stained face with cool lavender water, Diana felt sufficiently recuperated to accept her aunt's invitation to take a stroll in the rose garden, to examine the new varieties her ladyship had recently added to the collection which was the envy of the neighbourhood.

"Sir Rudolph is so pleased that I, too, am fond of roses," Lady Potter explained, as they wandered down a gravel walk lined with standard rosebushes already beginning to show colour in their first spring buds. "The dear man lives in fear that I will become bored with country life and hanker after London entertainment again. He has even offered to hire a house in Town this season if I wish it." Her ladyship chuckled at this evidence of her lord's affection for her. "Can you imagine, my love, exchanging what I have here for the often tiresome company of backbiting females whose first concern is for their own consequence?"

Diana looked around her at the masses of daffodils and crocuses still flowering under the newly budded beech trees, the borders of primroses and violets lining the walk, the sturdy stalks of larkspurs and foxgloves, and above all the promised splendour of the rose garden, and had to agree that country life was full of pleasures.

This rhapsodic mood lasted into the afternoon but was interrupted when the ladies, sitting over their needlework in the small morning-room at the back of the house, heard the sound of a carriage being driven round to the stables. A glance out the window was sufficient to drive the colour from Diana's cheeks and cause the haunted look to return to her eyes.

"The greys," she whispered, glancing beseechingly at her aunt. "Aunt Sophy, it's *him*. Please don't let him in. Oh, please! I can't see him. I simply *cannot* face that man."

Lady Potter rose and put a comforting arm around her distraught niece. "Calm yourself, my love. No one is going to make you do anything you don't wish to. But I do think you should give him a chance to tell you his side of the story, dearest.''

"There's nothing to tell. I saw what I saw," Diana replied darkly, but consented to return to her seat.

A few minutes later there was a discreet knock on the door and the Potter butler announced that the Earl of Rotherham had called to see Miss Wetherby.

Lady Potter rose and went to the door. "I shall see him, Eaton," she said, then turned back to Diana. "Think about what I have said, my dear. I cannot believe that you wish to be thought uncivil.''

Diana sighed and went to the window to look down into the stable yard where Sir Rudolph's grooms were busy rubbing down the earl's team of greys. The sight of these magnificent animals brought back bittersweet memories, and Diana was lost in her fantasies when she heard the door open behind her.

"That was a short interview, Aunt," she remarked without turning. "I trust you have sent that odious man about his business.''

A familiar crack of laughter made her whirl around to find herself, once again, transfixed by a pair of grey eyes, darkened with emotions Diana could not fathom.

Before she could utter a word, her aunt appeared in the doorway behind Rotherham, somewhat out of breath from having run all the way up the stairs in his wake. "My lord, this is most unseemly behaviour. I must ask you to leave at once." Lady Potter's voice shook with a mixture of indignation and amusement. One look at her niece's face, however, prompted her to pluck urgently at the earl's sleeve. "Diana is not feeling quite the thing this afternoon, my lord. Perhaps you would be so kind as to call at some other time?''

Rotherham gave a short laugh. "So I see," he murmured. Then he clasped both of Lady Potter's hands in his and gave her his most charming smile. "No, this won't keep. I beg of you, Lady Potter, allow me five minutes conversation with your niece. It is most urgent, I assure you.''

"I absolutely forbid you to do anything of the sort, Aunt Sophy," Diana exclaimed in a cold voice. "And as for you"—she glared at Rotherham—"nothing you may have to say is of the slightest interest to me, so you may as well leave immediately. Before I have you removed forcibly," she added with a certain grim satisfaction.

Eaton, the Potters' butler, had also followed Rotherham up to the morning-room and now stood behind his mistress glancing rather dubiously from Miss Wetherby to the earl. He obviously did not much relish being called upon to put such a distinguished visitor out by force.

During this dialogue, the earl had been inching her ladyship backwards out of the door. "Only five minutes," he pleaded again. "And I promise to behave with complete propriety. Have no fear."

Lady Potter, whose resistance was weakening under the influence of the earl's notorious charm, looked at her niece helplessly.

"If you abandon me now, Aunt, I shall never forgive you. *Never!*" Diana threatened.

"I'm sorry, my love, but I cannot allow any friend of Sir Rudolph's to be treated so shabbily. Five minutes, my lord," she murmured to the earl and retreated, closing the door behind her.

Disgusted at such a show of cowardice on the part of her nearest and dearest, Diana turned to gaze down into the stable yard where Jeremy, the earl's groom, was supervising the walking of the greys. She sensed that the earl had moved over to stand close behind her, but he remained silent for so long that Diana grew uneasy.

"I've brought your horse back," he said finally.

Diana was nearly surprised into turning her head, but caught herself in time. "If you mean Perseus, he's not my horse," she replied shortly.

"I've also brought the greys," he added casually, as if she had not spoken. "I thought you might like to take them out for a drive. They've been eating their heads off and could use the exercise."

The offer was tempting, as he must know only too well, Diana thought. But resolutely she hardened her heart. "No, thank you, my lord. I consider you perfectly capable of exercising your own horses."

A soft chuckle met this sally. "My, we are prickly today, aren't we, my dear?"

"How many times do I have to tell you—"

"Yes, forgive me. It comes naturally to the tongue where you are concerned, Miss Wetherby."

"Your five minutes must be nearly up, my lord."

"Then I shall hasten to tell you the two things I came to say to you, Miss Wetherby."

"And they are?" Diana continued to stare down into the yard.

"First of all, I want you to know that what you see is not always what it appears to be, my dear. Seeing is not always believing, you know.''

"I find that hard to accept, my lord," she replied calmly. "I see four grey horses down in the stable yard, for example, and you want me to believe that I am not seeing four grey horses? You must take me for a complete ninnyhammer," she chided him.

She had the satisfaction of hearing the earl snort impatiently at this ingenious remark. Surely, Diana thought to herself, this rake could not expect her to dispute the evidence of her own eyes.

"Now who is being deliberately obtuse?" he asked. "I recall that you accused me of that very thing only two days ago when I discovered you in a compromising tête-à-tête with Tottlefield. Or have you forgotten?"

"But I explained to you that we were not guilty of what you supposed, my lord," Diana explained crossly.

"Exactly, my dear. You assured me that the kiss you gave Tottlefield—the one I witnessed at least—was a sisterly one. And I believed you. In spite of all the evidence to the contrary."

"You did?" Diana was so surprised to hear this confession that she turned to face him. "You certainly gave no sign of doing so, my lord." No sooner had she said this than she realized her mistake.

"Well, I did," he said with a lazy smile. "I thought you must surely have taken my subsequent actions as a sign of my belief in your story, Miss Wetherby." A glint of unholy amusement leapt into his eyes as he observed the flush that rose to her cheeks at the mention of that particular incident.

"All I remember is that you behaved in an odiously encroaching manner, my lord. And I'll thank you to say no more on *that* subject." Unable to meet his quizzical gaze, she turned back to her observation of the yard below.

"I am quite cast down, Miss Wetherby," he said mournfully, but Diana detected a quiver of amusement in his voice. "I was convinced that I had made it quite clear that I believed you. And now, all I ask is that *you* believe *me* when I tell you that the little incident you witnessed last night was not at all what you imagine."

"And which little incident are you referring to, my lord?" Diana inquired sweetly. "There was so much going on as I remember."

"You know exactly which incident I mean, so don't play off your airs with me, Miss Wetherby," he replied sharply. "There was no mistaking your shocked surprise when you came upon me in the arbour in the company of a lady.''

"Oh, that's right! Now I remember," she said, schooling her voice to reveal a careless amusement she was far from feeling. ''I confess I was somewhat shocked that a lady—if indeed she was one—would allow herself to be caught in such a secluded spot with a gentleman of your rakish reputation, my lord. But after all," she continued, ignoring the choked exclamation from the earl, "at a masquerade it is difficult not to let oneself go just a tiny bit. I have to confess that I was guilty of a similar indiscretion, my lord, so I cannot blame her.''

Diana had turned to face the earl during this speech, the last part of which she had added out of the overwhelming desire to put him firmly in his place. As a result, she witnessed a change in his expression that made her wish she had held her tongue.

He gazed down at her, his eyes darkening to a slate grey, his lean face showing signs of anger. After what seemed an eternity, he asked softly, in a voice devoid of emotion: "Who was the gentleman?''

Wishing desperately that she could undo what now seemed to her a childish attempt at provoke the earl, Diana answered with as much coolness as she could contrive: "Oh, I cannot reveal names, my lord. That would betray a confidence. I would never dream of asking you to reveal the name of your lady, which I am convinced you would never do, now, would you?''

"You know very well who the lady was, Miss Wetherby," he replied coldly. "And if I am not much mistaken, I also know who your gentleman was. So don't try to bamboozle me, my dear.''

"How clever of you, my lord," she said in a low voice. "Because there was no gentleman. You see, it was all a hum. I merely said so in order to provoke you, that is all.''

"Well, you have certainly succeeded," he remarked coldly. "But if you think you can make a cake out of me a second time, you are sadly mistaken, Miss Wetherby. What a Johnny Raw I was to believe that Canterbury Tale of yours. Sisterly kisses, indeed.'' His lips curled contemptuously.

Unable to utter a word because of the huge lump which had suddenly formed in her throat, Diana could only stare at him in dismay. She realized she had herself to blame for the cutting things he was saying. Worse still, she had managed to involve poor Toby in her quarrel with Rotherham. Somehow she must make the earl believe that his friend was innocent.

"Please, oh, please do not blame Toby," she pleaded, taking a step towards him with the intention of laying a hand on his sleeve.

He stepped back abruptly and reached for the doorknob.

"Then it is Toby, after all," he said dryly—an affirmation rather than a question. A queer little smile softened his lips for a moment before he opened the door and was gone.

Diana stood rooted to the floor, her heart barely beating, her eyes glazed with unshed tears. That is how Lady Potter found her when she came bursting into the morning-room a few minutes later.

"My love," she cried, enveloping her dazed niece in a comforting embrace and urging her towards the settee. "Whatever did you say to Rotherham to make him charge out of the house in such a fury? He almost collided with me on the stairway and gave me the barest nod."

"Oh, Aunt Sophy, I have ruined everything," Diana wailed and burst into tears. Lady Potter, a bemused look on her face, sat for quite twenty minutes trying to console her niece and convince her that, although she had certainly acted unwisely to provoke a gentleman to such lengths, she might still repair the damage if she would but make a push to do so.

"No, that's past mending," she mumbled into her handkerchief as soon as the first flood of tears had subsided. "He thinks I want to marry Toby."

"And I gather you don't, dear?"

"Of course not," exclaimed Diana in a watery voice. "How can you be so n-nonsensical, Aunt? I d-don't want to m-marry anybody."

"No, of course you don't, dear. I can't imagine how I came to say such a thing." She regarded her tearful niece with affection. "And if you continue to ruin those lovely eyes with so much weeping, dear, I can tell you right now that nobody will want to marry you."

This information had the effect of precipitating another fit of tears, which Lady Potter set herself to stem by threatening to send her niece immediately up to her room without supper.

This admonition had the desired effect, and after a few gulping sobs, Diana asked miserably why gentlemen always managed to be such insensitive brutes.

"Because gentlemen are often unable to see what is right under their silly noses, my love," replied her aunt with a warm smile.

"We must constantly remember that they are often as puzzled by us as we are by them, dear. It requires a great deal of patience to deal comfortably with a man, my love, and I greatly fear that patience is not your strong suit."

Diana had to agree that her aunt was probably right.

"Run up to your room and wash your face, dear. And we may as well change for dinner since it is nearly five o'clock already. Sir Rudolph will be coming in at any moment, and it will not do to let him see you have been down in the dumps. Gentlemen do not like to be confronted by weeping females, you know. It makes them feel so helpless. Which of course they are, dear." On that note, the two ladies retired to their rooms.

The following morning, in response to an urgent message from Diana, Toby Tottlefield presented himself at Potter Hall and found her anxiously awaiting him in the library.

"Something dashed odd going on," he informed her bluntly, as soon as she had greeted him. "Hope you intend to tell me what it is, m'dear. Rotherham has got this queer notion into his head that I am getting riveted. Flew into the devil of a pucker last night and nearly bit my nose off when I assured him it was all a hum. Cut up pretty nasty again this morning when your note came, m'dear."

Diana looked at him anxiously. "Did you tell him what was in it, Toby?"

"Well, yes. As a matter of fact, I did. Nothing secret about it, was there?" Toby looked faintly aggrieved. "And how was I to know he would kick up such a dust just because I said you had asked me to come over to Potter Hall this morning?"

"Whatever did he say?"

Toby thought for a moment. "It's not what he said, m'dear, because he didn't say anything. But he flung out of the breakfast-room without so much as a by-your-leave. Dashed scrambling manners, I thought. And I would have said so, too, if Chatham hadn't reminded me that Rotherham acted in just that same fashion when the Standish female jilted him ten years ago. Stands to reason he's afraid she'll do it again, if you ask me."

This information did little to raise Diana's spirits; however, she made an effort to explain to Toby the events of the previous afternoon and her own part in Rotherham's misconception of his friend's impending nuptials.

"He believes I took you out into the garden and kissed you?"

he repeated in faintly shocked tones. "What demned impudence! I would never do such a thing, Diana. Word of a gentleman."

Diana could not resist smiling at this disclaimer of any real interest in her charms. "Of course you wouldn't, Toby. I know you too well to think that of you. Only if it were Arabella," she added teasingly, "you might be tempted to put decorum aside for a moment or two."

Toby looked crestfallen. "The occasion didn't arise, m'dear. Silly chit was hanging on that Frenchie's sleeve all night. Only managed to get one dance with her and all she could talk about was my cravat not being all the crack."

"Well, I have a particular favour to ask of you, Toby," Diana said coaxingly. "One which, I trust, will clear up this misunderstanding with Rotherham. For I am sure you don't want him to be forever ripping up at you over the breakfast table. Do you?"

"Of course I don't," exclaimed Toby energetically. "Dashed uncomfortable, I can tell you, m'dear. Not good for the digestion either if you ask me."

"Well, I know how you can put a stop to that immediately."

"You do?" Toby regarded her with suspicion. "What is it you want me to do?"

"Just make it quite plain to Rotherham that you want to fix your interest with Arabella and that you have no interest in me at all."

Toby thought for a minute and then shook his head dolefully. "That won't fadge, m'dear. He already knows I offered for you. In fact, told me to hedge off. Dashed queer start, that was." He regarded Diana thoughtfully. "Wondered at the time what his game was." An idea suddenly struck him. "He ain't thrown his handkerchief at you, by any chance?" When Diana shook her head, not trusting herself to speak, Toby shrugged. "I suppose not, at least not while the Incomparable is in the neighbourhood."

Her spirits shattered by this blunt evaluation of her chances of competing with the Incomparable, Diana swallowed hard and tried again. "Can't you say that you only offered for me because you felt sorry for me?" she suggested hopefully.

"Dash it all, Diana," Toby exclaimed, his chubby face turning a bright shade of pink. "Can't ask a gentleman to say anything that shabby. Besides it ain't true. I'm dashed fond of you, my girl, and I'd offer for you in a flash if I thought that's what you want. In fact, I think I'll do just that," he declared stoutly, heaving his considerable bulk up from the settee. "Just to let you know that the offer is still very much open, m'dear."

And before a startled Diana could stop him, Toby had ponderously gone down on one knee before her and taken one of her hands in his large grasp. He grinned at her. "Should have thought of this before, m'dear. Females being given to such romantic notions as they are."

"Oh, please, Toby," Diana started to say, undecided whether to laugh or cry at the ridiculous picture he presented, but he interrupted her.

"No, my dear Miss Wetherby. Let me do this right. Now, let's see," he mused, obviously searching for the right words.

Before he had a chance to begin his declaration, however, the library door swung open and Eaton, after a startled pause, announced Miss Arabella Chatham and the *vicomte* Duvalier.

# 17 .....

# The Chase

FOR AN INTERMINABLE moment the scene in Lady Potter's library remained frozen. Toby's mouth had dropped open, and he stared at the visitors with slightly protruding eyes. Arabella's face was a picture of shocked disbelief, and Diana had a shrewd notion that the last thing the pampered heiress expected to see was her long-standing admirer making a cake of himself at the feet of another female. The *vicomte* showed first surprise and then a contemptuous smile of amusement as he viewed the scene through his bejewelled quizzing-glass.

It was his faint snicker that broke the general paralysis. Toby struggled to his feet, his countenance overcome with a painful infusion of pink. Diana rose from the settee to greet her unexpected visitors, while Arabella, regaining the use of her tongue, inquired rather waspishly what Toby thought he was doing.

The *vicomte* laughed gently. "It should be obvious what our dear friend is doing, *cherie*. Pray do not embarrass the poor fellow any more than he already is." He turned to Diana and made her an elegant bow. "We seem to have come at a deucedly inconvenient time, my dear Aunt. Perhaps we should come back when you are not in the middle of such a tender scene," he added with a smirk.

Arabella, who had gone rather pale as the significance of Ferdinand's words sunk in, stared at Toby with a growing sense of disaster. It was one thing for her to flirt outrageously with every eligible bachelor of her acquaintance, and the *vicomte* had been by far the most assiduous and entertaining of these admirers, but it was quite another to find Toby—her Toby—down on his knees paying serious court to another. This discovery and the realization that perhaps she had, in her careless way, abused her dear friend and confidant once too often gave her a severe and unpleasant shock. Accustomed to Toby's loyal admiration from the time she was a young schoolroom miss, Arabella had taken it for granted that he was her very own gallant, who only awaited the day—now barely a month away—when she would turn eighteen, to declare the love she had taken for granted for so long.

The scene she had witnessed had jolted her out of her complacency. For the first time, it occurred to her to wonder whether a gentleman of Toby's elegance, reputation, and wealth would truly wish to marry a female just out of the schoolroom. Perhaps it really was brotherly affection he felt for her. Her Mama was, after all, always saying so. She suddenly realized that a lady of Diana's elegance of mind and air of consequence would suit him very well indeed. The thought caused a cold lump to form in the region of her heart.

With a visible effort, she pulled herself together. "Were you really making Miss Wetherby an offer of marriage, Toby?" she asked quietly, unable to keep a slight tremour out of her voice.

"Of course not, dearest," Diana replied with a quick smile, realizing that Toby was quite unprepared to answer such a question. "Whatever gave you that nonsensical notion?" she added, furiously racking her brain trying to think of a plausible excuse for Toby to be on his knees, clasping her hand in his, and not immediately finding one.

The *vicomte* gave a loud laugh but refrained from comment.

Arabella's face took on a belligerent expression. "You must take me for a flat, Diana. What else am I to think when I come in here and find Toby acting out a scene from some fustian novel?"

Grasping at this convenient idea, Diana saw a way out of the dilemma. "That's just it, my love," she replied gaily. "Some silly wager or other, I gather. Apparently Toby lost, so he had to come over here to act out a romantic scene from one of the latest novels." Seeing Arabella's doubtful expression, she added: "I can't say he was very convincing, dear. I could see almost from the start that it was all a hum. No doubt he is eternally grateful to you for interrupting him as you did. Although I expect that means you will have to do it all over again, Toby," she added, addressing herself to her tongue-tied suitor. "How droll! But practice makes perfect, sir. Next time perhaps you will be more persuasive."

It was clear that the *vicomte* was not taken in by this glib explanation, but Arabella cast a speculative gaze at her friend.

"Is that true, Toby?" she said, eyeing him with her steady blue gaze.

"Every word of it," stammered a relieved Toby. "But don't go blabbing to Dick that I didn't finish the scene, m'dear. I have no desire to go through *that* again. Wouldn't wish it on my worst enemy,'' he added for good measure.

Arabella did not look very convinced, but she said no more on the subject and the remainder of the visit passed agreeably enough. During the course of her conversation, noticeably more subdued than usual, Arabella let it slip that she was engaged to drive to Sherborne later that morning, in the *vicomte*'s curricle, to visit a fair which had opened in that neighbouring town.

"We are to meet Lady Chloe and a party of her friends at the Blue Boar in Melbury,'' Arabella explained quickly when she saw the disapproving look on Toby's face. "From there we will drive on to the Hog's Head in Sherborne.''

"In an open carriage?'' Diana inquired gently.

"I understand it is only ten miles from Melbury,'' Ferdinand put in smoothly. "And the day is so fine, I could see no harm in it. Besides,'' he added with a caressing glance at the heiress, "Miss Chatham has her heart quite set on it. Don't you, *ma petite*?''

What had yesterday seemed like such a marvellous lark to Arabella now appeared considerably less diverting, especially since she had begun to tire of Lady Chloe's managing ways. Now she came to think on it, it occurred to her that the whole excursion to the fair had been the Incomparable's idea after all, and how she came to have set her heart on it, Arabella was at a loss to remember. For a moment it flashed through her mind that she would be much more comfortable spending the day here at Potter Hall with Diana and Toby. The notion seemed strangely unlike her, however, and she quickly brushed it away, telling herself, with a queer little tug at her heart, that they seemed to go on much better without her.

Although the scene that morning had given Diana much food for thought, she was able to dispel most of her anxiety by confiding in Lady Ephigenia during their trip to the lending library in Melbury that afternoon. Her ladyship gave it as her considered opinion that Lady Chatham was far too casual in her supervision of a daughter as young and innocent as Arabella.

"It would serve her right if the poor child ran away with someone entirely ineligible,'' she remarked in her blunt way. "Not that I wish the chit any harm, mind you. She is a taking little thing, and we had all hoped to see her safely hitched to Toby before the year was out. From what you say, however, he is making no push to fix her interest, which is a great pity.''

She glanced speculatively at Diana as the latter tooled the yellow tilbury smartly down Melbury's main thoroughfare.

"Are you *quite* sure that he has not formed a *tendre* for you, my dear?'' she asked gently.

"Oh, absolutely,'' replied Diana calmly. "His heart is irrevocably lost to that silly chit who may only now be starting to realize how fortunate she is.''

This calm assurance that Arabella would eventually come to her senses and reward Toby for his unflagging loyalty was sadly disrupted upon Diana's return to Potter Hall. Upon entering the hall, she was informed by a flustered Eaton that Lady Potter was in the morning-room and had requested that Miss Wetherby come up to her as soon as she returned.

Her first glimpse of her aunt's normally serene countenance was sufficient to convince Diana that something untoward was in the wind.

"My dear!'' exclaimed Lady Potter, jumping up and coming to clasp Diana's hands in hers. "I have received some very disturbing news, my love. And I would have sent off to the village to fetch you, but I did not want to alarm the ladies at the Grange because it might, after all, be a Banbury story.''

Diana drew her aunt down on the settee and demanded to know exactly what news this was that had put her into such a dreadful pucker.

"This is not like you, Aunt Sophy,'' she chided her. "You are the one to whom I confided all my scrapes, remember? And you managed to get me out of them without so much as turning a hair. Or have you forgotten those good times we had together in Paris?''

"This concerns Arabella, my dear. I rather fancy that chit has no more sense than a peagoose and may have got herself into a nasty scrape. You were always much more up to snuff, my love.''

Diana's amusement faded. "What has happened, Aunt? Tell me quickly.''

"You had better hear it from Mrs. Teather herself, dear,'' replied Aunt Sophy, pulling the bell vigorously and instructing Eaton to request Mrs. Teather to step upstairs immediately. "She is the one who told me, just as soon as she got back from visiting her sick sister in Henstridge, which is near Sherborne, you know.''

"No, I didn't know. And what has Mrs. Teather's sick sister got to do with Arabella?"

"Nothing at all, dear. But her sister's second son—Thomas I believe his name is—is an undergroom at the Hog's Head Inn in Sherborne. Well, it seems he got leave to drive his aunt back to Melbury this afternoon. But just as they were leaving the inn, Mrs. Teather saw Arabella getting into a hired travelling chaise. She was accompanied by an elegant young swell, a foreign-looking gentleman—those were her very words—who can be no other than Ferdinand, don't you think, my love?" Lady Potter looked at her niece with apprehension.

"I would naturally assume so," Diana replied with a slight smile, unable to understand her aunt's distress. "He must have thought it was going to rain and didn't want to expose Arabella to a drive home in an open curricle."

"Oh, dear!" Lady Potter exclaimed in distraught tones. "I only wish that had been the case, my love. But Mrs. Teather recognized Arabella, you see, and had the foresight to send her nephew back into the inn to discover who had hired the chaise and what its destination was."

"Well?" Diana raised an expectant eyebrow. "Don't keep me in suspense forever, Aunt, I beg you."

"It was the *vicomte* all right, but the chaise was not hired for Melbury, dear. Their destination was Bath."

As Diana absorbed this information, her colour receded and she jumped up to pace the floor nervously.

"You cannot mean this," she burst out. "Are you sure that Mrs. Teather did not mistake the matter?"

At that moment Mrs. Teather herself entered the room and was able to corroborate, with a wealth of detail, the story imparted by Lady Potter.

"Put me in a fair taking, it did, miss," said that motherly woman who claimed acquaintance with Arabella since her birth. "There was no mistaking her. I'd know that sweet young lady anywheres, I would. And I can't tell you how it shook me up to know she was gallivanting up to Bath without anyone the wiser."

"Did she see you?" Diana wanted to know.

"No, my dear. She didn't look too much up to snuff. Kind of dazed if you know what I mean. I figured she must have been tired or something. By the time Tommy found out where they were going, of course, it was too late for me to speak to her. The chaise had gone by then."

Lady Potter thanked her housekeeper, and after they were alone again, demanded to know what her niece thought they should do.

"Sir Rudolph will not be home till after dinner this evening, my dear, which is provoking of him because he is bound to know just what should be done in such a case. Perhaps we should consult Lord Rotherham?" she suggested cautiously.

"Certainly not," Diana exclaimed. "I know exactly what must be done. If you will let me borrow your chaise, Aunt, I will drive over to the Grange and consult Toby. He is the most nearly concerned in the matter and can be trusted to do what is right without kicking up a dust." She did not mention that she intended to bring Arabella back safely even if she had to go all the way to Bath to do so.

Twenty minutes later, Diana was on her way to the Grange in Lady Potter's new chaise. She had changed into a travelling dress of brown velvet and had brought her warm pelisse, her reticule, and several rugs in case the weather turned cold.

The Grange lay a scant five miles from Potter Hall and Diana spent the time thinking how she could get Toby alone at such an hour when the guests at the Grange must already be gathering in the drawing-room before dinner. She was by now quite determined that the only course to take was to pursue the couple with all possible speed, and she was depending on Toby to accompany her.

Fortham examined her suspiciously from under his grizzled eyebrows when he swung open the huge door and informed her stiffly that the family was dressing for dinner. Upon learning that Miss Wetherby requested only a few words in private with Mr. Tottlefield, the butler glowered at the levity and scrambling manners of the younger generation and informed her, disapproval heavy in his voice, that he doubted that the gentleman would care to come down with his toilet only half complete.

Having consented, rather unwillingly, to send up a message to Toby, Fortham put Diana in the library to await his pleasure.

She had not long to wait. Five minutes later Toby burst into the room, still wearing his breeches and riding coat, and demanded to know what urgent matter had brought Diana over to the Grange at that hour.

Diana wasted no time in pleasantries. "It's Arabella," she said curtly. "I have every reason to suppose that she has run away with my nephew. I have come to seek your company in bringing her back safely."

Toby stared at her in astonishment, then a hopeless grimace spread over his ruddy face. "Just as I thought," he said dejectedly. "She has quite cut me out and is determined to marry that Frenchie nevvy of yours, m'dear. So be it," he added in lugubrious tones, staring out the window at the encroaching darkness. "There's nothing more to be said, if that's what she is set on."

This lack of resolution made Diana bristle with indignation. "If that's all you can say, sir," she exclaimed impatiently, "then you deserve to lose her."

"It appears that I already have," was his mournful reply.

"Fiddle!" Diana retorted angrily. "I have every reason to believe she was taken by some trick or other. And I intend to find out," she added militantly. "So get your coat, Toby, and come with me at once."

Finding himself addressed in tones that reminded him forcibly of his mother, a strong-willed woman who ruled her offspring with a rod of iron, Toby automatically obeyed Diana's orders. So it was that a few minutes later they descended the front steps together after assuring an incredulous and outraged Fortham that they would not be dining at the Grange that evening. Toby thought it appropriate to add that if his hostess should inquire, she might be informed that they were on their way to Bath.

The vile headache and queasiness, which had overtaken Arabella at the Sherborne Fair shortly after she had partaken of some light refreshments at one of the colourful booths was, she thought, a fitting climax to a dreadful day. Although wild horses would not have dragged it from her, she had to admit to herself that the ludicrous scene she had witnessed so recently in Lady Potter's library still rankled. She had sworn to put Toby out of her mind and to concentrate on enjoying the drive to Sherborne in the *vicomte*'s smart curricle and the wondrous sights of the fair she had so been looking forward to.

By the time they were no more than halfway to Sherborne, however, Arabella discovered that Toby's unexpected perfidy had quite spoiled her day. Neither the enchanting country scenery nor the flattering attentions of her handsome companion seemed to lift her spirits out of the mood of flat sullens into which they had fallen. Time and again she tried to throw off this unaccustomed fit of melancholy, but in the end she was forced to pretend an interest she did not feel in the risqué stories with which Ferdinand regaled her.

When they arrived at the fair, things were a little better, and Arabella was genuinely diverted by the Fat Lady, the one-hundred-year-old Dwarf, the Dancing Pigs, a play involving Pirates and Saracens in deadly conflict, and other freak shows designed to appeal by their strangeness and originality. However, by three o'clock she was quite weary of the bustle and noise and willingly accepted Lady Chloe's suggestion that the two of them retire to one of the private booths and send the *vicomte* to procure glasses of lemonade for them.

It was after she drank the lemonade, which was bitterer than she liked, that Arabella began to feel decidedly ill. When Lady Chloe blamed the heat and the dust for her indisposition, and suggested that the best thing would be for the *vicomte* to accompany her back to the Hog's Head to rest, Arabella was only too eager to comply. But when they reached the inn, she felt so much worse that she begged Ferdinand, in a voice that would have softened a heart less self-centered than his, to take her home.

The *vicomte* was all compliance. Leaving her to the ministrations of the kindly wife of the innkeeper, he went off to hire a more comfortable carriage, one which—he assured her with a slight smile—would be less taxing on her poor head.

Overcome by this unexpected kindness, Arabella had no hesitation in allowing herself to be assisted into the hired travelling chaise and settled in a comfortable position with a cushion under her aching head and a cloth dampened in lavender water to cool her forehead.

Since the *vicomte* had, in the interests of propriety, hired a hack to ride beside the carriage, Arabella had the chaise to herself and was soon lulled into a fitful slumber by the rhythmical swaying of the vehicle.

When she opened her eyes some time later, she was surprised to see that it was getting dark outside and that the chaise had stopped. Her head was still throbbing but her dizziness had almost disappeared. Gingerly she sat up and looked out of the window.

They seemed to be in the yard of a posting-house and from the bustling and shouting she gathered that the team had just been changed. She did not seem to recognize the inn and this bothered her. Why did they need to change horses when Melbury was less than ten miles from Sherborne? she wondered.

At that moment the *vicomte* came out of the inn and when he saw she was awake he came quickly to the carriage window.

"So, my dear, you are quite recovered I hope," he smiled ingratiatingly. "I have ordered a glass of lemonade for you, *cherie*."

"What are we doing here?" she asked petulantly.

The *vicomte* glibly explained that one of the wheelers had gone lame before they had gone more than a mile from Sherborne and they had had to drive slowly until they were able to change horses. "We should still get you home in time to change for dinner, my dear," he remarked casually. "So drink up your lemonade and we'll leave immediately."

Arabella was thankful for the cool drink because her throat was strangely parched, and she drank it down without protest and settled back drowsily as the chaise pulled out of the yard and rolled away at a smart pace.

When next she awoke, her migraine seemed to be much worse and on top of it she now felt decidedly feverish. It was pitch-dark outside and the chaise was rattling down a cobbled street. This alarmed her, and she was about to cry out to the coachman when the vehicle suddenly swung into another inn yard and came to a grinding halt.

Such was her distress that she made little protest when the *vicomte* flung open the door and urged her to step down from the chaise. Supporting her trembling frame, he guided her into the inn where he had bespoken what appeared to be the only private parlour in the house.

Once the curious landlord, intrigued at the presence of two obvious members of the *ton* in his lowly establishment, had laid out the table and promised to send in refreshments, Arabella asked querulously where they were and why they had stopped again.

"Don't distress yourself, *cherie*," Ferdinand replied smoothly. "The coachman mistook the road in the dark and has landed us at a place called Bruton. Luckily I was able to obtain rooms for us—"

"Bruton?" Arabella cried in dismay. "Why that is halfway to Bath! How can he have made such a silly error?" She stared at the *vicomte* suspiciously. "I don't believe it," she breathed, holding the damp cloth to her aching head. "You have planned this all along, haven't you? Oh, how could you?" she wailed. "I insist that you put up fresh horses and take me back to Melbury immediately."

The *vicomte* only smiled. "You are in no condition to travel further tonight, *cherie*," he explained patiently, sitting down beside her on the rather lumpy settee and taking her small hand in his. "You have been very sick, my love. But you have me to take care of you now, *cherie*, so there is nothing to fear. You will feel much better after a bite to eat and a good night's rest. And tomorrow we can decide what to do; whether to go back to Melbury and face the disagreeable scene your family will undoubtedly make, or go on to Bath and get married there."

Arabella had stared at him in growing horror during this smug speech. His words had gradually made it clear to her that her predicament was much more serious than she had imagined. "I have no wish to marry you, sir," she said as calmly as she could, snatching her hand from his grasp. "And furthermore, I am not hungry and my headache is much better. So oblige me by taking me home immediately."

The *vicomte* continued to smile. "You are such an innocent, my love. That's what I like about you." He attempted to take her hand again, but Arabella drew back angrily.

"Don't you dare touch me," she hissed, jumping up and glaring down at him in a brave attempt to hide her consternation at the fix she was in.

He rose lazily and moved towards her, his triumphant, cynical smile growing wider. "It's no use fighting me, *cherie*. As a gentleman of honour, I shall be obligated to marry you if we spend the night here together. And I do not intend to shirk my duty, my love, so put your mind at rest. Besides, you will make an excellent wife once you have learned to control your temper, *cherie*." His gaze slid down her slim form speculatively. "I am quite looking forward to our wedding night, my dearest," he added caressingly, slipping an arm around her waist.

Fury and panic drove Arabella to lash out blindly at that smiling face and make a dash for the parlour door. As she grasped the doorknob she felt herself roughly caught up and deposited back near the hearth. "Oh, no you don't, my pretty one," Ferdinand growled, both arms firmly imprisoning her. "Come now," he wheedled, "you are going to like this."

His breath was hot on her cheek as he ran his lips seductively down her face to her mouth. Arabella shrank from his touch and turned her head away, closing her eyes against this frightening attack from a man she had thought of as a friend and admirer, ready to do her every bidding. His fingers gripped her chin roughly and forced her head up. Just as Arabella had given up all hope of escaping this most unwelcome embrace, she heard the door burst open and felt the *vicomte*'s arms literally torn from around her.

Several resounding smacks and the clatter of broken dishes and falling furniture made her open her eyes. The table and several chairs lay on their sides, broken china and glass littered the floor, and in the midst of this confusion, the *vicomte* sprawled on his back, blood oozing slowing from an ugly gash in his forehead. Over him, poised to administer another felling blow, stood a large gentleman in a many-caped greatcoat, his back to Arabella.

Recognizing those broad shoulders and large form, Arabella breathed a sigh of relief. "Toby! Oh, Toby, I'm so glad you're here," she whispered. "I've been so silly, so very silly. I never imagined . . ."

At her first words, the gentleman had turned, and now he stepped purposefully across the litter of broken china to clasp Arabella in a bearlike hug. "Are you hurt, my precious?" he murmured against her golden hair. "Did that Frenchie harm you, sweetheart? I'll kill him if he did," he added savagely, glaring at the prostrate *vicomte* over Arabella's head.

"Oh, Toby!" exclaimed Arabella, snuggling closer to him and rejoicing in the feel of his arms about her. "That won't be necessary, my love. He doesn't matter at all now, does he?" She looked up at him with tears of happiness shining in her eyes.

"Happens you're right, my dear. Happens you're right," Toby replied, dropping a kiss on her forehead before turning to wink solemnly at Miss Wetherby who had appeared in the open doorway and stood surveying the wreckage with a twinkle of amusement in her eyes.

# 18 .....
# The Last Stand

LADY EPHIGENIA GLANCED for the third time at the ormolu clock on the ornate mantelpiece in the Blue drawing-room where her guests were assembled for dinner. The hands had already inched their way past the hour of six and Toby Tottlefield had not yet put in an appearance. She had quite decided that she would wait no longer when Fortham entered the room and, making his way deferentially to his mistress's side, bent his creaking old bones to whisper in her ear.

After a startled glance at her butler's frozen countenance, Lady Ephigenia instructed him to put dinner back fifteen minutes. Leaving Lord Forsdyke to entertain Lady Chatham, she made her way to the end of the room where her nephew was exchanging hunting reminiscences with Captain Chatham.

"Christopher, dear," she said a little breathlessly. "I have just received a piece of astonishing news from Fortham. I can't make head or tail of it." She glanced nervously up at him, and the earl, recognizing that his aunt was truly disturbed about something, took her frail hand in his and squeezed it encouragingly.

"Tell me all about it, love," he urged.

Captain Chatham made as if to move away, but Lady Ephigenia stopped him with a gesture. "Don't go, Dick. You should know this too, I expect. Since you are also one of Toby's friends. I can't understand why he would do such a thing." She paused and seemed to be lost in revery, her crimped curls bobbing as she shook her head absently.

"What did Toby do, love?" the earl inquired gently.

"Oh, he ran off to Bath just before dinner," she explained earnestly. "I wonder what was so urgent that he missed his dinner. Not like Toby at all now, is it?"

"Bath?" the earl repeated in amazement. He gave a short crack

189

of laughter. "No, that's not like Toby, Aunt. You must have your story all wrong, dear."

"Oh, no. Fortham was quite adamant about it. But what really worries me, dear, is that Diana went with him."

It was Chatham's turn to let out a laugh. "Well, it looks as though good old Toby came up to scratch, after all. An elopement of all things! Who would have thought our Toby had so much romance in his fat soul?"

Rotherham gave his friend a cold, fulminating look. "Don't be ridiculous, Dick," he snapped.

"What else could it be?" the captain ventured to ask and was quelled by another murderous glance.

"You must be misinformed, Aunt," Rotherham insisted. "I will speak to Fortham myself. And don't worry your head about this, my love; it's bound to be all a hum. Come on, Chatham," he added and left the room precipitously.

He found the butler in the front hall and after listening to Fortham's account of Miss Wetherby's arrival, her insistence on speaking with Mr. Tottlefield alone, and the odd circumstances of their hurried departure in a travelling chaise, Rotherham's face was a study in granite.

"Going to Bath, he was, my lord," the old retainer insisted.

"Did Mr. Tottlefield actually say so?" demanded his employer.

"Yes, my lord. He said that if her ladyship should enquire, she should be told he had gone to Bath. His very words, my lord," exclaimed the old retainer, his bushy eyebrows working up and down in acute agitation.

"How long ago was this?" snapped the earl.

"Miss Wetherby arrived just before half past five," Fortham replied soberly. "They were gone by half past. In a tearing hurry they were too, my lord. A tearing hurry."

"Thank you, Fortham. Send round to the stables to have my curricle and the greys at the door in ten minutes."

Before the old butler had a chance to ask his master if he should hold dinner for him, the earl was halfway up the stairs, followed by Captain Chatham.

By the time the two gentlemen descended again, dressed in greatcoats and high-crowned beavers, Jeremy had the greys waiting at the front door. The earl jumped into the vehicle and gathered up the reins, waiting impatiently for Chatham to join him.

Fortham, who stood at the top of the shallow stairs anxiously observing his master's eccentric behaviour, ventured to ask, in a voice that trembled with disapproval, what he should tell her ladyship.

"Tell her we have gone to Bath," the earl replied curtly and gave Jeremy the signal to release the greys who sprang forward eagerly, leaving Fortham to stare after them in bewilderment.

The landlord of the White Stag was inclined to express himself rather forcefully when he surveyed the devastation wrought by the large gentleman in the inn's only private parlour. His wife, who came bustling up from the kitchen at the first sounds of the rumpus, was even less reticent in speaking her mind.

"I'll have none of these goings-on in my 'ouse," she declared darkly, standing at the threshold of the parlour, arms akimbo, suspicion writ large on her homely features. "This is a respectable 'ouse, this is," she added, quite inaccurately but with a good deal of conviction. "And I don't mind tellin' you, ma'am," she said, addressing herself to Miss Wetherby, "that I don't take kindly to young girls bein' 'ugged and kissed." She glared accusingly at Toby, who hastily withdrew his arms from around Arabella's small waist. "Or to young gentlemen havin' their lights darkened in my establishment," she continued, frowning at the still prone form of the *vicomte*. "All this is most irreglar, if you get my meanin', ma'am. And as for this, this . . . ." Words failed her as she made a theatrical gesture at the disordered room. "Well, it just ain't what I'm used to, ma'am," she finished angrily, her corpulent frame quivering with indignation. "You can be very sure of that."

"Oh, I am quite sure of it," Diana assured her soothingly. "But there is absolutely nothing here that is irregular, as you call it. Quite the contrary. This is a particularly happy occasion."

The landlady looked at her in astonishment, bereft of speech.

"Wouldn't you agree, Arabella?" Diana added, smiling affectionately at that young lady.

"Oh, yes!" Arabella cried, running to fling her arms around Diana with unrestrained enthusiasm. "But, Diana, however did you know where to find me? I was in such a scrape, you have no idea."

"I think I do, dear," Diana said hastily, unwilling to have Arabella blurt out her story in front of their hosts, who were both agog with curiosity. "But it's a long story and Toby and I will tell you all about it over dinner."

She turned to the landlady with a smile and said with all the authority she could muster: "If you will be so kind as to have this room swept up and lay the table again, I am sure we are all ready to enjoy a bite to eat. In the meantime, Arabella, you and I will go upstairs to tidy up," she added, taking her charge by the hand. At the door she turned and regarded her nephew. "I suggest you do the same, Ferdinand. You look decidedly under the weather."

Twenty minutes later, when Diana entered the parlour again, she found the broken dishes gone, the furniture restored to its place, and the table again set for dinner.

"I seem to have convinced our formidable landlady that there is nothing irregular in our party," she remarked to Toby who stood before the hearth, a glazed look of happiness still on his cherubic face.

"Yes, indeed, m'dear," he murmured absentmindedly. "Of course, it helped when I told her to put the cost of the broken china on the reckoning, and to bring up a bottle of her best brandy." He smiled dreamily as Diana settled herself in a straight-backed chair near the fire. "I will never be able to repay the debt I owe you, m'dear," he said awkwardly.

"Nonsense, Toby. You owe me nothing. It is reward enough to see you and Arabella in complete accord at last."

He came over to her chair and took one of her hands in both his large ones. "You are a true friend to us, m'dear. But you cannot deny that if it hadn't been for your insistence, I might have allowed that nephew of yours to run off with her. I shudder to think of it. Although I must say he might have chosen a less disreputable inn, don't you?" he added in disgust. "This one is definitely not of the first stare."

Diana could not help letting off a peal of laughter at this remark. It was so like Toby to focus on the most trivial aspect of their adventure. As she gazed up at him, a wave of affection for this gentle, warmhearted man brought a sudden lump to her throat. To gain the love of such a man must be every woman's dream. She hoped that Arabella knew how very lucky she was.

Impulsively she reached up and placed an affectionate kiss on Toby's plump cheek. "Let me be the first to wish you happy," she said mistily.

An angry oath caused them to jump apart and turn towards the door. Before either of them realized what was happening, the Earl of Rotherham had sprung across the room, sending the table and all the china flying, and landed Toby a facer with such force that it sent him reeling backwards, knocking over a chair before coming to rest on the floor, a dazed expression on his ruddy face.

Diana gazed in dismay as Rotherham stood over Toby, his face white and drawn, his lips curled in a sneer, his fists clenched menacingly.

"Dash it all, man," Toby mumbled, gingerly probing a rapidly swelling jaw. "This ain't Jackson's Saloon. And I never did show to advantage against you, Chris. Besides, not at all the thing to start a mill in front of the ladies. Never would have thought it of you." He looked up at his friend, suddenly aware that all was not right. "Something bothering you, old man?" he inquired with an innocence that caused the earl to grind his teeth.

Before he could say anything, however, their ears were assailed by a piercing scream as Arabella, entering the parlour to join her new fiancé for dinner, was greeted by the alarming spectacle of her loved one sprawled on his back among the broken dishes, a rather large bump protruding from his bewildered face.

"Oh, what have you done?" she cried, rushing over to push the earl violently out of her way and throw herself on her knees beside Toby. "You brute!" She glared up at Rotherham, whose face showed a puzzled frown. "How dare you hit Toby. I hate you!" she cried vehemently, tears running down her lovely face. "Oh, Toby, my dearest," she crooned, "let me kiss it better, love."

This tender scene was interrupted by the landlady who burst into the room, her face red with suppressed fury. "Well, I never!" she exclaimed, casting an agitated glance at the scattered china and overturned table. "Not again! I'll have you know, sir," she shrilled, addressing herself to the earl, "that this is a respectable 'ouse, this is. And—"

"Yes, we know," interrupted Diana, barely able to suppress a bubble of laughter that threatened to overcome her. "This is not what you are used to. But I beg you will conquer your disgust long enough to send up a large beef steak for I very much fear we have another black eye on our hands."

"Oh, no!" cried Arabella, the horror of this fate bursting upon her. "How could you do such a nasty, wicked thing to Toby, who never hurt anybody? What a monster you are!" she spat at the earl. "Don't you agree, Diana?"

"Yes, dear. An absolute, irrevocable, dastardly monster," she agreed with evident relish. "No doubt about it, love."

"Who's a monster?" asked Chatham, coming into the room at that moment.

"Dick!" his sister cried tearfully. "Look what that wretch has done to darling Toby. I shall never forgive him. Never!'' She dipped her lace handkerchief into a bowl of water thoughtfully sent up by the landlady, who had succumbed to Diana's entreaties and gone in search of a remedy for Toby's eye which was turning an interesting shade of blue.

"There, love," she murmured, gently bathing Toby's face with the damp cloth. "I absolutely refuse to invite him to the wedding, so it's no use you insisting, dearest, because I won't do it."

"Whatever you say, m'dear," Toby agreed mildly, his eyes half closed in blissful enjoyment.

Arabella threw a quelling glance at the earl, who had stood as if rooted to the ground during this outburst.

"And we will not name our firstborn after him either, shall we, love?" she remarked, much taken by the severity of this punishment.

"Of course not, my love," Toby responded, a smile playing across his face as he gazed adoringly up into Arabella's blue eyes.

"What's all this about weddings and firstborns?" Chatham demanded loudly. "And, Arabella, get up off the floor. It's not seemly for you to hang over a gentleman in that hoydenish fashion. Even if it's only Toby."

"Ah, Dick, old man. Just the fellow I need to see," Toby said, suddenly becoming aware of the crowd standing around listening to Arabella's artless chatter. "Help me up, Dick. We need to talk. Matter of utmost importance. Won't wait. So let's go into the taproom and . . . What the devil?"

The cause of this exclamation was standing in the doorway, his face puffy and one eye closed, swollen, and definitely black.

"I have come to make my apologies, dear Aunt," said the *vicomte* stiffly, addressing Diana. "I fear I cannot stay to have dinner with you, much as I would like to, but I find I am not in the mood for pleasantries."

Toby let out a guffaw. "That's pretty obvious to everybody, my lad. And if you take my advice, you'll go back to Paris and leave Miss Wetherby alone. You've caused her enough trouble already. And if I catch you anywhere near Miss Chatham," he growled, putting a protective arm around that trembling damsel, "I won't answer for your life, my fine buck."

"Oh, Toby!" sighed Arabella. "How very brave you are, love."

Revolted by this spectacle, the *vicomte* made a brief bow and disappeared, leaving Chatham, equally revolted but with no possibility of escape, to invite Toby to follow him into the taproom.

"I will go too," declared Arabella, hanging tightly to Toby's arm.

"Not suitable, my love. We won't be but a minute or two."

But Arabella was not so easily put off. "It's about me, isn't it?" she asked ingeniously. "Well, I want to be there, too."

"You really shouldn't," put in Diana, wishing at all costs to avoid a tête-à-tête with Rotherham, who had been regarding her fixedly for some time. "Come upstairs with me while they clean up this room and set the table again."

"You go if you like, Diana, but I intend to go with Toby," Arabella replied mulishly, but with such an enchanting smile at her admirer that he relented instantly and bore her off with him to the empty taproom.

In the resulting confusion, Diana was able to slip up to the small bed-chamber her nephew had hired for Arabella. The events of the past few hours had left her emotions chaotic and her nerves raw. She had been particularly upset by the unexpected arrival of the earl and his unprovoked attack on Toby. She desperately needed a few minutes respite from the overcharged emotional atmosphere she had experienced downstairs.

Soaking one of her handkerchiefs in fragrant lavender water, she lay back on the narrow bed and covered her aching eyes with the cool cloth. The relief was almost immediate and she allowed herself to retreat into a dreamworld in which a tall man with slate-grey eyes was smiling at her in the most enticing way.

She heard the door open and close softly, but she was reluctant to rouse herself. The moment she did, she knew Arabella would burst into a torrent of confidences on her newly discovered state of affianced bride, and Diana was not quite ready to endure such happiness in another. After a few moments, however, unable to lose herself in her fantasies again, she sighed and resigned herself to Arabella's exuberant chatter.

"Are you happy, dearest?" she asked softly, knowing full well that Arabella would need no further encouragement.

"Not yet, my love, but I soon hope to be," responded a deep masculine voice from somewhere above her.

Diana's eyes flew open and she let out a faint gasp. The Earl of Rotherham was leaning negligently against the bedpost, his arms crossed against his broad chest, his slate-grey eyes smiling at her in the most enticing way.

For the briefest of moments, Diana felt she must have relapsed into her dreamworld. When the impropriety of the scene hit her like a bucket of cold water, she scrambled off the bed and stood glaring at him, speechless with indignation and something else that seemed to have made her knees singularly unsteady.

The room suddenly appeared to have shrunk in size, and although he stood at least four feet away from her, his presence was overpowering. She caught the familiar scent of his shaving lotion, the pleasant aroma of horses on his hunting jacket.

Abruptly she realized she had been staring at him for several minutes, caught in the web of his magnetism. She stepped backwards, a wave of colour invading her pale cheeks.

"This is my bed-chamber, my lord," she said stiffly. "Whatever can you be thinking of?"

"I don't think I'd better tell you what I'm thinking of, love. At least not until we have reached a certain understanding." His smile widened into a grin.

"I must request you leave immediately," she stammered, caught off guard by the implications of his words. "At once, if you please," she added with growing fury at the impertinence of this man who seemed to think he had only to smile at her in that totally devastating way and she would agree to his improper proposals.

"I find myself to be very comfortable here, my dear. Extremely cosy, in fact. Although I could suggest several ways of making ourselves even more cosy," he added, a lazy smile twitching his lips.

"I am not interested in any of your suggestions, my lord. Especially since they are bound to be most improper."

He raised an eyebrow in surprise. "What have I ever done to deserve such harsh words from you, Miss Wetherby?"

She looked at him warily. "It's no use trying to gammon me, my lord. Everyone knows you are a rake and a libertine."

He let out a crack of laughter. "You are mistaken, my dear. If I were really a libertine, I would have taken advantage of our isolation here to press my licentious attentions upon you."

"I don't doubt it for a minute," she retorted. "In fact, it surprises me that you have not done so," she added without thinking. But no sooner had the careless words left her mouth than she regretted them, and the amused chuckle which met this sally made her blush hotly at the interpretation he had obviously read into her reckless remark.

"I see I have disappointed you, Miss Wetherby, and will endeavour to live up to my reputation." He advanced towards her with a purposeful glint in his eyes.

Diana looked around the small room helplessly. There seemed to be no possible escape, and even if there had been, she was not at all sure she would have welcomed it.

"We are expected downstairs," she began weakly as Rotherham took both her hands in his, held them against his chest, and looked down at her with an expression which nearly undid her resolve to remain firm in the face of improper proposals from libertines.

"Are you hungry, my love?" he murmured solicitously.

"Oh, yes. I'm quite starved," lied Diana, who could not have swallowed a morsel at that moment if her life had depended upon it. Furthermore, she wished he would not call her endearing names; it was most unsettling.

"So am I, love. But not for food." His voice was a mere whisper, and Diana told herself quite firmly that she had no interest at all in knowing what he was hungry for.

"What for, then?" she heard herself asking in a breathless voice that didn't sound at all like the Miss Wetherby she knew.

"Curiosity will be the ruin of you, my sweet." He laughed, slipping one hand around her waist and tilting her chin up with the other. "Here, I'll show you," he murmured, and brushed a chaste kiss on her upturned lips.

"Does that feel like the kind of kiss a libertine would give you?" he teased.

"No, it doesn't at all," Diana replied daringly, and even to her own ears her voice sounded full of disappointment.

"Well, how about this?" He laughed and brought his lips down with more pressure, moving them against her mouth caressingly.

He lifted his head reluctantly and smiled fondly at her. "Well? Does that feel more like it?"

Diana lowered her long lashes to hide the laughter in her eyes. She knew she should not be doing this. To allow a gentleman to take such liberties was highly reprehensible and sure to invite just the kind of improper proposal Lady Chloe had implied was all she could hope to receive from the earl. But while her head told her to withdraw from such a compromising position, her heart insisted that one more kiss was not going to make her any more depraved than she already felt. Besides, after one more such kiss, she might almost be resigned to a life of spinsterhood.

So she kept her eyes lowered and replied somewhat breathlessly, "Better. Definitely better, my lord. But still not q-quite what I had imagined it could be."

"You adorable witch." The earl laughed, now thoroughly on his mettle. "I'll teach you not to torment me, my sweet tease." And if the rough, tempestuous embrace to which she was instantly subjected left any doubt in Diana's mind that the earl could be anything but a libertine of the worst sort, she would never have admitted it. But for some quite inexplicable reason it no longer seemed important.

"Diana! Oh, Diana! What are you doing?"

She realized an astonished voice was calling her from the doorway, and Diana felt herself suddenly bereft as the earl released her and turned to face Arabella who was gazing at them in half-shocked amusement.

Toby, appearing behind her, took one look at the occupants of the room and said rather caustically: "M'dear, you have an alarming propensity to ask the most obvious questions."

"He was kissing her," Arabella exclaimed rather unnecessarily and much to the embarrassment of everyone present.

"Yes, dearest," Toby said patiently. "No need to shout it out over the rooftops, though. Not at all the thing, m'love. None of our business either, come to think of it."

"Oh, but it is, Toby," countered that damsel. "Don't you see? We can have a double wedding now. I would like that beyond anything. Wouldn't you, Diana?" She paused and looked at Diana oddly, as if a thought had just occurred to her. "You *are* betrothed, are you not, Diana?" she inquired apprehensively.

Diana gathered together the shreds of her tattered dignity. "No, as a matter of fact, I'm not," she said in a low voice, aware that Rotherham was finding the whole scene vastly amusing.

"But, dash it all." Now it was Toby who looked at them with a puzzled expression on his face. "I could have sworn—"

"Don't you want to be?" Arabella inquired candidly, oblivious of the consternation she was causing her listeners. "Then what were you about, Diana, letting Rotherham kiss you like that?" she demanded.

"That's enough, m'dear," Toby interrupted quickly. "Let's go down to see what that old harridan has set out for our dinner. I'm starving." And without further ado, he hustled Arabella out and shut the door.

"Yes, Diana," said Rotherham as soon as the door closed behind them. "What were you about, my love? Letting a libertine kiss you like that? And you not even betrothed to him, my dear. How shocking of you." He took both her hands in his again and drew her to him. "Trust Arabella to put her finger right on the crux of the matter." He kissed each finger on her right hand slowly and deliberately. "Don't you want to be, sweetheart?" he asked after a short pause.

Diana refused to raise her eyes. "What? To a libertine? No, thank you, sir," she replied tartly.

He was now kissing each finger on her left hand. "How about a reformed libertine?"

"How would I be sure he is reformed?"

"You would have to take his word for it, love."

"The word of a libertine?" She laughed, daring to glance up to scan his lean face. What she saw there made her heart skip joyously.

"The word of a gentleman libertine; a *reformed* gentleman libertine. What do you say, love?"

"Well, that's a difficult question to put to a maiden lady of advanced years who knows very little about libertines, reformed or otherwise," she said solemnly. "But, hypothetically speaking, if such a *reformed* libertine were to ask me such a question, I would certainly give it my careful consideration," she said evasively. Then added impulsively: "Only if he were not reformed beyond recognition that is."

Rotherham laughed and pulled her roughly against him. "I don't think there is any danger of that happening, my love," he exclaimed, kissing her thoroughly to prove his point. Then he pulled away and looked down at her seriously. "Enough joking, my dear. Tell me you will marry me, love."

Diana looked at him with equal seriousness. "Why should I?" she asked softly.

Astonished by the unexpected question, Rotherham gazed at her for a moment before a slow smile started in his eyes and curled his lips. "Because I love you, dearest. Why else?"

"It's not because of that silly wager, is it?" she demanded, and he knew from her tone that this was the key to their future happiness.

"No," he said truthfully. "But I can't regret it, because it gave me you, my love. Little though I thought so at the time, I was really the winner, not the loser of that wager.''

"Promise me you won't ever again accept a wager for another maiden aunt.''

"Promise me you'll marry me.''

Diana looked up at him, her eyes filled with love. "I promise." She smiled.

"Why?'' he asked, although he already knew the answer.

"Because I love this particular reformed libertine.'' This confession was greeted with another embrace which left her breathless.

"Then let's go down and set Arabella's mind at rest by telling her we are betrothed.''

"Not until you promise—''

"Not to wager for another maiden aunt? That's a promise I certainly intend to keep. One maiden aunt is quite enough for any reformed libertine, my love. Believe me.''